**THE WHIRLWIND OF WASHINGTON
SWEEPS UP A GALLANT GIRL IN
FRANCES PARKINSON KEYES'
MOST TOUCHING STORY**

ANNE CHAMBERLAIN CONRAD
*Her small-town background did not
prepare her for the challenges of
being a Senator's wife; she was nearly
defeated by the relentless demands until
help came from an unexpected place.*

NEAL CONRAD
*He found his beautiful and beloved young
wife even more an asset to his soaring
career than he could have guessed.*

CLARENCE HATHAWAY
*A wise older counselor to Neal and Anne, his
loneliness drove him dangerously close to his
young friend's wife.*

Frances Parkinson Keyes

Queen Anne's Lace

AVON
PUBLISHERS OF
DISCUS • CAMELOT • BARD

AVON BOOKS
A division of
The Hearst Corporation
959 Eighth Avenue
New York, New York 10019

First Avon Printing, December, 1969

Contents

PREFACE

to Queen Anne's Lace

There is a story back of the story of QUEEN ANNE'S LACE.

In the middle twenties, Liveright published a novel entitled REVELRY, by Samuel Hopkins Adams, which was a thinly veiled indictment of the Harding Administration. Horace Liveright, who was then President of the firm which bore his name, sent me an advance copy and asked me to write a review.

I had greatly admired the previous work of Samuel Hopkins Adams; in fact I still feel that his novel entitled SUCCESS—which also had a firm foundation on fact—is the best one I have ever read with journalism as its predominent theme. So I felt very sure that I would find REVELRY a worthy successor to this. Moreover, I was understandably flattered at being considered, by that time, enough of an authority on the political and social scene in Washington to write an intelligent review.

But I had known President and Mrs. Harding personally and I was fond of them both, as indeed I believe was almost everyone who had been associated with them in the early twenties. Mrs. Harding and I had been fellow members of the Ladies of the Senate, so I had seen her, at least once a week, at our Senate Ladies' Luncheons, as well as often on other occasions, since most Senators and their wives frequented interlocking circles, if not actually the same ones. Harding's Inauguration was hailed with hopeful enthusiasm, and the rays of sunshine which suddenly slanted across his face while he was delivering his address, were regarded as symbolic of brighter days to come. The sight of the White House gates, so long closed against visitors, and opened wide as soon as the exercises were over, was also regarded as a happy sign, nor was it misleading. Hospitality, necessarily reduced to a minimum during President Wilson's long illness, was again freely and elegantly dispensed; and the following year, the Washington Arms Conference, which brought distinguished participants and visitors from all over the world, highlighted entertaining at the White House and in the Diplomatic Corps. As I said myself, in writing later about this period, "Never did an administration begin more buoyantly. Never did one end more shamefully."

But when REVELRY was published, Washington—at least that section of it in which I lived, moved, breathed and had my being—was still inclined to look back on this period with some disillusionment, but with more sorrow than shame. The magnificent eulogy of Harding, delivered by Charles Evans Hughes, then Secretary of State, before a distinguished gathering that filled the House of Representatives to the last seat, epitomized what all of us would have liked to say and none would have been able to express in so masterly a manner. Moreover, the integrity of Mr. Hughes has never been questioned, and it is inconceivable that he would have knowingly condoned misconduct in others. With his eloquent words still ringing in my ears, I wrote Mr. Liveright an indignant letter. Indeed, I think I may go so far as to say that it was the only consciously discourteous letter that I have ever written anyone. Nothing would induce me to review that horrible book he had sent me, I stated unequivocally. I considered it inexcusable, however you looked at it. In the first place, it was slanderous. What was almost as bad, from the viewpoint of honest reporting, it was riddled with inaccuracies. It was all too plain that the author knew nothing whatsoever about social and official Washington. Some day I would write a novel on that subject myself, which would at least be basically truthful.

Of course I did not expect an answer to this outburst. But life is full of surprises. By return mail I had a letter from Mr. Liveright, as courteous as mine had been rude. He appreciated my candor. Under the circumstances he would not expect me to write a review; but when I wrote the novel I had in mind, he would be very interested in seeing it.

At this stage, two editors had convinced me that I would never succeed as a novelist; but for my own satisfaction, as I went hither and yon writing the articles, which were successful, about current events, I yielded to the impulse, in such spare moments as I had, to write a novel about social and official Washington, or rather the aspects of this with which I was familiar. I realized then that my knowledge was not comprehensive and of course I realize this much better now; but at least the story was basically true.

I made no effort to market it. In fact, almost no one knew of its existence except my eldest son, who in those days frequently traveled with me as my secretary and not infrequently caught me working on it, and who then offered criticism, advice or encouragement, according to his mood. It was not until I was offered an assignment by GOOD HOUSEKEEPING, which would keep me in South America for at least a year, and I realized I would have to stop writing about current events for DELINEATOR that it occurred to me the material might be used as a serial; and it was not until the very eve of my departure, when Oscar Graeve, the editor of DELINEATOR, and Eleanor Carroll, the Associate Editor, were holding a final conference with me, that the question of a book came up.

"Who is going to publish this?" Oscar asked, making notes.

"Why—I don't know that anyone is."

"*You don't know that anyone is!*" he repeated in a shocked voice. "Do you mean to sit there and tell me you haven't made any arrangements for book publication?"

"Yes. That's what I mean to tell you."

"But you can't expect us to print a story as a serial that isn't important enough to interest a book publisher! Something will have to be done about this right away."

"Very well. But then you'll have to do it. My ship"—

11

and I looked at the clock—"leaves before business hours tomorrow."

"But haven't you any ideas? Any suggestions? Any preference?"

I considered for a moment. "Well," I said, "publishers don't think much of me as a novelist—you know that. But Horace Liveright did tell me, five or six years ago, that if I ever wrote a novel about Washington he'd like to see it. He's probably forgotten all about it or, if he hasn't forgotten, he's probably lost all interest. But it wouldn't do any harm to find out."

The next morning I sailed happily away, according to schedule. When I was three days out at sea I received a cable:

DELIGHTED TO PUBLISH YOUR NOVEL—WITH WHOM SHALL WE NEGOTIATE—HORACE LIVERIGHT

I cabled a brief reply:

WITH ME WHEN I GET HOME

The next morning there was another cable:

UNWILLING TO AWAIT YOUR RETURN—BOOK PUBLICATION SCHEDULED FOR MONTH SERIAL ENDS—PLEASE ADVISE

I began to think that soon the Atlantic would be strewn with cables. By this time my eldest son had ceased to function as my secretary and had become a full fledged lawyer. I decided, as I have many times before and since, that I had better wash my hands of the whole thing and let him take over. I cabled his name and address. The sea became calm again.

So that is the story back of the story of QUEEN ANNE'S LACE—before publication. There are also several stories, which I hope and believe are equally worth telling, about what happened to it after publication.

From the very first installment of its appearance as a serial, it attracted attention. Rumors almost immediately began to circulate to the effect that it was actually the story of President and Mrs. Coolidge, very thinly disguised. This rumor gained impetus when Mr. Coolidge descended from a train, in which he and his wife were traveling westward, to inquire solicitously if the *Delineator* were for sale at the station newsstand. On being informed that it was, he allegedly purchased two copies, so that he and Mrs. Coolidge could read it simultaneously—an almost unheard extravagance on the part of this economical gentleman! Then he returned with the magazines to the Pullman drawing room, where both Coolidges remained engrossed with the story until they reached their destination. Whether or not there is any truth in this tall tale, I cannot tell; but if the two Coolidges really believed—which I doubt—that they had inspired my story, certainly nothing about it displeased them, for we remained the best of friends until their deaths. It is my honest conviction that they realized the facts: namely, that I had written a story which was true to official Washington, as I had known it over a period of years, but that this was intended as a composite portrait and not a photograph of any specific person or persons.

Nevertheless, another rumor became even more widespread than the one about the Coolidges: that the story was autobiographical. I had some rather amusing experiences in connection with this. On one occasion, a lady, who was a complete stranger to me but apparently a faithful reader, came up to me at a reception and, putting her hand affectionately on my arm, exclaimed, "My dear, I can't help telling you how much I admire you for rising the way you have above your background. No one would ever guess to meet you that your father was an ignorant, shiftless farmer and your mother such a slattern that she never took her hair out of curlpapers until late in the afternoon! Or that you had no education except in a village one-room school!" For a moment, I gazed at her speechlessly, unable to grasp what she was talking about; then I realized that the "background" she believed to have been mine was indeed that of my heroine, Anne Conrad. As gently and tactfully as possible, I disillusioned her, telling her that my father had been head of the Greek Department at the University of Virginia and that my mother, who was then still living, could, at any time of her life,

13

have posed for a fashion plate. As for my education, that had taken place partly at two very famous private schools in Boston, partly in Europe and partly in the charge of a German governess who was a graduate of the Sorbonne. While she lived with us, all my lessons were in either French or German, so that I had had the advantage of growing up tri-lingual; when she left us, it was to become the governess of Gladys Vanderbilt. I would have loved to be able to take the credit of nobly rising above my background but, as a matter of sober fact, I had hard work living up to it.

However, I freely admitted that I believed all authors, either consciously or unconsciously, put some aspects of their own experiences and their own emotions in their books, though usually in a form very different from the real ones and that I had unquestionably done this in other novels I had written and, also, in QUEEN ANNE'S LACE. In this story, moreover, there were several episodes that were like some in my own life and frankly based on these: the first dreadful days "At Home" as a senator's wife; the first night that Anne took election returns over the telephone, hour after hour, because her husband refused to go near the instrument, but wanted frequent reports; the frank enjoyment in the general Washington picture, as it unfolds in a privileged circle and, specifically, the impression made by a typical Washington dinner party. And certainly no one who was present in New York at the great Democratic National Convention of 1924 or even who listened to accounts of it over the radio—for this was when radio first came into its own—needs to be told that this was my model, with absolutely nothing changed but the names of the candidates, for the national convention described in QUEEN ANNE'S LACE. I attended the real one from start to finish and heartily echoed the statement made by the inimitable Will Rogers at the end of it that he would consider covering the next war on a straight yearly basis, but that he would never again agree to cover a National Democratic Convention—though, as a matter of fact, both he and I did so.

The first printing of QUEEN ANNE'S LACE in book

14

form was for only 1,500 copies. Those were the days of the great depression and publishers were understandably cautious in presenting a new author. But this edition was exhausted almost overnight and copies of it now have considerable value, commercially as well as sentimentally. The book was quickly reprinted and as Julian Messner, then vice president of Liveright, was kind enough to write me, "In a bad year, your story goes steadily on and on, selling more and more." Indeed, it was the first of my novels to go beyond the category of those which represent a modest profit to both publisher and author and enter the category of potential best-sellers. It has never gone out of print and, in hard cover trade editions, it has done as well in both France and England as it has in the United States, where it has also been published in abridged form in *Omnibook* and without abridgement by the Dollar Book Club. The reception of its first edition in paperback was so gratifying that it seems logical the reception of its second edition will be even more so.

FRANCES PARKINSON KEYES

The Finished Design

CLARENCE HATHAWAY, who, as everyone knew, was to be the next Ambassador to Great Britain if the President-elect had his way—and the President-elect was accustomed to having his way—emerged from the impressive doorway of his residence, and stood for a moment, slender cane hanging from slender wrist, sleek silk hat and spotless gray gloves in slender hand, sleek dark hair—slightly crisp, slightly gray, over the temples—uncovered, looking up and down Sixteenth Street, before he signified his consciousness that a gleaming Hispana Suiza waited before him, a chauffeur in maroon livery at the wheel, a footman similarly attired holding open the door.

He could hardly be blamed for pausing to survey the scene before him with satisfaction. It was a perfect spring morning of sparkling freshness, and a magnolia tree, top-heavy with bursting buds, gleamed pink against the grill-work of the basement windows; a small, vividly colored bird, perched on its topmost branch, was singing as if he would slit his throat; crocuses were pushing their way through the delicate green of the tiny lawn, fringed with daffodils, in front of the house; and from the marble balcony on the second story an American flag flew stiff in the breeze and shone in the sun. From the neighboring embassies and legations other flags were flying—French, Spanish, Swiss, Cuban, Polish—how glorious they looked, the tri-color, the crown, the cross, the bars, displayed in honor of the Stars and Stripes! Gravely, Hathaway saluted; there was nothing artificial, nothing self-conscious

17

about the gesture; he had the elegance, the poise, the graciousness that made such an act seem natural and lovely; the chauffeur and footman, shaken from their stiff correctness, faced the American flag and saluted in their turn; Hathaway turning to them smiling.

"A fine day for the President, Jarvis—a great day for all of us!"

"Yes, indeed, sir; Squires and I 'ave been remarking it."

Hathaway nodded, smiled again, paused again, set one slim foot, shod in patent leather topped by a pearl-gray spat, on the step of his car.

"The Shoreham, Jarvis. We're stopping there for the Attorney-General-designate and his mother, and Governor and Mrs. Hildreth."

"Yes, sir. Very good, sir. It's a great honor for us to be taking them, as Squires and I 'ave been remarking, sir."

The dignitaries in question were already standing on the steps of the Shoreham as the Hispana Suiza slid to a silent stop in front of the hotel. Hathaway alighted and greeted them in turn.

"Good morning, Mrs. Griffin. Well, how does it feel to be the mother of a Cabinet-member? You've not kept Roy in very good order, but from now on—you must allow him no wild habits, mind! Mabel, you look as fresh as a May morning—or a March morning, I ought to say! *What* a day! Made to order, if one ever was! Made in Heaven, Anne would say—bless her heart!"

"I wonder how she is this morning?" The new Attorney-General, a thin, timid-looking man, quite evidently under the domination of his belligerent mother, spoke anxiously, and with a slight lisp, which his evident nervousness intensified.

"Oh, she's finely," announced Mabel Hildreth, settling herself comfortably in the corner of the car. Both the Governor and his wife bore unmistakable signs of long-continued rural prosperity, over which a slight veneer of recent official importance lay somewhat insecurely; but there was something very likeable about their rather round and florid faces, and Mrs. Hildreth retained traces of a girlish bloom which, though somewhat faded, must once

18

have been very lovely. "Look out, George," she went on, "you'll get your coat-tails terribly crushed if you sit that way—and my, but you look hot already. Why can't you be like Clarence here? He never turns a hair, no matter what he has to dress up in— Well, Anne called me up herself at eight o'clock this morning—she says she's going to telephone her friends herself *always*—well, of course she won't—can't—but it's nice she feels that way about it. Her dresses are here *at last*—. Mr. Goldenburg brought them over from New York, himself, on the midnight. And Anne says they're perfectly lovely."

"I haven't heard what she was to wear," interposed Mrs. Griffin eagerly.

"Why, *lace* of course! Venetian point, so old that it's fawn-color, combined with tan georgette and silk, this morning. Rose-point and white satin this evening. Neal wouldn't hear of anything less—"

"I don't quite see—" began Mrs. Griffin but the lively Mabel, who had the habit of interruption, broke in upon her.

"Oh, look at those beautiful horses—aren't they perfectly matched! And they're fawn-color, too! Are they— are they something special, Clarence?"

"Yes, indeed. It's the cavalry from Fort Meyer that acts as escort to the delegation going to the White House to meet the President."

"The President!" exclaimed the Griffins and the Hildreths together; and they sat quietly, awed to unaccustomed silence, which Hathaway made no attempt to break, as the car swung around the Treasury Building and sped down the cleared width of Pennsylvania Avenue, banked on either side with good-natured, orderly crowds. The official permit, displayed on the windshield, took it swiftly past the saluting guards at the Capitol; and here the host, as he guided his guests through the revolving doors, issued a few directions.

"You fellows join your respective colleagues now in the waiting-rooms—you're for the floor of the Senate, as of course you know. I'll take the ladies to the gallery, see them safely to the platform where they'll rejoin you after

19

the exercises in the Chamber, and then find them after the President's address and look out for them during the parade. See *you* again for luncheon at the White House!"

The dingy old Chamber was filling fast as Hathaway and the two ladies took their places in the gallery. The balconies were, indeed, overcrowded already, only one vacant seat, in the front row of the Senators' gallery, apparently remaining unoccupied. On one side of this sat a lovely young girl, her golden curls uncovered; on the other a slim boy with ruffled hair and a wide, disarming smile, which he was bestowing impartially in response to greetings from every direction. They both caught sight of Hathaway, and waved to him enthusiastically, a welcome which he acknowledged with evident affection.

"Nancy and Junior are missing nothing," he whispered to Mabel Hildreth. "I shouldn't be surprised if they had been here for an hour already!"

Mabel nodded, her eyes on the Vice-President. This functionary was presiding for the last time, while final appointments were being made, Senators who were retaining their seats delivering eulogies upon Senators who had failed of reëlection, and the vanquished replying to these grandiose tributes. Hathaway called his companions' attention to the large clock under the press gallery and directly over the Vice-President's seat; and as they looked at it, they saw that its hands, which had stood at one minute of twelve, were turned back until these pointed at half-past eleven again.

"The new Congress begins at twelve," he told them, "by that clock. It doesn't matter what time it is outside. You may see the hands set back three times. This session can't end without all these little frills and furbelows."

At last the gavel descended. The Democratic Senators surged across the aisle, and took their places on the east side of the Chamber, with the Republican Senators and the Senators-elect, the visiting Governors, and the Cabinet members-designate. Mabel Hildreth, assisted by Hathaway, discovered her husband; Mrs. Griffin, without assistance, discovered her son. It was a supreme moment. The members of the House of Representatives, filing in, took their places behind the Senators on the east side, and behind the members of the retiring Cabinet and the Diplomatic Corps, gorgeous in gold braid, gold lace, gold medals, on the west side. The judges of the Supreme Court rustled forward, their black robes, voluminous as hoop skirts, billowing about them and the ranking military and naval officers who were placed near them. All these dignitaries made an impressive showing; but towards none of them did either of the two ladies allow their fascinated gaze to wander. Governor Hildreth and the Attorney-General-designate were, as far as they were concerned, the only two men on that crowded floor.

The Speaker of the House and the Vice-President-elect were, in turn, escorted to seats beside the Vice-President. The applause, which, though technically forbidden had rung out again and again unchecked, was quickly, voluntarily hushed; then it resounded again, echoing and reëchoing.

The President-elect had entered the Chamber, accompanied by an escort of three Senators and three Congressmen, and had taken his place in front of the raised platform where the Vice-President sat. And, when he had done so, he lifted his eyes to the Senators' gallery, just as a lady, with a soft full cloak partially covering a dress of heavy deep-cream lace, came down the aisle and took her place in the vacant seat between the golden-haired girl and the shaggy-haired boy. For a moment she sat with her head bent, her drooping hat with its delicate plumes concealing her face. ("She is praying,") Hathaway said to himself, choking a little. Then she looked up, and across the Chamber, meeting the President's eyes; seemed to steady herself; and, putting her arms around her children, rose with them to accept the tribute of applause which rocked the room. It came from every side; from the Senators' gallery and the Diplomatic gallery and the Press gallery; from Cabinet and Court and Congressmen. Not until she raised her ungloved right hand, with a gentle gesture which at one and the same time acknowledged and checked the outburst, did the tumult lessen. Then she gathered the folds of her cloak around her, and with com-

21

plete composure, grace, and dignity, reseated herself. She had smiled, bowing, in every direction, she was still smiling—a smile very like her son's in its frankness, ingenuousness and charm, although a little more restrained; but, somehow, her eyes did not seem for an instant to have left the President's face.

"Neal told me that when he took his oath of office as Senator," Hathaway whispered, in a voice that shook, "he was almost overcome, when he looked up and saw Anne sitting in the gallery and—and found he could go on, after all. After that, he never came into the Chamber without instinctively looking up to see if she were here. He did it today—did you notice? . . . No woman ever had such a tribute in the Senate before. I wonder whether any ever will again."

His companions were only half listening to him. It did not matter. It did not matter, either, that the retiring Vice-President was making one of the most remarkable speeches that had ever been delivered in the Chamber, or that the new Vice-President, having been duly sworn in, was trying in vain to re-create the impression which his predecessor had made; that a message calling the Senate to special executive session was being read; that new Senators, repeating the same oath of office as the Vice-President, were "taking their seats." The President's own speech was the next thing that mattered; and after a long time—an eternity it seemed to Hathaway—suddenly, the Senate was adjourned, and the occupants of the galleries, hurrying to the doors, were rushing through the corridors and down the staircases. Steering his charges towards the stage, temporarily erected over the east steps of the Capitol, where the President was to take his oath and make his address, he turned them over to an officer, with hasty instructions that Mrs. Griffin should be taken to her place beside her son, and Mrs. Hildreth to her place beside her husband. Then he directed his own steps to the open space directly in front of the platform which had been roped off for the specially invited guests who had been in the Senate Chamber, but who did not have seats on the stage.

For the second time that day he paused and stood contemplating the scene before him, almost oblivious of the crowd that surged about him, before he took his seat. Far beyond the reserved space where he stood, over the park extending between the Capitol and the Congressional Library, was massed the waiting multitude, silent, calm, expectant. The wind which had whipped the embassy flags to tautness earlier in the day had died down; and the Stars and Stripes, standing between the Corinthian columns of the Capitol's façade, fell in quiet folds, as the rich draperies of some royal room might have fallen. The temporary stage had been designed by a master-mind, and executed by a master-hand; its harmony with the architecture of the Capitol was complete. Corinthian columns, replicas of those behind it, supported it; and on eitner side of them rose enormous vases, filled with scarlet carnations and snowy lilies. The national coat of arms, laurel-wreathed, surmounted the platform; and looped about it were long festoons of laurel, to which were fastened laurel-wreathed shields. The platform was crowded, and the sun shone full upon it; a shaft of this fell as if straight from heaven, upon the President's lifted face, as he emerged from the mass behind him, and stood revealed between the white columns, beside the black-robed justice.

"Anne will say that was another omen!" the thought flashed through Hathaway's mind, and instantly, as if by telepathy, he heard the man beside him saying, "Lord Almighty! *Did* you see that sun?" Hathaway glanced at the speaker—a stout, matter-of-fact looking person, certainly not the sort given to superstition. Then he looked up at the lady in fawn-color. She was sitting very close to the President now, the folds of her cloak falling softly about her slim form, her earnest eyes fixed on his face, as they had been in the Senate Chamber. He had taken the oath, the Justice had stepped back, and the President had begun his speech. He was talking about transient policies and about permanent peace, about the constitution and the World Court, about law and order, and economy and freedom. This was sane, able, conservative,—what had been expected of him. Gradually, a greater earnestness, a greater power, crept into his words; his strangely youthful,

23

vibrant face became beautified, it glowed as if from some inner light; the impassioned eloquence which had first made him famous had never been so lambent before. He was speaking about America, about her heritage, about her future, about her place on earth. He visioned and revealed his country, personified as a steadfast figure, with never-failing courage and never-faltering faith, standing tranquil and mighty in the midst of dangers, or moving serenely and powerfully forward, a leader of enlightenment in a sorrow-stricken world.

"Lord Almighty!" exclaimed the stout person sitting beside Hathaway again, "I've always been patriotic, but no one ever made me feel this way about America before. I'll say we're going to have a great President—one of the greatest. He talks about the United States as if it were *real*, a person a—a woman. Like a man might talk about some one he was in love with—" Hathaway turned towards him.

"It is real," he said, "to the President. That's why he makes it seem real to you and me. You're right—he's making a great speech, one that will live. And the person who made all that real to him is his wife."

"Lord Almighty!" exclaimed the stout person for the third time. "You don't say so!" He leaned eagerly forward, as if fearing that he might lose a single one of the syllables which fell, clear as crystal, from the President's lips. He sat, breathless with admiration, mopping tears of honest emotion from his eyes, until the last sentence had been spoken, until after one lingering look towards the people beneath him, the President had turned, and with the lady in fawn-color beside him, had disappeared from the platform. Then the stranger spoke to Hathaway again.

"I'm from the West," he said, a trifle apologetically, instead of in the proud tones with which the average Westerner proclaims this fact, "so I'm not acquainted much here. My nephew—he's in Congress—got me this seat. I'll thank him to my dying day. Lord Almighty! What a speech! What a *man!* I hope you'll excuse me for asking, but from the way you spoke—do you know the President?"

24

"Yes," said Hathaway quietly, "I know him rather well. I'm—if you'll excuse me—on my way to lunch at the White House now, and I must find my motor and some friends of ours whom I've promised to take there with me after the parade."

The Westerner's chagrin at losing his newly found acquaintance was tempered by his excitement at the evident importance of this slim, sleek-haired, "dudish" personage. (Later, when the account of Clarence Hathaway's appointment to the Court of St. James, accompanied by his picture, was printed in every metropolitan daily in the United States, the Westerner's pride doubled and redoubled as he told his "home town" that he "knew the Ambassador.") He laid a detaining hand on Hathaway's sleeve.

"I don't want to keep you, of course," he said, apologetically, "but I want you should tell me just a word, before you go, about—about his wife. You said—"

Hathaway smiled, and shook his head. But he stopped for a moment before he moved away, the crowd closing in on him as he went.

"I couldn't tell you about her in a week," he said. "I couldn't tell you if I stayed here all day, trying. Nobody could tell the real story, as it ought to be told, about the part a woman has in her husband's career, from very humble beginning through long, hard, drab, uneventful years, and on to ultimate supremacy. It's a part very different from what's popularly supposed, a part not only misunderstood, but underestimated. Nobody could do such a story justice, though dozens of able biographies will be written about the President; but somebody ought to try. Not only because then the American people might appreciate—partly at least—their President's wife. But also because hundreds of women, who are longing to help their husbands, but feeling that they are failing to do so, would find consolation and encouragement in the story of Anne Chamberlain."

"Why don't you write the story yourself?" persisted the Westerner. "Or, if you can't do it yourself—I presume you're a busy man—why don't you find someone else who will? Someone you could trust to make a try at it, anyways. Lord Almighty, man! Don't fade away from me like that!"

For the Westerner found that he was speaking to the crowd in general, and not to one person in particular. He was also being looked at curiously, and he himself looked about in some bewilderment. He had agreed to meet his nephew in the latter's room at the House Office Building; from there they were going to see the parade together. It was late already and he ought to hurry.

"Just the same," he said to himself, as he scurried, panting, across the park, "I hope I put an idea into that slick-looking fellow's head, and I believe I *did*. I believe he heard me after *all*. I believe he'll get somebody to write that story!"

PART ONE

The Bobbin and the Thread

CHAPTER I

"Anne—Anne—where be ye?"

It was the third time the shrill, insistent call had pene-trated to the hot little attic room. Twice the girl who heard it, unfastening her crumpled print dress and pulling out hairpins, had disregarded it. Now she jerked open the door and answered.

"I'm upstairs—undressing."

"Hev ye fed the hens?"

"Yes."

"Did ye fasten the gate after ye?"

"Yes."

"Hev ye put them clothes ter soak I told ye couldn't wait till next week ter be washed?"

"Yes."

"Well, don't ferget I want ye should wring 'em out the first thing in the mornin' and iron 'em after dinner."

"I won't."

"I ben lookin' at the string beans. I think there's enough ter start cannin'. Couldn't ye come down an' pick a few afore it gits dark?"

"Oh, *Mummer!* It's late now! I've barely time to get ready before George'll be here! I'll pick them tomorrow night."

There was a silence fraught with disapproval.

"Won't that do?"

"I s'pose so. Seems to me 'twould be a good thing to

27

can 'em when they're fit, but I know that don't count none in your jedgment when you want to go to a dance."

Mrs. Chamberlain retreated with a sound of shuffling footsteps. She wore carpet-slippers in the evening to rest her feet, putting them on in the afternoon about the same time that she took her hair out of "crimpers"! Anne had seldom seen her mother tidy at both ends at once.

She bit her lip, and went on with her undressing, tossing her coarse cotton chemise, petticoat and stockings after her dress on the pine bedstead, covered with a dingy patchwork quilt, that was crowded under the eaves, and kicking her tattered shoes under it. The cheap little alarm clock, ticking away on the pine bureau, warned her that she must hurry. She snatched up the broken comb that lay beside it, and drew it through her tangled mass of yellow curls, with swift, impatient strokes, so that the snarls hissed and broke. Then, pulling it tautly away from her small ears into a tight flat knot on the top of her head, she fastened it securely, and filled the heavy, cracked white basin from the heavy cracked white pitcher.

A sculptor would have used her as a model for a bathing nymph, with a delighted prayer of thanksgiving to Providence for giving him so perfect a subject. For she was slim and straight and supple, as exquisitely white-skinned as she was finely formed, except for the tan on soft forearm and softer neck. But to herself, she was simply a hot, tired girl, hastening to make herself clean and cool to go out with the young farmer whose place adjoined her father's, and whom both had long taken for granted she would eventually marry. She would have liked to feel, naturally, that she could make herself beautiful as well as clean and cool; but that seemed almost too much to hope. However, she did her best. She dusted herself with talcum powder from a highly colored can stamped in an "oriental design," and rubbed her neck with "rose perfume" from a still more highly colored bottle, decorated with a crimson flower which bloomed brightly on one side, and a pink ribbon which was tied around its neck. These toilet perquisites had been purchased, at the total expenditure of fifty cents which she could ill-afford to squander, on her latest trip to Wallacetown, and she knew they must be reserved for great occasions only, if she were to justify her extravagance to herself. But this really did seem a sufficiently great occasion. Then she put on her "best underclothes," made of lansdowne, embroidered—by herself—with sprays of forget-me-nots, and trimmed with crocheted lace which she had made herself; her one pair of silk stockings, originally white, but grown yellow from many washings, and carefully darned; two of the darns—one on the instep and one just above the heel—showed, but that could not be helped; black patent leather slippers, somewhat cracked and shapeless, came next; then a pink silk muslin dress, with a knot of black velvet on one shoulder, and a black velvet sash, made from an old "sacque" of her mother's, carefully steamed, pressed, and recut—she had read in the "Symposium of Styles"—which her friend Mabel Buck loaned her from time to time, since she could not afford to subscribe to a fashion magazine herself—that "a touch of black was always very Frenchy." Last of all, she loosened and rewound her hair, and added another knot of velvet to its shining coils.

"I'm glad I've got some flowers to wear," she said to herself, as she surveyed the results of her efforts in the small, blurred glass over the washstand. "I *will* have a *real* flower garden some day, even if Pupper and Mummer do think it's a waste of time and space. I know the sweet-peas are almost a failure, because I got them in so late, but I'm sure there are enough so that I can manage. I haven't picked them for three days on purpose."

She was down the steep narrow staircase in one swift rush of color and motion, across the kitchen, out of the rusty screen door half hanging on its hinges, and punctured by holes whose uneven edges curled shaggily back, over the scraggly yard to the still more scraggly garden. The one line of scanty sweet-pea vines, growing close beside the flourishing string-beans, was completely stripped of blossoms. Anne, holding her skirts carefully around her, dashed from the garden to the narrow front porch, where, their labors for the day ended, her parents and her two small brothers, Sol and Sam, were taking their ease in un-washed relaxation.

"Who picked my sweet-peas?" she demanded accusingly. "You all knew I was saving them for tonight, and they're gone."

"I picked 'em," announced Mrs. Chamberlain, rocking heavily. "I took 'em down to the cemetery an' put 'em on your Aunt Sarah's grave. They're settin' there now, in a preserve jar, side of some nasturtiums and candy-tuft Ella Wiley brought. They look real handsome. It's just three years ago today sense your Aunt Sarah passed away. I presume ye've ben so took up thinkin' about this dance ye're goin' to, ye ain't thought of the dead. Maybe ye'd like to go down and take 'em off the grave," she ended with supreme scorn.

"I would, if I had time," the girl burst out fiercely. "You knew how much I wanted them—and they're mine, anyway! I bought the seeds, and planted them, and I've tended them. They won't do Aunt Sarah any good, and they were all I had!"

Her mother remained entirely unmoved; clearly, the matter of the beans still rankled; but her father glimpsed something of the tragedy of her disappointment.

"Shucks, Nannie—what does a few flowers matter? Ye're the greatest hand to take on, over nothin'. If ye hev to hev flowers, there's some roses left still on that bush down the lane by the medder. They're kinder gone by, but I guess they'd answer. 'Twouldn't take ye long to run down there and see."

"Sol, you go! I'll get my skirts all dusty!"

"Hold 'em up an' ye won't. I can't pick flowers, roses leastwise. The pesky thorns stick inter me so, I get to hollerin' an' let go, an'—"

"Sam, won't *you?*"

Sam gave a deep groan, reminiscent of too much supper. "Them cucumbers I et don't seem to lay jest right," he objected graphically, "or mebbe 'twas the blueberry pie. The crust wuz kinder heavy. Yer pies ain't nothin' extra, Nan. I'd rather set still for a spell than go weed-chasin'. I ben workin' hard all day, anyway. I—"

30

"All right! You just wait till I ever help you with anything again! Either of you! You'll see—"

She was gone, a blur of pink and gold, past the chicken-yard, with its sagging wire, and the foul pig pen with its rotten trough; through the creaking gate to the malodorous barnyard, where half a dozen lean "grade" cows regarded her with dumb resentment. Then down the lane to the meadow where the grass, a poor crop which should have been mown a fortnight since, was still standing, sparse and dry. The rose bush clambered, prickly and parched, over a decaying fence. It was, as her father had said, not far. But Anne hated the white powder of dust on her shiny black shoes, the tiny beads of perspiration which, with her haste, gathered on her face; most of all she hated the laziness and indifference on the part of her family which had made her quest necessary.

"They might do something to help *me*, once in a while! But they never do, never! When I do all I can for them! It isn't fair—"

In her anger, she attacked the unoffending rosebush with more vehemence than caution, and pricked her finger. She whipped it swiftly to her mouth. But she was not quick enough; a drop of blood had fallen on her bodice, just above the waist-line.

"Now I've got to get something to cover *that*—and there aren't enough roses— Oh, what *shall* I do?"

"Why don't you take some of that white flower growin' on the other side of the fence, in the medder, and put it with yer roses? It's kinder large—that'll cover up yer spot."

Anne wheeled about. George Hildreth, who was to take her to the party, was standing beside her. His blond hair lay wet and sleek away from its uneven part, and his round, red, and rather flat face shone with soap and scrubbing. His blue eyes, usually somewhat vacant in expression, beamed in anticipation. He was dressed in his best, a garnet pin in his spotted tie, a monogram buckle on his belt, chocolate-colored shoes. Evidently he had arrived during her absence, and on being informed where she had gone, had welcomed the opportunity of greeting her apart from the gaze of the assembled family, and had followed her. Unconsciously, she had spoken aloud, and he had heard her.

"You look great anyway. I don't see why you should worry about flowers."

"Do you honestly think so?"

"Well, I guess I do!"

There was not the slightest doubt of the earnestness of George's admiration. Anne veered away from a more tangible proof of it.

"But those flowers *would* be pretty. Could you climb through the barbed wire and get me some, or would you hurt your clothes?"

George hesitated, torn between his desire to serve, and his consciousness of the twenty-nine-fifty, earned by the sweat of his brow, which he had so recently expended on his new "pepper and salt" suit—"the latest in collegiate apparel"—as he had been assured when he had bought it in Wallacetown, and which he was now wearing for the first time.

"Would it take too long to go round by the gate? We could let down the bars and go round inter the medder. We could both go."

"Oh, George, you're just like all the others! You never can do anything *quick!*"

"Now, Anne, don't get mad. I only thought—"

"Oh, I know what you thought—the same as I know what Pupper and Mummer and Sol and Sam think! You've got about as much action between you as Aunt Sarah!"

"Why, she's been dead three years—"

"I *know* it. That's what I *meant!* You can't even see *that!*—come on then, we'll go round by the gate."

"Honest, Anne"—

"For Heaven's sake, *come on!* Do you want to get to that party before they start playing 'Home Sweet Home'?"

"I don't care, Anne, so long as I can be with you."

He put his arm about her. She did not actually shake it off, but her lack of mental response to his caress was so marked that a physical withdrawal would really have been less chilling.

"Well, I do! I want to dance every dance! And then there won't be half enough!"

"I know you like to dance, Anne, and you know I always want you should have a good time, but—"

"Help me pick some of these flowers, then, so we can start."

For a moment they pulled away, silently, at the white blossoms. Then Anne laughed—laughed so joyously that George realized, with a bounding heart, that her vexation must be passing.

"Do you know the name of these flowers?"

"No—I never heard. I've seen 'em always, growin' in medders, an' along roadsides where the crops an' soil ain't none too good. They're kind of a pest, I s'pose—but they're pretty. They don't seem to belong, someway, with the dust and weeds and rocks. They're kinder like lace."

"That's what they're called—Queen Anne's Lace. It's funny, isn't it, my name, I mean, and wearing them, and finding them in a place like this, and not having anything else pretty—"

She held a spray up against her face, smiling as the soft white blossoms brushed her cheeks. Then she broke off the stems, and twisting them in the thorny roses, thrust them into her belt.

"I don't see nawthin' funny about it," said George stolidly, "but they look nice, the way you've fixed 'em. You're awful sweet, Anne—couldn't you give me a kiss before we start for the dance?"

CHAPTER II

GEORGE did not get his kiss, but as he had not expected it, he was not unduly disappointed. Anne was always "offish." She hated to be "pawed." She flung away from him impatiently, and started, on a run, back up the lane. George followed at a more leisurely pace, chewing a piece of grass as he went—at this rate, they would never be married—he was making no progress at all. And he wanted to marry Anne, very much. He grew warm all over, at the very thought of it. But he never seemed to be able to think of the move that would help his cause along.

When they were seated in his new top-buggy, with its slim, rubber-tired wheels, and were actually on their way into Hamstead, Anne relaxed a little, and they fell into casual and friendly conversation, without reference to his lover-like advances, which he made no further effort to resume. But with dogged perseverance he sought to win his point by other means.

"Are you pretty well through haying?" Anne asked noncommittally.

"Yes, Saturday night'll see it done."

"You've had good luck, haven't you?"

"Fine. And the oats and corn's comin' along great, too. I don't know as I ever had a better year. And my creamery check keeps a-mountin' and mountin' straight along."

Anne made no direct response to this boastful statement, with its hidden thrust at her father's lack of prosperity in dismal contrast to her suitor's abundance.

"I'm thinkin' some of throwin' out a bay-winder in the

34

dinin' room an' puttin' in a furnace. An' a bathroom. There's space for one beside the parlor-chamber."

"That would be nice, wouldn't it? Why don't you un-brick the fireplaces, too, and throw away the air-tights? Everyone's doin' it down in Hamstead."

"Well, mebbe I will. It ain't a bad idea. The house needs paperin' an' paintin' too. It'll look real good when I get it all fixed up. I cal'late I could get all them improvements done by late fall."

Again Anne gave no sign that she had drawn the obvious conclusion.

"You aren't honestly figurin' on teachin' another winter, are ye?"

"I think I better. It's hard to get girls to come to these district schools 'out back.' And ten dollars a week helps out a good deal."

"It helps out yer *family*. I don't see that *you* get much outer it."

"Well, *somebody's* got to see that the taxes are paid, and that we don't starve, at least."

"Yes, and that somebody'll be you, just as long as you'll do it. There are two good husky young 'uns, and an able-bodied man an' woman just settin' back and lettin' ye."

"George! Don't you dare criticize my family!"

"I shall, too—if yer so dead set on teachin', ye could keep on after we was married. You could do all the house-work there is in my house with one hand tied behind ye, convenient like it all is. And you could hev all the money ye earned to spend on yeself—clothes an' books an' a pianner."

He had scored at last. He saw it, and pressed his advantage.

"Ye've always wanted ter travel. We could take a real nice trip this fall. I could plan the work so's I could git away for a spell after the crops is all in, an' before the cows begin to freshen." George was suddenly conscious of a slight conversational indiscretion, and blushed; but Anne, apparently, had not noticed it. She was thinking about the trip, and George went on eagerly, "We could go to Niagara Falls, or Montreal, or Boston."

35

"Oh, George, everybody goes to those places. Everybody that can afford to."

"Well, where do you want to go?"

"To New York. And—and Washington."

George gulped with surprise. But he was game.

"All right. To New York and Washington."

"Especially Washington."

"Why on earth—"

"I don't know. But I'm crazy to see it. I think I'd like to live there."

"For Heaven's sake, Nan! Why you haven't a chance in the world, any more'n I have, of ever livin' anywhere but in West Hamstead."

"I know it. But I wish I had."

George saw his rosy dreams vanishing into thin mist. He sought to recapture them.

"But it'd be worth somethin' ter go. Mebbe we could go more'n once."

"Well—"

"Nan!"

"Let's talk about something else for a while."

"Oh, Nan, please—"

He leaned forward, laying his hand earnestly on her knee, trying to look into her eyes. She put her own hand over his, gave it a friendly pressure, and then shook her pink skirt free of it.

"I can't, George," she said with equal earnestness. "Honestly, I can't. I know how much you'd try to do for me, and I do like you. But it isn't enough."

"It's a lot more'n you've got now."

"I know—when I said it wasn't enough I didn't mean that I wouldn't be lots more comfortable than I've ever been before. I know I would. I meant that I somehow couldn't look at things the way you do. We're at swords' points half the time. And then I don't care enough."

"You just said you liked me."

"I do. But I don't love you. That is, I don't believe I do. I don't like to have you touch me, and I certainly never wanted to touch you. If a girl's in love with a man, I think she does."

36

George blushed again. Anne seemed to have less mental than physical reserve.

"That's a long way from feeling you'd be glad to marry a man. And it's further still from feeling as if you'd die if you couldn't."

"It—it would all come out all right, you'd see."

"It wouldn't. I couldn't make you happy."

"I'll take that risk."

"And I couldn't be happy myself. *I won't* take the risk."

"Won't you think it over some more?" asked George miserably. "You know how it's been with me, ever since we was kids. I'm a good provider. You shouldn't never lack nothin'. And I'd be a kind husband. We *would* be happy. If ye can't say yes, don't say no neither. Not for a while, anyways. That's not askin' much of ye."

Anne hesitated. She had no wish to be needlessly unkind, and she was really fond of George. He was, as he said, not asking for much.

"All right," she said at length, "I won't say 'no' yet, if you won't pester me. And if you won't talk about it any more tonight.—Have you heard what there's going to be for music at the dance?"

George settled back in the buggy with a sigh of mingled relief and triumph, slapping the reins over the horse's back as he did so.

"The Wallacetown Band's goin' to play," he replied. "Four pieces. I bet it'll be slick. I hear there's a number comin' down from there to go to it. Roy Griffin has got company. A feller he knew at college, named Neal Conrad, is visitin' him, so they're gettin' up a party. Conrad's come up from Hinsboro where he lives, in one of these new-fangled horseless carriages. I don't think much of them."

"Don't you? Where have you seen one?"

"I ain't seen one. But I've heard tell."

"In the postoffice, sitting around the air-tight with a lot of other mossbacks who never saw one either, I suppose," said Anne scornfully. "Oh, George! Don't you *see?* It's just as I said! We never look at things the same way! *I* believe that horseless carriages are going to be a great success, and revolutionize transportation."

"I do wish you wouldn't use all the long words there are in the dictionary like that. I can't keep track of what you really mean."

"I mean I think they're going to make a great change in travel, and work, and pleasure. I wish I had a chance to go out in one."

"Well," said George sarcastically, "mebbe Neal Conrad will ask ye to. Roy and him are comin' down to the dance in his. That's what I started to tell you."

The words were hardly out of his mouth before he repented them. He had put an idea in Anne's head that might much better have been left out of it. Of course, it was not probable that this city-dude would take any notice of her, but it was possible. He recalled that she knew Roy Griffin, just slightly, of course, but still well enough for him to ask her to dance. And Roy Griffin might introduce his friend, and then—Anne was so pretty, and so smart, and such a good dancer—he inwardly cursed his stupidity, and they drove on in silence.

The "ball" had not been in progress half an hour before his worst fears were realized. At first everything went well. The town hall in Hamstead was looking its best, decorated with festoons of colored crêpe paper, the electric-light globes hanging from the pressed-steel ceiling shielded with large crêpe paper flowers; big bunches of sweet-peas had been placed on the window sills, and on the table where the pressed-glass punch-bowl filled with grape-juice-lemonade and surrounded with paper cups was standing. The Wallacetown Band was grouped about the square piano near the stage, opposite the lemonade table, and was already beginning to "tune up" as they entered. George surveyed the scene with satisfaction. He had paid for their tickets, fifty cents apiece, while Anne withdrew to leave her knitted shawl in the dressing-room, and exchange a few joyous, whispered confidences with her best friend, Mabel Buck, who was waiting for her there; when she returned, he sat down beside her, to scrawl his initials at frequent intervals over her "program" with the small tasseled pencil attached

38

to it. The first and last dances were his by unwritten law, of course, because he was her escort; but he wanted to secure as many as possible in between these before the Hamstead fellows, who had come to know her when she was going there to High School, butted in. He had to hurry. David Noble and Austin Gray were already crossing the floor in their direction, and others would follow close upon their heels.

"Don't take too many," whispered Anne, who was watching developments quite as carefully as he was, but with other ends in view, "you don't want to make the whole town think we're engaged."

"Why, of course I do! Everyone knows we're keeping company! Now, Anne—"

"If you say another word about it tonight, I won't dance with you *at all*— Hello, Austin, hello, David, I'm awfully glad to see you.—Yes, I've got most of them free. George, do give me back that program. Goodness, you've written your name all over it. Have you an eraser?"

"No," said George doggedly, not deigning so much as a nod towards the intruders.

"Then I'll have to get another program."

"I've an extra one," cheerfully volunteered Austin's younger brother, Thomas, who had joined the group. "That's right, let's start all over again. I want the Schottish, Anne, there's no one dances it so good as you. Both numbers that are schottishes, one before the intermission and one afterwards. And the Portland Fancy. And the second waltz— Hello, Roy."

"Hello yourself. Hello, Anne."

"Oh, Roy, I'm ever so glad to see you! It's ages since you've been down."

"I know. But I've been awfully busy. Say, what have you got for a feller?"

"There doesn't seem to be much left but a 'Paul Jones.' "

"Shucks! You'll get whistled away from me in about two seconds! Well, I'll take that, and how about the first extra?"

"Fine."

"I've got a friend here, I want him to meet you."

39

"I'd love to."

"I'll get him right away—"

But the Wallacetown Band had begun to play the strains of the opening waltz. Even Anne's independence of spirit did not permit her to question George's right to that, without an instant's delay. She rose, shaking down her skirts, and thrusting her program into her sash, slipped into his arms. But she smiled back at the deserted group over her shoulder. She was perfectly satisfied. Roy, she knew, would not forget.

CHAPTER III

THE second dance was the "Paul Jones," and Roy came promptly to Anne's side as soon as the music for it began. Roy was not especially popular, either in Hamstead or in Wallacetown, where he was well known and to West Hamstead—"out back"—he never went, so, by repute, he was not popular there, but branded as "stuck up." He had gone to Harvard, and had graduated from the Law School there as well as completing his academic course with considerable success. He had spent a summer in Europe, and part of a winter in California. He was an only child, and had inherited a comfortable fortune from his father, a prosperous hardware dealer, who had been immensely proud of him, and had wanted him to have "advantages." It was owing to his father's death that he had returned to Wallacetown, and settled there to practice, in order that his mother, who was too old to be uprooted from her native element, need not be left alone. He was a good son, and a good citizen, and he was rapidly proving himself to be a good lawyer. But he was insignificant-looking, "pindling" the neighbors had always called him—slightly built and anemic, his glasses, shielding his near-sighted eyes, always hanging half way down over his nose. He lisped a little. Anne liked him, because he lent her books, and talked with her about the glimpses of the great world which he had had. And he liked Anne, recognizing her beauty and brains and spirit. But she did not stir his senses, and he felt himself slightly above her, though he was careful—more careful than he was toward many other persons—not to let her see this. The Chamberlains were a "shiftless lot" and the thrifty Griffins looked down upon all such. It did not occur to them that good could come out of Nazareth.

It was known in the village that Roy had made fashionable friends while he was away at college, but they seldom visited him, largely—though this was not known—because he seldom invited them. When they did come, it was only for a night or two, and he generally took them "up to the mountains" on a driving trip, so Wallacetown saw nothing of them. He lived quietly along from year to year, alone with his mother, who did all the housework, exquisitely and precisely. His law-office was in the ell of their house; by means of this arrangement Mrs. Griffin could always be sure that it was in perfect order, and that the clients were respectable.

Into this well-ordered household, Neal Conrad burst without warning. He was "motoring through" to see some wealthy clients of his own, who were spending the summer in the mountains, and "simply had to see good old Roy." The terrified horses who skitted wildly to one side of the dusty road at his approach were not more taken aback by his sudden appearance than were the Griffins. But when they recovered from the first shock of his unheralded arrival, and the further shock of the discovery that he intended to spend several days with them, they accepted his presence with a mild joy and a satisfaction that was by no means mild. Neal "had a way with him," and he "was making a name for himself." This important combination was difficult to resist; after he had gone, it would be agreeable to refer to him, casually but frequently, in conversation with the neighbors.

Roy had meant to tell Anne something about his guest as they twirled about together; but the whistle blew for the forming of the ring before they had had time to exchange a dozen words, and they immediately lost sight of each other in the maze of the "grand right and left." When the whistle blew for the second time, Anne found herself facing a stranger; sensed, instinctively, that it must be *the* stranger; and was caught up swiftly and swung into a quick-step without the exchange of a word.

It was only a minute, of course, before the man spoke

to her. But in that minute she became crowdingly conscious of a number of strange sensations. He was so startlingly different from any of the men she knew. His haircut was different, and his collar, and his tie, the shape of his blue serge coat, the texture of his spotless white trousers. He had a square jaw and square shoulders; and he held her so easily, yet so firmly—so closely. He did not seem in the least concerned because they had never met, or at a loss to know how to talk to her.

"What fun this kind of a dance is! Gets everyone acquainted, the very first thing—I'm Neal Conrad, a friend of Roy Griffin's—I'm visiting him."

"I—I thought you must be Neal Conrad."

"So you'd heard about me in Hamstead? Well, I *must* be getting famous!" They laughed together, and Neal's firm hold became still a little closer as he turned her around.

"I've known Roy a long time. He promised to introduce you to me."

"Well, I should hope so! I'd be terribly disappointed if he didn't."

"But there wasn't time before the party began," Anne went on, completing her sentence as she had intended before this astonishing person interrupted her.

"We must make up for lost time now then—darn it! There goes that whistle!"

"You said this kind of a dance was great fun!" exclaimed Anne, laughing again.

"Well, I've changed my mind. It's a darned poor kind of a dance. We were just getting nicely started—but I'll see you later."

The grand right and left had already begun again. They took their places in it tardily, and Anne, at least, self-consciously. It was accounted nothing short of a crime to hold it up, and she knew it. George, as she approached him, showed a face as black as a thunder-cloud. But her own conscience ceased to trouble her when she saw that he was guilty of trying to cheat, by going rapidly until he reached her, and then signaling for the whistle. She quickened her own pace, and sped by him without a glance. When the

43

"Paul Jones" finally ended, she was dancing with David Noble. She admitted that she was thirsty and turned with him to the lemonade table.

Neal Conrad meanwhile had sought out his host without delay, and taken him impatiently aside.

"Who's that girl I danced with the first time the whistle blew? I didn't even have time to get her name."

"How should I know? I wasn't watching you."

"Well, she said she'd known you a long time and that you had promised to present me. I wish you'd hurry up and do it."

"I've known all the girls here a long time, and I've promised all of them that I'd introduce you to them. You're THE EVENT of the evening."

"This girl," continued Neal, not in the least discouraged, "had on an awful pink dress trimmed with black velvet bows, and she'd been using cheap perfumery. But she danced like a featherweight angel, and she was a raving, tearing beauty. You don't often see a blonde with any pep, but she had it. Now, do you know whom I mean?"

"I've known whom you meant all along," lisped Roy, enjoying his little joke. "It's Anne Chamberlain. She's over there by the table now, drinking lemonade with David Noble."

"Come on," said Neal briefly.

The necessary formalities consumed very little time. At the end of them, declining David's invitation to join in their refreshment, Neal asked to see Anne's program.

"I'm awfully sorry. It's all filled."

"Nonsense!"

"It is, really," she said, blushing. "Ask David."

"Anne's program is always filled," her partner corroborated.

"But I wish it wasn't," she added, blushing more deeply still.

There was not the slightest doubt of her sincerity. Neal regarded her with amusement.

"What shall we do about it?" he asked.

"I don't know."

"Well, I do. I'm going to ask the band to add two more extras. And they'll both be mine. Don't forget."

"I shan't," said Anne ecstatically. "But do you think the band will be willing to play them?"

"I think so. In fact, I'm perfectly sure of it. Then—what do you usually do during the intermission?"

"Why—I wait for it to be over."

"Of course. But where?"

"Right here," she replied with growing bewilderment.

"The worst place you could think of. Why don't you come and sit it out with me in my motor?"

"Where?"

"In my motor. The horseless carriage, you know."

Anne hesitated. Such a suggestion had certainly never been made in Hamstead before, because it was the first time that anyone had stopped there with a horseless carriage. Therefore she had no precedent for either accepting or declining the invitation. But she knew perfectly well that local etiquette demanded she should refuse.

"Fine," said Neal heartily, quite as if she had given him a swiftly affirmative answer. "I'll come for you. Now I must go and speak to the band."

The first of the extras, which, without the slightest apparent difficulty, he succeeded in persuading the band to interpolate, came just before the intermission. It was a waltz—"The Beautiful Blue Danube." Anne had never heard it before, and when she asked Neal its name, he looked at her again with unconcealed amusement as he told her. It was then that she first noticed his eyes—gray-brown, almost yellow in certain lights, flecked with black, merry and warm and flashing, and at the same time oddly penetrating.

"It was written by quite a famous Austrian composer—Strauss. The best thing he ever did. Listen to it, don't talk, and *dance* it. If you've never waltzed to it before, you don't know what dancing can be."

She had never known before what dancing could be! That was true enough, whatever the music was, far truer than he guessed. Or did he guess? She hoped he did not—feared he did—then longed to tell him so herself. But she

45

was speechless. A silence no less insidious than the sensuous strain of the singing melody bound her. She could not break it, not even when, at the last lingering bars, his encircling arm tightened for an instant and then relaxed its hold, and she felt his fingers on her bare elbow, guiding her lightly.

"Out this way. To the left, under those maple trees. Ought you to have brought a wrap?"

"No."

"Let me help you. The seat is rather high."

(What was the magic in those strong, white hands, so different from any hands that had ever touched her before?)

"Do you mind if I smoke?"

"No."

"Perhaps you'll join me?"

"Oh, no!"

"That wasn't fair. I knew you wouldn't. I only wanted to hear you say it."

"Why?"

"I don't know. But I like your voice. Where did you learn to use it so well?"

"I never learned at all. I've just kept trying— I've thought about it, I mean, and practiced by myself. And I love beautiful English. But I've never heard much."

"Where did you go to school?"

"In West Hamstead, at the district school until I was old enough to go to High School. I teach the district school myself now."

"And you went to High School—"

"Here in Hamstead. I lived with Mummer's Aunt Sarah. She was an old lady, a cripple. She was awfully good to me. She let me come and live with her and work for my board and go to school. If she hadn't I'd have had to go out as hired help when I was thirteen."

"Are—are your parents dead?"

"Oh, no. But they've never seemed to prosper. Pupper's had hard luck always, and Mummer isn't strong." Anne hesitated a moment, and then continued, in a burst of confidence, "I'm afraid you won't say anything about loving to

46

hear me talk again, after hearing me call them Mummer and Pupper. But I did when I was a little girl, and when I learned that I ought to say Mamma and Papa, they wouldn't let me change. They thought I was trying to put on airs. I guess Roy Griffin is the only person around here who calls his mother 'Mamma.' "

"Did you think of 'Father' and 'Mother'?"

"Yes—but they didn't like that either."

"I see—so you've never been away from Hamstead?"

"Well, of course I go to Wallacetown. On errands. And once in a while to a show. And I've been down the valley as far as the state line once. That's the only time I was ever on a train."

"Wouldn't you like to go further away than that?"

"Wouldn't I like to? What do you suppose?"

"Well, I suppose you would. So why don't you? Why don't you let me come and take you for a nice long drive up through the mountains in my automobile?"

Anne was speechless. It was impossible—and yet it had happened. For the first time in nearly an hour, she remembered the existence of George. And only because it would be such a satisfaction to tell him that his jeering prediction had come true. Then her heart smote her. George would be hurt, terribly hurt, by the mere knowledge that the invitation had been extended. If she accepted it, he would be stricken.

"I could come for you right after breakfast," Neal went on, "then we could stop in Wallacetown and pick up Mrs. Griffin and Roy. We could have lunch at some hotel. We could go a long way in a day, you've no idea. Then I'd bring you back in the evening."

"Oh, I can't, I can't!"

Neal flung away his cigarette, and looked at her curiously in the moonlight. There was real anguish in her voice.

"Well, don't take it that way, even if you can't. But why can't you?"

"You have no idea how much work there is for me to do at home. Mummer didn't like it tonight because I came away without starting the beans for canning. And there's extra washing to do this week."

"We could go on Sunday."

"On Sunday?"

"Yes, why not?"

"I don't believe you understand our ways. We never go anywhere on Sunday."

"Well, couldn't you, for once?"

"No—even if I thought it was right, I have to play the organ in church and teach my Sunday-school class, and—"

"Wouldn't somebody else do that for you, just once?"

"No one ever has."

"That's no sign no one ever would. You might ask."

She tried to shake herself free from the lure of his suggestion.

"I—George wouldn't like it at all if I did."

"Who is George?"

"George Hildreth. He lives on the next farm to ours."

"I see. Are you engaged to him?"

"No, but—"

"But he wants you to be?"

"Yes. I've known him for years. He brought me here tonight."

"Three cheers for George!" said Neal heartily. "I don't believe you really intend to marry him, though, do you?"

"No, but—"

"Then wouldn't it be a real kindness, in the end, to let him find that out right away?"

"Perhaps, but—"

"Do you know how many times you've said 'but' to me tonight."

"No, but—"

They both laughed. It seemed, somehow, very easy for Anne to laugh with Neal Conrad. And in the course of her laugh she recovered herself somewhat.

"I may as well tell you. I couldn't possibly go with you to one of those big hotels. I haven't anything to wear."

She was afraid, then, that he was going to laugh at her instead of with her. But he did nothing of the sort. He regarded her with less amusement than before, and something very like tenderness.

"You don't need to dress up, you know. Haven't you a simple little serge suit of some sort? It's cool, motoring."

"No."

"And you couldn't get one?"

"No, I couldn't afford to buy one. And anyway, I wouldn't know what to buy. I wouldn't know what was suitable."

Neal saw that he was facing real heartbreak, frankly confessed. He veered away from it with consummate tact.

"Well, we could take a picnic lunch and eat it by the roadside. Then you could wear anything you happen to have. What you'd wear to church, as long as we're going on a Sunday. How would that do?"

"I don't believe it would do at all."

"Why not?"

"It just wouldn't."

A scraping and booming sound began to float through the open windows of the town hall. Clearly, the band was preparing to recommence its ministrations. Neal's time was growing short. He leaned over, and took Anne's hand, which somehow she could not seem to withdraw, and spoke to her very earnestly.

"Look here—you're not refusing because you think I'm trying to be fresh, asking you to do this when I'd never met you before?"

"N-o-o."

"For I'm not. If you'd rather, we won't say anything more about the ride until I've called on you several times, and all that. This is Thursday. I could come twice before Sunday, anyway. Tomorrow evening and Saturday evening. You're willing I should come to call, aren't you?"

"Y-e-e-s."

"The only trouble is, I can only stay here a few days. I'm on my vacation, but it's got to be a pretty short one. I'm a lawyer, you know, in Hinsboro. Roy and I were classmates in college, and through the law-school. We roomed together one year. He'll tell you, or your family, anything you'd like to know about me. I'm doing pretty

49

well—quite well. But this is the first vacation I've ever taken, and I can't afford to leave my office too long now. I mustn't take any chances. I've worked too hard, building up my practice, to let it slide. You see that, don't you?"

"Yes."

"And before I go away, I'd like to see something of you —a good deal of you."

Anne's heart had bounded from her fluttering breast to her throat. She could not answer him. Inside the hall, the leader of the band was beginning to call the numbers of the Portland Fancy. Thomas Gray would be hunting for her, and George—

"Won't you please say you'll take that drive?"

It was no use. She could not struggle against his insistence. She could not struggle against her own longing. Somehow she found her voice.

"All right," she said breathlessly. It was barely more than a whisper, but Neal, hearing it, knew that she would not change her mind. "Yes, I'll go."

CHAPTER IV

THE motoring party took place, not without violent opposition from more quarters than one.

In the first place, neither Mrs. Griffin nor Roy was in the least enthusiastic about it. Neal broached the subject to his friend on the way home from the dance, and Roy objected to it with more vigor than Neal would have supposed him capable of displaying in regard to any subject.

"You asked Anne Chamberlain to go up to the mountains with you! Good Heavens, Neal, you don't know anything about the girl at all!"

"Well, suppose you tell me something."

"She comes from one of the most worthless families in the whole town."

"Well, she's come a long way then. You don't call *her* worthless, do you?"

"No, I rather like Anne."

"Good! I like her very much; and she's darned attractive."

"You must have seen plenty of good-looking girls."

"I have. And plenty of bright girls. And plenty of girls with lots of go to them. But I never saw one that combined all those qualities so thoroughly in one and the same person. I got her to tell me a little about herself. She said her father had had hard luck, and her mother wasn't strong."

"Hard luck! the kind of hard luck that comes from never doing any hard work! His farm is going to rack and ruin, it's mortgaged, and he's head over heels in debt besides. His barns have never been painted, and it must be twenty years since his house has. As for Anne's mother

51

being delicate—well, she weighs about three hundred and fifty pounds, and she may have heart disease or kidney trouble. I shouldn't be at all surprised. If Anne hadn't worked her fingers to the bone and taught school besides these last two years, I don't know how they'd have lived. There are two little brothers that have to be fed and covered—you couldn't call them clothed."

"And you think a girl with that much spunk isn't worth knowing?"

Roy stared at his friend with growing astonishment. Neal had not only been swiftly hit. He had been hit hard.

"I didn't say that she wasn't worth knowing. But—why, she doesn't even know how to dress!"

"She knows that she doesn't know. And that being the case, she'll learn. Give her time. She can't be much over twenty."

"She isn't quite that."

"Then you just wait and see what she'll look like by the time she's thirty! You don't object if I at least *ask* your mother to go with us?"

"You can ask her. But I know she'll refuse."

"Surely she wouldn't expect me to insult the girl by inviting her to go off on an all-day trip with me without a chaperon!"

"Good Lord, Neal! You don't need to invite her at all."

"But I have. And she's accepted."

"Then you both ought to be willing to take the consequences."

"Look here, Roy, I thought you were a friend of mine. You're not acting much like one."

Roy felt a pang of contrition. He was a gentle creature.

"I'm sorry, Neal. I shouldn't have spoken as I did. Anne's a nice girl. Everyone admits that. I'd be as sorry as anyone to see her get into trouble."

"It's inconceivable that she should get into trouble," said Neal icily.

"Yes, of course. What I meant was—go ahead and ask Mother. I'll say what I can to her, too."

"Thank you," said Neal, still coldly.

Because of his repentant spirit, Roy said even more to

his mother than he had intended. But in spite of this intercession, Neal found her adamant when he first approached her.

"I couldn't think of it, Neal. It would make talk, going on a Sunday."

"It's the only day the poor girl *can* go. She works like a dog all the rest of the time."

"And I don't know her at all. It wouldn't seem natural starting off that way with a stranger."

"Why, I should think you'd like to get acquainted with her. She and Roy are such good friends."

Roy's mother looked at her guest for a moment with bewilderment, and then with growing terror. What was he suggesting? That her precious child, the only companion of her declining years—*Roy*—and one of *those Chamberlains!* It was unthinkable!

"I'm trying to cut him out. I thought perhaps you wouldn't mind. But of course—"

Neal went into his bedroom and shut the door carefully behind him. He stood looking at the neat bed with its starched, frilled, pillow-shams and stiff white spread, at the picture of the funeral wreath hanging above it, and the woven dog with the blue ribbon around its neck on the rug near by, and laughed. All is fair in love and war. He knew that he had won. When he emerged, Mrs. Griffin accosted him, and asked what he would like to take along for a lunch. She could make a veal-loaf, and she was quite a hand at an angel cake.

Anne, meanwhile, was having difficulties, too. She decided that it would be wiser to take the bull by the horns, and tell George about the invitation at once. They were no sooner settled in the rubber-tired buggy on their way back over the hills than she broached the subject.

"George," she said, "do you remember what you said to me on the way in? About Neal Conrad asking me to go out with him in his horseless carriage? Well, he has."

George gasped and then sputtered.

"The fresh city guy! I hope you give him all that wuz comin' to him."

"I told him I'd be pleased to go. You suggested it your-self! Why should I think you'd mind, after that?"

"You knew I was only jokin'."

"You weren't joking. You were jeering. Trying to get even with me because I'd said you were behind the times."

"Are you goin' just to get even with me?"

It would have been welcome tidings, she knew, if she had said she was. But she was too honest.

"Partly—a little. But mostly because I want to. I've never been to the mountains."

"I'll take you to the mountains."

"You've had plenty of chances to ask me, and you never did. It's too late now."

"Are you goin' off all alone with this feller?"

"Of course not. Mrs. Griffin and Roy are going too."

"Wal, you went outside an' set with him quite a spell, I noticed. Did he kiss you?"

"Of course not. He's a gentleman."

"He's a man," said George darkly.

"I think you're awfully vulgar and—and insulting. I don't believe he even thought of such a thing."

"You know darned well he did."

"Well, then, it's all the more credit to him because he didn't do it! It's more than you would have done, with the same chance!"

"You ain't comparin' me an' him, are you?"

"I am not. There's no comparison possible."

They were actually quarreling. The evening on which George had counted so much was turning out worse than a failure.

"I think you've acted real mean," he mumbled.

"I don't care if you do. If you say another word, finding fault, I'll jump out of this buggy and *walk* home!"

She meant what she said, and George knew it. There was nothing to do but relapse into sullen silence. Not an-other word was spoken during the six-mile drive. They even parted without saying good-night.

It was after two when Anne slipped into bed. An hour later before she fell asleep. But she was up again at five, and by seven the "extra wash" was on the line, and she had started picking the beans. While they were cooking, she ironed. And when the dinner dishes were dried and stacked away, she asked her father if she might take the team and drive to Wallacetown.

"Land sakes, Anne, can't you never set still? I sh'd think you'd be glad to lay down an' take a nap, after bein' out all night, ef you've done up all the work yer ma wanted you sh'd do."

"I need to do some errands."

"I was kinder thinkin' of mowin' the medder this afternoon."

"Oh, Pupper, you *know* you weren't! It's no kind of a hay-day!"

"I s'pose you think you know more 'bout farmin' than I do. That's just like a woman—wal, go ahead, ef yer so set on it."

She escaped before he could change his mind, without even waiting to put on a fresh dress. She could only pray that neither the Griffins nor Neal Conrad would see her in Wallacetown. It was half-past one already, and it would take her until nearly three to reach Wallacetown. The bank closed at that hour, and the bank was her first objective. She reached it barely in time, and presented herself at the cashier's window.

"I want to draw some money out of my savings-bank account," she said breathlessly.

The cashier, who had known her a long time, looked at her dumbfounded.

"You don't mean to say you're going to cut into that money your Aunt Sarah left you?" he asked without stirring.

"That's exactly what I mean. I want fifty dollars. If I don't spend it all, I'll bring part of it back."

"Why, Anne Chamberlain, you don't mean to tell me that you're going to take it out and *spend* it! When you haven't but three hundred altogether, counting interest."

"Oh, Tad, please hurry!"

Still protesting, he counted the notes into her hand— five crisp, new bills. She had never seen so much money, at once, in all her life before. She tucked it into her shabby little purse, thrilling at the crackling sound which it made. Then she sped down the street to Mr. Goldenburg's store, stopping to look into the window as she reached it. The display consisted mostly of hamburg edging and seersucker, which was being sold by the yard at a reduction. But back of these attractive wares, three headless "dummies" stood, draped with white muslin dresses, and above them ran the legend, "Special Bargain Sale. Marked down to $9.98."

A white muslin dress had not been included in her calculations. But, as she looked at these, she suddenly saw herself clad in one, when Neal came to call that evening and the next—if he really did come. It was the kind of thing a girl ought to wear, under such circumstances, she saw instinctively, sheer and snowy; that the material was coarse, and the lace trimming coarser, did not matter. The crude color of her pink dress, the heaviness of the black bows that adorned it, seemed hopelessly hideous to her all at once. If she bought a white muslin dress, it would mean buying white shoes and stockings, too, and the right kind of a slip, but she felt too reckless to care—if necessary, she could draw out more money. She unlatched the shopdoor, and walked in. By good luck, she encountered the proprietor himself, a kindly Jew who had been in Wallacetown only a few years, and who had prospered there.

"Vel, vel, if it ain't my liddle frent Anne Chamberlain! Vat can I do for you, my dear?"

"Oh, Mr. Goldenburg, I want to buy such a lot of things! I've just drawn fifty dollars out of the bank, and I'm afraid it isn't enough. If I run short, will you trust me until I can go back and draw some more? The bank's closed for the day now."

"Vel, now, I tink I could. But you shouldn't take out your money, yust to spend, like this. You goin' to get married, *hein?* To dat flat-faced poy, George Hildreth?"

"No—it isn't like that at all." She hesitated, blushed, and finally decided to confide in the merchant. "Have—have you met Roy Griffin's friend, Neal Conrad?"

"I seen him. I know apout him. Dat's a smart young man."

56

"I met him at the dance in Hamstead last night. He—he invited me to go to the mountains with him and Roy and Mrs. Griffin in his horseless carriage. And—he said he might call tonight."

"Oh, is dat so? Vel, dat's anoder story, Anne. I'm real pleased to hear it. Don't you worry apoud your liddle savinks. You puy yust vad you need, and ven you pegin to teach school again digs fall, you pay me pack a liddle at a time, *hein?* I dake the fifdy dollars now an' the rest lader on."

"Mr. Goldenburg, you're as kind as—"

"Now, now—vat vas you tinkin' of virst?"

"A suit. A—a 'simple little serge suit,'" quoted Anne, "have you anything like that?"

"Of course I haf. Dark blue. Dat's vat you vant. Dvendy-fife dollars." He paused. "Id's geddin' on late in de summer. Ve'll say dvendy. An' a vide shirt-vaist to go mit-maype doo, so you could keeb nice an' clean. An' den you'll valk down to Miss Lynn's and puy vun liddle blue an' vide hat."

"Yes," breathed Anne, "that's it. But I must have some shoes to go with it from you first."

"Sure. Nice dan oxfords. An' silk stockings de same color. An' gloves."

"And—and could I try on one of those white dresses at the same time?"

An hour later, she was on her way home again, her new possessions tucked securely under the seat of the rickety buggy. She had spent seventy-five dollars. But she did not begrudge a cent of it. She was deliciously happy.

The family were already at supper when she slammed the kitchen door behind her. "Wal, here ye be at last," her mother said heavily, looking up from the cold pork and maple syrup she was eating. "I sh'd think you might have ben here to help me git supper."

"I left everything all ready."

"Ain't yer goin' ter set down?"

"No, I'm not hungry. I'm going in to dust the parlor, and then I'm going to dress."

"George must be comin' over," chortled Mr. Chamberlain, pouring his tea into his saucer, "I shouldn't be a mite surprised ef they wuz t' settle everything up ter-night."

Anne had decided that it would be wiser to say nothing about her new acquaintance until his arrival was imminent. There would not be much time, then, for explanations. Unfortunately, however, she ran too close to the wind. The disorder in the parlor was worse than she had expected. She had had no time to go in there that morning, and she had counted overmuch on its being kept sacred from intrusion, according to New England tradition. Aunt Sarah's haircloth set, her wax flowers under glass, her "Rogers group" and her wool carpet were all in there; so were the crayon portraits of Mr. and Mrs. Chamberlain, taken at the time of their marriage, a kaleidoscope, and a set of views of the White Mountain to be viewed through a double magnifying-glass, on a small teetering stand. Unfortunately, nothing was sacred to Sam and Sol, and their mother was too indolent to interfere with them. They had spent the showery afternoon looking at the kaleidoscope and the views, and chasing each other around the furniture. The pictures hung awry from jostling; the tidies on the backs of the chairs were disarranged; the photographs were scattered about; the carpet was tracked with mud; it took Anne some moments, in spite of the speed with which she worked, to put things to rights. She was not half dressed when she heard the chugging sound of the horseless carriage, and, from her window, saw it come to a noisy and violent stop in front of the house. There was nothing to do but leave the situation for Neal to manage, while she hurried as fast as she could into the new muslin dress. After all, he was probably entirely capable of managing it.

She did not overestimate his resourcefulness. Hat in hand, he advanced, smiling pleasantly, towards the porch where, as usual, the entire family, with the exception of Anne, was gathered.

"Good evening," he said with the utmost friendliness. "This is Mr. Chamberlain's house, isn't it? Is this Mr. Chamberlain? And Mrs. Chamberlain? And Sol and

Sam?" He shook hands heartily all around. "I'm Neal Conrad, of Hinsboro. I'm visiting Roy Griffin in Wallace-town, and I had the pleasure of meeting Miss Chamberlain at the dance in Hamstead last night. So I ventured to come and call."

His cordiality and composure were contagious. Mr. and Mrs. Chamberlain spoke with one breath.

"Pleased ter meet yer. Won't yer sit down an' make yer-self ter home?"

"Thanks, I'd be glad to—unless—unless the boys would like to come out and take a little spin with me first?"

Sol and Sam sprang to their feet simultaneously.

"Say, Pupper, kin we? Oh, Mummer, let us!"

"It's perfectly safe, I assure you. Perhaps you'll *all* come?"

Mr. and Mrs. Chamberlain exchanged glances, and Mr. Chamberlain sighed heavily. With obvious disappointment, her husband spoke for both.

"Thanks kindly. I guess me an' Mummer'll set here. We're kinder tired after a hard day's work, but the boys kin go, if they're a mind ter."

When, fifteen minutes later, the horseless carriage dashed into the yard again, discharging its owner and his guests, the latter beaming, their countenances smeared with chocolate, Anne was just coming out of the front door. It was so perfectly timed, that the hand of the Lord seemed to be in it. Perhaps it was. For something told Anne, who of course had overheard everything, to wait in her room after she finished dressing, until Neal's return. He advanced towards them all, without appearing to single her out.

"Well, we had a fine little ride—the first of many, I hope— Good evening, Miss Chamberlain, it's nice to see you again— I'll accept your invitation to sit down now, sir, if I may."

"It's cooler inside," said Anne.

"Oh, I don't mind the heat."

Apparently Neal had no intention of seeking the seclu-sion of the parlor. He did not seem in the least anxious to see her alone. Anne was puzzled and a little hurt. The conversation was general. Neal talked a good deal himself, to be sure, but he made the others talk, too. Even Mrs. Chamberlain stirred from her apathy to tell him about Aunt Sarah's last illness, while Mr. Chamberlain and the boys became enthusiastically loquacious. At the end of an hour, when Neal rose to go, they all urged him to stay a little longer.

"I'm awfully sorry, but I promised Mrs. Griffin I'd get back early. She's nervous about this car of mine. Imagines I've run over the side of one of your mountains if I'm gone long. However, I'll come again, if I may."

"Wal, thet's what I call a nice feller," remarked Mr. Chamberlain, as their guest, waving one hand high above his head, disappeared in a cloud of smelly dust. "Lots of good horse sense, and real smart an' pleasant, too. Why didn't ye tell us about him, Nan?"

"I didn't have time," said Anne, chokingly. Then, without another word, she dashed upstairs, and flung herself, still dressed, on her bed, crushing her fresh new finery. She was terribly tired, bitterly disappointed. Neal hadn't seen the parlor, the one presentable place she had in which to receive him, and which she had worked so hard to make tidy. He hadn't noticed the clothes on which she had squandered her savings. He hadn't said a word about their trip, or even made a definite reference to coming the next evening. Nothing had gone right. She buried her head in her limp and lumpy pillow, and stifled her sobs. And so she fell asleep.

She awoke rested, and consequently hopeful. Probably he would come again, and this time everything would be all right. She ironed out her dress, put sweet peas in the parlor, baked and frosted an extra cake, made lemonade. Again the fates were against her. Neal appeared, as she had hoped, and was cordially welcomed—by Mr. and Mrs. Chamberlain, Sol and Sam. But George had arrived before him, and had taken possession of the parlor and of Anne.

She escaped, of course, long enough to greet Neal. But for a second time, he declined her invitation to come in.

"Mr. Hildreth would never forgive me," he said laughingly, "and I'm sure the boys want another ride. This time

I shan't take no for an answer from your father and mother, either. Do come, Mrs. Chamberlain."

Anne's mother, who had been torn between her fear that he might not renew his invitation, and her hope that he would, rose with assumed reluctance.

"Wal, ef yer so dead set on it," she puffed, "mebbe I might as well. Jest a short ways. An' don't drive too fast. It would put me all of a tremble ef ye should."

They were gone. Anne fed George with the lemonade and cake. He devoured both with relish, and she sat dumbly beside him, only shaking her head when he urged her to join him, listening intently for the return of the motor.

At last it came. Everyone was laughing, and Neal was coming up the scrubby walk with a small boy hanging on either hand. At the rickety gate he paused. Anne could see and hear him plainly.

"No, I don't believe I better come in," he was saying. "You know what I told you about Mrs. Griffin's nerves. I don't like to disturb her. But I've been wondering— She and Roy and I have decided to take a little ride through the mountains tomorrow, and I thought possibly you'd let your daughter come with us. We'd take good care of her. You've seen for yourselves that there really isn't anything to be afraid of in a horseless carriage. Would you have any objections?"

Again Mr. and Mrs. Chamberlain exchanged glances. "Why, no," said Mr. Chamberlain at length, when he thought he had understood his signals correctly, "I dunno's I would. I think 'twould be a real pleasant change for her. Don't you, Mummer?"

"Wall, I dunno's I've any objection either, ef Anne would like ter."

"Suppose we ask her."

Sol and Sam, preceding him, burst screaming into the parlor, too excited to brook delay.

"Say, Nan, what ye think? Mr. Conrad wants ye should go to the mountings with him! To-morrer! Gee, but yer lucky. Say, Nan, bring us home a balsam, will ye?"

Suddenly Anne saw it all—the tact, the skill, the kindness with which Neal had managed everything. And she had doubted him— Oh, how stupid, how wicked she had been! She went towards him, blinded with contrition, with gratitude, with joy.

"I've just been asking Mr. and Mrs. Chamberlain," he said blandly, "whether they would have any objections to your going to the mountains with the Griffins and me to-morrow—provided, of course, that you would like to go. They've been kind enough to give their consent. Would it be convenient if I came for you about nine?"

"Yes," said Anne.

She could not, to save her life, have said another word. She stood still watching the others as they swarmed about him, while he cranked the car and climbed into the high seat. Then she went back—to the parlor and George. There was one piece of cake left, and a little lukewarm lemonade at the bottom of the pitcher, swimming above undissolved sugar and a few seeds.

"I guess I *am* a little hungry and thirsty after all," she said gayly, "I'm going to finish these myself, if you don't mind."

CHAPTER V

ANNE was waiting for Neal in the yard when he appeared, promptly at nine, the following morning. He insisted on going to the porch and chatting with the family for a few minutes; then they started off. At first he was entirely occupied with gear-shifts and brakes; but soon he turned to her gayly.

"This is fine! You don't know how pleased I am!"

"It's fine for *me*. You've been simply wonderful, arranging it all, and making it look so easy when it was really hard."

"Oh, that was nothing— Did you get someone to play the organ and teach the Sunday-school class?"

"Yes."

"I thought you would— Do you mind if I tell you how nice you look?"

"Of course I don't mind. Why do people always ask you if you mind when they have something pleasant to say, and remark, 'I think you ought to know' when they're going to tell you something perfectly horrid?"

"I don't know. But they do, don't they?" Neal laughed. "Well, then, 'perhaps you won't mind' if I tell you, too, how lovely you were these last two evenings. You look just like a white rose in that muslin dress."

"Oh, do you really think so? I'm awfully glad! I bought it Friday, in Wallacetown, from Mr. Goldenburg. And these clothes, too. Was this what you meant by 'a simple little serge suit'?"

"Exactly. And the hat is corking, too—I've been doing some shopping myself. I've bought two of those new bottles that keep things hot or cold, whichever you like. Have you seen one?"

"No, but I've read about them in advertisements."

"Well, today you'll see them in action. We're going to have hot coffee and iced tea. Mrs. Griffin has put up a wonderful lunch; and it's a perfect day. I should say we were having good luck all around."

"Well, I should say we *were.*"

The Griffins, armed with hampers, jars and wraps, were all ready to start when Neal and Anne reached Wallacetown; and Mrs. Griffin, taking in Anne's attractions with one swift glance while the introductions were going on, was not long in deciding that Roy must be rescued, at any cost. She insisting on sitting on the back seat with him, while Anne resumed her place beside Neal in front. And every time Roy leaned forward to speak to the girl, his mother called his attention to something by the roadside. Roy, thus besieged, soon abandoned all efforts at conversation; and Anne, apparently, forgot him entirely. Not once did she turn around, without being first addressed; for that matter, she did not talk much to Neal either. Her rapture at the sensation of swift motion, like imagined flying, her eager astonishment at the beauty of the scenery, her joy in being with Neal, were all too great for utterance. They reached the famous "gorges" in time to go through them before luncheon. Mrs. Griffin was sure the walk would be too much for her, and besides, she wanted to get things ready for their meal. So Roy dutifully remained behind to help her. Once or twice, hungrily, he took a stealthy glance at his watch, realizing that Anne and Neal were certainly not hurrying, that they must indeed have lost all track of time.—At last they reappeared, flushed and laughing. Anne had taken off her coat, and Neal was carrying it over his arm; the delicate skin of her neck and arms showed pink and soft through the sheer white of her shirt-waist; her hair was curling in moist tendrils around her face. Roy thought, miserably aware that it was now too late for the thought to do him any good, that he had never seen her look so pretty before—or else he had, stupidly never realized how pretty she was. She had brought back some little souvenirs—birch bark canoes, a balsam pillow, a red pennant, and was arguing that *she* ought to pay for them, that Neal simply mustn't spend so much for her; and Neal was insisting, teasingly, that this was his party.

Still contending, they sank down on the grass beside the Griffins. The contents of the magic bottles were tested and declared delicious; so were the veal loaf and the angel cake, and all the other goodies which Mrs. Griffin had cooked with such skill, and wrapped in paraffin paper with such exquisite care—stuffed eggs, chicken sandwiches, sugared doughnuts. At the end of the feast, Neal produced from a hiding-place in the car two large boxes of candy, one blue and one lavender, gayly festooned with ribbon; and while the ladies were opening these, with exclamations of surprise and delight, he lit a cigarette. Roy did not smoke; his mother did not approve of it.

After a lazy half-hour they removed all traces of their feast from the shady little nook, and Neal suggested that they should ride down to "the Lake" and row a little while.

"Oh, I'm terribly afraid of boats!" exclaimed Mrs. Griffin, shrinking back. "And Roy doesn't know how to row. I've always been afraid to have him learn, because he might drown. But you take Miss Chamberlain, Neal. We'll wait for you here. I might get a little nap."

The row took even longer than the walk, and it was late afternoon before they started on their way home; twilight when the Griffins were deposited at their front door, and Anne and Neal on their way back over the hills to West Hamstead. As it grew darker, the stars came out, softly and gently, and below them, in the river valley, the mist hung like a bridal veil. At the last mile, a great golden moon swung slowly into sight above the distant blue of the mountains. Neal brought the car to a stop, and spoke a little huskily.

"I've got to go away in the morning," he said, "I've stayed longer than I should already. Of course I'm coming back. You know that. But I don't want to say good night yet. Couldn't we take a little walk somewhere together before I leave you at your house?"

Anne hesitated. He laid his hand over hers, as he had done on the night of the dance.

"Please," he said as he had said then, but in a voice which shook a little this time. And again she found herself powerless to refuse.

"We could let down the bars and go through this pasture to the lane that runs out to the meadow back of our barn. No one will see us. And it's very quiet and lovely there."

"Yes. That's it."

He helped her out of the car and opened the bars. Together they passed into the cool greenness of the pasture, dotted with little pointed fir trees, shadowy with the feathery elms and maples that bordered it, drenched with the heavy evening dew of midsummer. A whippoorwill was singing, unseen; but except for this, the air was freighted with warm, pregnant silence, sweet with the scent of the August fragrance.

"I'm afraid you'll stumble and hurt yourself, it's so dark where the moonlight doesn't strike. May I put my arm around you?"

"Yes."

They were in the lane now, near the rosebush with its sharp thorns and falling petals. Was it possible that it was only four nights before, Anne asked herself, that she had stood in this same place, which now seemed so mystically lovely, in rage and rebellion? In rage and rebellion, while now . . . Neal could feel her young body, quivering with rapture, beneath his encircling arm.

"What is it, Anne? Tell me!"

"I was only thinking . . . I came here, the night of the dance in Hamstead, to pick some flowers to wear to the party. Mummer had taken the sweet-peas I was saving and put them on Aunt Sarah's grave. They were all I had."

"You poor child!"

"So Pupper suggested the rosebush. I got all hot and

66

dusty, hurrying, and then I pricked my fingers . . . there weren't enough roses anyway. George followed me down here, and asked me why I didn't mix them with some of those flowers growing in the meadow."

"I noticed them at the dance, of course."

"Do you know what they're called?"

"Certainly I do—Queen Anne's Lace . . . by Jove!"

How quickly he had sensed the symbolism which had eluded George entirely! In the moonlight, she could see the expression of his face as he turned from her to the field of stirring grass studded with the fragile white flowers on their slender stems, and back to her again—the tightening of his mouth, the softening of his eyes. She caught her breath.

"It grows where the soil is very poor. The farmers think it's just a weed—an awful pest."

"Because they can't see how beautiful it is. Anne— Anne—my darling!"

His arms had tightened about her like bands of steel. He bent and laid his face against her hair, then suddenly, with a little cry, his lips brushed across her cheek, seeking her mouth, and found it already upturned to the hard, hot kisses which he pressed down on it. They clung to each other, two clean, passionate young creatures, fused in the white flame of their first great desire . . .

Neal was the first to recover himself. He drew away from Anne gently, with a caress that he might have given to a child. Then he took her face between his two hands.

"Look at me, Anne."

"I am looking."

"I didn't mean that this should happen—not for a long time yet. Not because I didn't love you—"

"I know you love me—"

"But because I didn't want to hurt or even startle you—"

"You haven't. I love *you*. It would have killed me, not being sure."

She thought he was going to take her in his arms again, to kiss her until it hurt, as he had before. Instead, he knelt down in the long grass, and bowed his head.

"Anne," he said, so softly that she could hardly hear him, "Anne, you are a queen—a queen in disguise, a fairy changeling perhaps, but a queen just the same. Will you help me earn the lace for you to wear?"

CHAPTER VI

A LITTLE over a month later, Anne and Neal were married.

He did not allow their sudden betrothal to interfere with his plans. The following morning he started off in pursuit of his wealthy client. Four days later he returned, with the report of complete success in his venture.

"That meant five hundred dollars to me—to us—," he told Anne, "and we'll need it. You mustn't think of me as some kind of a fairy prince, even if you are a queen."

"I don't," said Anne, flushing.

"You do, too. You know you do. Bless you! But I'm not. I'd be willing to bet that George Hildreth's got twice as much salted away as I have, this very minute. Sure you don't want to change your mind?"

"Neal—I wish you wouldn't."

He saw that her love was so strange to her still, so sacred, that she could not jest about it.

"All right, dear, I won't. But we must talk over the practical side of things. Because I want to marry you right away."

"Yes. That's what I want, too."

"Anne, I wish you wouldn't," he mocked, lightly. "You have no idea how hard it is for me to behave when you speak to me like that. But we ought to straighten out a few important details first, as I said. . . . I've got a good practice, for a fellow my age, and it's growing. I'm earning a fair income. And I've saved something. Not an awful lot. I worked my way through college, and ran into debt, a little, while I was getting started. That's all cleaned up. We can begin clear, with something ahead and something be-

69

hind us. But we've got to begin small. I'm afraid you've been misled by the automobile. I got it second-hand from a man who owed me money and couldn't pay. And it's the best investment I ever made, since it brought me to you. I thought I'd try and rent a little place we could live in this winter, and we could look around together, after we were married, for something better. I'd like to buy or build a little house for our very own, right away. It's poor economy, in the long run, to pay rent."

"Yes. I see that."

"Shall I go ahead, as soon as I get back to Hinsboro, and see what I can find for temporary quarters then? Are you willing to leave that to me?"

"Of course I am. And I'll get ready, too. Clothes and linen. Of course I can't have much. But I've a little legacy from Aunt Sarah. I'd rather spend it on my trousseau than anything I can think of."

"Well, that's settled then. Now—where would you like to go for our honeymoon?"

"Anywhere, with you."

"What would you say to Washington?"

"Oh, Neal, how did you guess! I've longed and longed—"

"Well, so have I. So that's settled, too. And we won't stint on that trip, either. We'll have a good time.—I don't believe I've told you—I'm tremendously interested in politics. Even more than in law. I'm a member of the City Council in Hinsboro now. Perhaps some day I can go further."

"Oh, *Neal!* I'm sure you can."

"Anyone can be President, you know," he said teasingly.

"*You* could."

"Well, perhaps I can be mayor. But we'll have a look at the White House anyhow. Maybe it won't appeal to you, and that would settle it," he laughed. Then, changing the subject abruptly, "Another thing we mustn't economize on is your ring."

"Honestly, I don't need an engagement ring. I shouldn't mind a bit—"

70

"Nonsense. Let me hold your hand a while, so I can measure your finger."

Neal's second visit was even briefer than his first. But in the course of it he had a long talk with his prospective parents-in-law, whom he found stunned but acquiescent—and then insisted in announcing the engagement in the *Wallacetown Bugle*. Having thus burned all his bridges behind him, he departed to tell his own father and mother of his impending plunge into matrimony.

He had adroitly contrived to avoid much discussion of the Conrads with Anne. He knew, all too well, how bitterly they were bound to oppose the match, but he hoped, as far as possible, to keep this knowledge from her. Mrs. Conrad came from one of the oldest families in the country, and she never forgot it or allowed any one else to forget it; she belonged not only to the Daughters of the American Revolution but to the Colonial Dames; to the Episcopal Church and the Wednesday Sewing Circle. She subscribed to the *Atlantic Monthly* and the *Boston Transcript*. All humanity, to her, was divided into two classes—those who were "refined" and those who were not; the display of all human emotion was to her "disgusting"; she was fond of the words, "good breeding," "culture and tradition." She lamented the passing of the standards of the days of her youth, so infinitely superior to those of more recent times, and doubted whether any girls were "nice" any longer. Her husband's standards were much like her own, and his sense of self-importance quite equal to hers, though, like herself, he depended largely on the past to establish his claim to distinction. He had never made much headway in his profession as an architect. Both were distinguished-looking, in a lean, cold way, which helped to maintain the impression which they were anxious to create. They had very little money, but they contrived to keep up appearances in a way that was almost uncanny. No one outside the family guessed the bitter, biting economies that went on inside the spreading house on the most select street in town. Their elder son, Arthur, an unmarried clergyman, and their widowed daughter, Harriet, lived with them, as well as Neal. By pooling their resources, in this way, their income went much further than it otherwise would have done. Harriet had very pronounced views, all Neal's decision of character without his charm. She believed, long ahead of the times, in prohibition and woman's suffrage. She also believed in the depravity of the Latin races, and all members of the Roman Catholic Church, and in the infallibility of the Conrad family. Her husband had committed suicide by jumping from a sixth story window while they were on their honeymoon.

When Neal burst in upon his family, they were already gathered around the one reading lamp in their living-room after their evening meal—they always referred to it as "dinner," but since there had been no guests, as indeed there seldom were, it had in reality been a very frugal supper. He kissed his mother and sister dutifully, but without enthusiasm, and told them, immediately, of the fat fee which he had captured in the course of his vacation, and the promise of further revenue from the same source. Then he told the rest of his story.

"I knew you'd think that was good news. But I've got some that's better yet. I'm going to be married."

There was a moment of ominous, horrified silence. Then a simultaneous exclamation.

"Married! To whom?"

"A girl named Anne Chamberlain."

"I don't know any one by that name," said Mrs. Conrad, endeavoring to recover herself somewhat.

"You wouldn't. I met her while I was gone. She lives in a little place called West Hamstead."

"My son—are you really telling us this in earnest?"

"I certainly am."

The Conrads exchanged terrified glances.

"Then I must ask you to explain yourself."

Neal's worst enemy could hardly accuse him of a lack of eloquence, on any theme or on any occasion. And this time he outdid himself. The results, however, were even worse than he had feared.

"Do you expect us to admit this engagement if we are questioned?"

"Certainly. It's been announced in the *Wallacetown Bugle* already." He noticed his mother's shudder. "I shall see that it's in the *Hinsboro Times* tomorrow."

"And you expect us—your father and I, your brother and sister—to go to the wedding . . . to receive this—this —person."

"My *fiancée*. Very soon my wife. Of course."

"Perhaps you were thinking of bringing her here to live."

"I wouldn't be so cruel to her."

He had scored. His mother attempted to draw blood in her turn.

"Have you thought what the withdrawal of your contribution to the family expenses is going to mean to us in our old age?"

"Harriet and Arthur aren't so very aged. It wouldn't hurt either of them to get out and hustle a little, as I've had to do."

"Neal! do not degrade us—and yourself—with vulgarity! I suppose your language—and your conduct—are the result of your political associations. You should never have allowed yourself—a gentleman, by birth at least—to be drawn into them."

"Then why are you so proud of the fact that one of your great-great-grandfathers was a Colonial Governor? Politics are more decent now than they were then, by a long shot."

He got up suddenly, and stood with his hands on the back of his chair, facing them.

"Look here," he said abruptly, almost violently, "I've had a long drive, and I'm tired. I'm going to bed. But I'll tell you this much, and then we won't discuss the subject again. I'll continue my usual subscription to this household just as long as you're decent to Anne. Not a second longer. It may not be very aristocratic to bargain, but I notice that none of the rest of you seem to want to work, and I don't believe you want to go hungry. You better think it over."

There was no hint of this battle, however, or of his own victory, when he wrote to Anne. She took his letter out

73

into the pasture when her day's work was over, to read and reread, pressing it to her lips each time she did so.

"Dearest—darling—sweetheart—" it began.

"I can't find any name lovely enough and loving enough to tell you how I feel about you.

"I miss you so terribly that I'm doing everything I can to shorten our separation. I've found a little home for us. It's the upper story of a house belonging to a friend of mine—he's had it fixed up for a flat, to rent, with an entrance and stairway of its own. It's very small—just a living-room, bedroom, bathroom, and kitchen, but we could manage in that for this winter, couldn't we? It's sunny and clean and new; he and his mother have never used that part of the house—and there's a gas stove and a set tub in the kitchen. The furniture's rather awful—mission oak in the living-room and a brass bed, and so on, but I don't mind if you don't.

"I've been to a stationer's, and asked him to send you some samples of wedding-invitations. I thought perhaps it would be easier for me to attend to that than for you. Write me which you like best, and a list of your friends whom you want to invite, and I'll have the cards addressed and sent out from here.

"Do you think you can manage a church wedding? And is there a church parlor or something of the sort in which we could have a reception afterwards? Of course my family and some of my friends will want to come up, and I realize how little room there is in your house? But do just as you think best. I've asked Roy to be my best man. I think that's only fair, considering that he introduced us. Bless his heart! good old Roy! My brother Arthur would like to assist in the marriage ceremony, and I should like to have him, if that would be agreeable to your own minister and to you. And of course I want George Hildreth to be one of the ushers.

"I want you to have your ring to wear right away, so I'm going to forgo the joy of putting it on myself. It started to you by express this morning—a solitaire diamond in a Tiffany setting. I know my mother is sending

74

you something, too, with a letter welcoming you into the family.

"I wish I could kiss you tonight, over and over again, as I did that time down by the rosebush, and feel you in my arms. But I will before long. And meanwhile you know that I love you with all my heart and soul, and that I am counting the days that must go by before you are my wife.

"NEAL."

Anne wrote back:

"Dearest Neal: The ring came this morning, and fits perfectly. I put it on right away, and have it on now. Of course it's the most beautiful thing I ever saw in my life. I never dreamed that I should ever have anything like it, and of course I shouldn't have had it, if it hadn't been for you.

"Your mother's letter came too, and a lovely brooch which she said had belonged to your great grandmother, and which she had kept for your wife ever since you were a little boy. I put that on, too, though it looks strange with my percale dress. There is a big garnet in the center, then a row of pearls, then a row of turquoises, then an openwork design in gold. I suppose you've seen it. It's beautiful, too, but of course I like the ring best. I was very much surprised that your mother should give me a present. It was awfully kind of her.

"I've chosen the sample for a wedding-invitation that I like best, and I'm sending you a list of my friends' names. I shouldn't have known I ought to do this if you hadn't told me about it. There never has been a wedding in the little church here, but we can have ours there, if you wish. I'm afraid you'll be disappointed, for it's very bare and plain and small, but we'll do our best to make it as pretty as possible. Mr. Hains, our minister, would be pleased to have your brother Arthur take part in the ceremony.

"I think the little flat will be wonderful. I love mission furniture and brass beds.

"What do you think? Mr. and Mrs. Goldenburg have invited me to go to New York with them! Mr. Goldenburg takes a trip every year at this time to buy his fall stock, and he's going to help me make my money go a long way in getting my trousseau. I'm going to have a real wedding dress, and a veil, and orange blossoms. We're leaving Monday, so send your next letter to me at the Waldorf Astoria Hotel, New York City. I think we'll be gone a whole week. I simply can't believe it's true. Next to getting engaged to you, it's the most wonderful thing that ever happened to me.

"George feels terribly. He hardly looks at me when I meet him, and he won't speak to me at all. But Roy and his mother have been awfully kind. Mrs. Griffin has given me half a dozen teacups, and Roy has given me a set of Shakespeare in four volumes. I've put them on the parlor table where I can go and look at them often.

"I wish I could write letters like yours. Of course I can't. But just the same, you know how much I love you, and that I'm wishing all the same things that you are wishing, and counting the days, too.

"With a heartful of love,

"ANNE."

To Neal, the next few weeks represented a period of worrying over details, and surmounting difficulties. But to Anne, it was a month of enchantment. The drab, workaday world, was, after all, such a beautiful place, and the people in it so transcendently kind and generous. Her class at High School, and her Sunday-school class sent her wedding-presents—a silver pickle-fork, a cut glass "sugar and creamer"; Mabel Buck made her a set of crocheted mats; even George sent her a present—a huge lamp, hand painted in pink roses, on a gilt stand and with a fringed shade. Then the presents began to come in from Neal's friends and relatives, presents beyond anything she had ever imagined: a little chest of flat silver, smooth, shining knives and forks and spoons, six of each, a large silver bowl from the mayor of Hinsboro and his wife, a silver sandwich-plate from the City Council; a lemonade set from the mother and son whose house they were to share; innumerable pretty trifles from his classmates at college and his legal acquaintances that looked to her like priceless treasures. But, after all, no one gave her as much as the Goldenburgs, no one was quite so thoughtful. First, Mr. Goldenburg went through his old stock, and found appropriate wedding-raiment for Mr. and Mrs. Chamberlain, Sol and Sam: a "stylish stout" not quite so stylish, to be sure, as when it was laid in, three years before, but still undeniably stout enough for Mummer; a "gent's guaranteed two-thirds wool," that needed the guarantee to convince the doubtful, but Mr. Chamberlain was not inclined to be doubtful; two "schoolboys' special," so special as to have attained no great vogue, but beautiful to the eyes of Sol and Sam. Mr. Goldenburg let them have all these things on credit, though no one knew better than he the state of Mr. Chamberlain's finances. Then he went through his stock again, searching out bargains for Anne . . . she could have those towels just as well as not, there were imperfect threads in them, but they would look nice when she had embroidered them. Those handkerchiefs, those aprons, were badly soiled, but she could wash them out; that pleated wool skirt, those shoes and shirtwaists, were discontinued lines, but if they happened to fit her . . . he let her pay him for them, to save her pride, but they cost her next to nothing. After the invitation to go to New York was extended by Mrs. Goldenburg she lay awake all night, trembling with excitement; and when they were actually on their way, they all three put their heads together and made out a list of her household needs.

Half a dozen sheets, half a dozen pillow slips, a pair of blankets, a quilt, two spreads; two dozen bathroom towels —that would be plenty, with the odd ones Mr. Goldenburg let her have; one half dozen each glass and kitchen towels; three dozen napkins; three table cloths—"You won't use doze much; these new-fangled mats, d'oylies dey call dem, safes lots of vashing; put doze down, my tear." Then the clothes, more entrancing still; six nightgowns, six of each undergarment beside the "bridal set"; a kimono, two pairs of shoes, a dozen pairs of stockings, three gingham dresses for house wear; a dark blue silk for afternoon wear; a dark blue coat that would "fit in" both with that and with the serge suit already purchased, a hat to match; the wedding dress itself, white *crêpe de chine*—that was to serve, later on, for all occasions where "best" was required. "Oh, Mr. Goldenburg, I'll never be able to buy all that with three hundred dollars—you know that's all I have left." . . . "Yes, you vill, my tear, you'll see. An' I'm goin' to speak to some of my pizness frents apout you. One in de caterin pizness, he'll send you up a nice little lunch by express, one florist, ve'll talk to him apout de decorations for de church."

The visit to New York was one of rapture from the beginning to the end of the five days that it lasted. Anne had never been in a hotel before—had never seen an elevator, a menu card, a bell-boy or twin beds; she had never ridden in a subway, or attended a play in a theater. There was a bathroom of sorts in Mabel Buck's house and Anne had used the tin tub, bound with water-soaked wood, when she had visited Mabel, sharing the luxuries of the Buck family; but this was her first experience of white-tiled perfection with running hot water, and a tub of solid porcelain, for her own exclusive use—for Mr. and Mrs. Goldenburg actually had a bathroom off their bedroom, too! She made mental notes of everything, gleaning fresh bits of knowledge from each new experience. How much this trip was doing to prepare her for the still more wonderful one to Washington with Neal! He was not going to find her ignorant, after all, of all the niceties of life which he knew, as she had feared. Only once was she cowed by a waiter or bewildered by finger-bowls or uncertain how to follow an usher. Mrs. Conrad would have shuddered at the thought of the Goldenburgs as social mentors, just as she would have thought a marriage hardly legal when the bride brought to it an outfit as meager as Anne's; but to the girl, both seemed more than adequate; they seemed almost God-given.

The Goldenburg's had lost a daughter, Rachel, who would have been just Anne's age if she had lived. Mrs. Goldenburg finally confided this to Anne, her beady eyes brimming, her plump hands twitching; and Anne in turn confided it to Neal when after a three weeks' absence he returned to West Hamstead, and stood amazed at all that had been accomplished while he was gone.

"So they're doing all this for me in her memory! Just think of it."

"I believe they're doing it partly in her memory, but largely because they love and admire you. The Jewish race appreciates qualities like yours. But anyway, they're doing it, whatever the reason is, and I shan't forget. Perhaps I can do them a good turn some day."

"Neal—would you mind very much—do you suppose it would be possible—for me to keep on teaching after we are married?"

"Of course I'd mind. I wouldn't hear of it for an instant. Whatever put such an idea in your head?"

"I don't see how my family is going to get along without what I'm earning," she faltered.

Neal did some swift calculating. His contribution to the expenses of his own family had been seventy-five dollars a month, nine hundred dollars a year. Of course, now that his board and laundry would no longer come out of that, what he gave them would be clear gain, except for his share in taxes and insurance; but he had made a bargain and he must stick to it. If he added this burden of Anne's to his own, they were going to be a good deal straitened in consequence; but that, as he saw it, was what he ought to do. They were in the same boat, as far as their dependents were concerned; and he intended to do the rowing.

"You've been earning ten dollars a week?"

"Yes."

"How many weeks are there in the school year?"

"Thirty-eight."

"Three hundred and eighty dollars—well, we'll manage to find that much some way. Don't you worry."

"You mean *you'll* send it?"

"Of course—why, Anne, darling, don't take it that way—"

For she was crying—shedding glad tears that sprang from a heart overflowing with gratitude and adoration.

"There, there—why, it isn't anything at all—I'll be earning so much a few years from now that I shan't even notice it. Then I'll pay off the mortgage on the farm, and your father can get a fresh start and—now, Anne . . ."

Neal's general satisfaction received only one setback: The revelation that the "organ" which Anne played in church was not an organ at all, as he understood the term, but a "reed organ." No bridal music worthy of the name could be achieved on such an inadequate instrument. But again, Anne's genius for making friends bore fruit. The leader of the Wallacetown band agreed to transport a square piano over the hills at his own expense and to play it himself on the all-important day, accompanied by a violinist and a 'cellist.

Mrs. Griffin, in an outburst of hospitality, offered to take the entire Conrad family into her house, and to entertain them throughout the period of their stay; and she proved so perfect a hostess, so thoroughly "refined" so far removed from anything that was "disgusting" that the Conrads' worst forebodings melted away at once, almost as the perfect biscuits and flaky pies she made melted in their mouths. She set a much better table than they could either afford or conceive. There was nothing to rouse their forebodings, either, when Anne appeared in the flesh to take supper at the Griffins' and be presented to them soon after their arrival. She was wearing her white muslin dress, and even Mrs. Conrad was forced to admit that there was nothing wrong with her appearance. The dress was cheap, of course, but it was suitable and it was becoming; and the girl's excellent figure and natural style set it off. There was no denying that she was good-looking—well, Neal might be forgiven for thinking her beautiful. Her skin and her teeth were both perfect. Those counted for more, really, than those great dark blue eyes with their fringed lashes, and the masses of soft golden hair. And her manner was not awkward at all, or bold; on the contrary, she was rather silent, a little shy, but perfectly polite, perfectly self-possessed. In the seclusion of their own apartment, afterwards, they confessed to each other that she was not so very dreadful, after all . . . though of course they did not say as much to Neal.

Their forebodings were not roused the next day either. The September morning dawned cold and crisp and clear, mellowing into golden warmth before noon. The drive over the hills, through silent, shady roads, with glimpses, at every clearing, of the blue-massed mountains in the distance, was beautiful enough to stir more senseless souls than theirs. The little church which was their destination stood high above the clustering houses around it, austerely white, strong in the simplicity of Puritanism. Inside, boughs of fir and spruce, mingled with bows of maple and oak had been spread behind the pulpit and over the windows; sprays of roses were lifted in front of the green masses, and tied on the pews. A very unhappy-looking young man, with a hurt and puzzled expression on his kind, flat face, was waiting to receive them, to take them to their places in front, on the left; he seemed anxious that everything should be right, that they should be comfortable and pleased. The orchestra was playing the wedding march from Lohengrin very acceptably. The strange country minister, standing beside Arthur, had a fine head, something gothic and serene about it; Neal, paler than usual, but handsomer than ever, chin and shoulders squarer than ever, came in with Roy, who was trembling visibly with nervousness, but correct to the last trifling detail of costume and custom; Mabel Buck began her progress up the aisle. The Bucks were well-to-do, and proud to have their daughter invited to take part in the wedding; her filmy, pale pink frock, her wide lacy hat, left nothing to be desired in the attire of a maid-of-honor; her costume had been selected from the latest Altman catalogue, and did full justice to that establishment.

And then came the bride, crowned with orange blossoms, white lilies and roses in her hands, a mist of tulle around her . . .

Ten minutes later they were all in the church parlor. Congratulations were being received and kisses exchanged. The wedding breakfast over which Mr. Goldenburg, resplendent in frock coat and gray trousers, was presiding,

81

left nothing to be desired; it was in the same class with the roses, more of which appeared on the tastefully laden table. His "pizness frents" had done him proud. So, he reflected, had the girl in whose future he had invested. He sized up the Conrad family with one or two swift, appraising glances.

"Dey took on apout it when de poy told 'em, and now de're disaboinded pecause dey can't fint more vault!" he muttered shrewdly to himself. "Dey hat petter not make her unhappy, dat liddle Annel put even if dey do she'll come out on top, yust de same, py and py. A great lady—twendy years from now, maype—put a great lady, some day!"

But alone in her little attic room for the last time, no thought of possible future greatness for herself entered Anne's head. Her thoughts were all of Neal, who, in her mind, was so great—so glorious—already, that nothing could magnify him in her eyes. Mabel helped her change from her snowy bridal raiment to the "simple little serge suit," enhanced with a new blouse of matching blue and a new early fall hat. In the open fitted bag—one of Neal's wedding gifts to her—was everything she needed for that night—the lacy nightgown with its white ribbons, the pale blue kimono and bedroom slippers, fresh handkerchiefs; her suit case and trunk were already locked and strapped. Her tiny new gold watch—Neal's other wedding gift—was ticking away at the end of its long fine chain, securely tucked in her belt. Neal was waiting for her outside, in the horseless carriage. They were to motor to a famous inn, nestled in the heart of the hills fifty miles south, and spend their first night there, lingering on for another day or two if it suited their fancy, then taking an express to New York which connected with a midnight train to Washington. A drawing-room was to be engaged as soon as they decided when they wanted to go. The horseless carriage would then be shipped by freight to Hinsboro. The careful plans for her comfort and happiness had all been perfected by Neal—

Anne closed her bag, and turned to kiss her friend.

"I'm not going to say good-by. We'll see each other

often. My marriage isn't going to make any difference. After Neal and I get settled I want you to come and visit us. Neal says the living-room sofa makes into a sort of bed. Mabel—will you do one more thing for me?"

"Of course, honey-bunch."

"Take this bag down to Neal, and tell him I'll be there in just a minute."

Slightly surprised at being dismissed, but without objections, Mabel departed. Anne closed the door carefully behind her and locked it. Then swiftly, she knelt beside her bed.

"Oh, God," she prayed aloud, "please make me worthy of him! I don't know how to say it. I don't even know how to think it, but Neal is so wonderful, and good and great, that I *feel* he's going to rise to high places. Help me to go with him, show me the way. So that he won't leave me behind, so that we can be together always. For Christ's sake. Amen."

PART TWO

Knots and Tangles

CHAPTER VII

Two weeks later, their wedding journey over, Neal and Anne began their homemaking together in the little four-room apartment in Hinsboro.

The trip to Washington had been everything that they both had dreamed of and hoped for and more. To a sophisticated traveler, the capital city in early September, emptied of official and resident society, and sizzling in the damp and sultry heat, is at its worst; but Anne and Neal were neither sophisticated nor traveled; and to them it seemed as beautiful as a vision of a white-pillared Paradise. They went through the Treasury Building and the Army and Navy Building, wearily but persistently; through the Corcoran Art Gallery, puzzled but eagerly. They went by boat down the Potomac to Mt. Vernon, and spent a day there, wandering through the mansion and garden, resting on the shady lawn overlooking the river; and they spent another day at Arlington and Alexandria, instead of trying to crowd all three into one expedition. They climbed to the top of the Washington monument, lingered before the picture of Pocohontas in the Rotunda of the Capitol, surveyed the beautiful chamber of the Supreme Court, sat for a few minutes in the vacant gallery of the House of Representatives. It was here that Neal gave voice to his only regret.

"If Congress were only in session! I'd like to see these fellows in action."

"You will some day."

"Yes, we'll come again."

They crossed the green park to the new Library of Congress recently opened, glittering with mosaic, gorgeous with Pompeian red—it was good to find that they could lunch there, for half an hour passed by, and still they had not half seen it all, the endless corridors, the wide, shallow-stepped staircases leading on and on to new wonders. They were so tired when they reached the hotel that night, that they could not study the map they had bought or read in their guidebook about what they had seen that day and intended to see the next, but tumbled off to bed like sleepy children, the ruby-colored balloon which Neal had bought for Anne, in sheer excess of joyousness, from an itinerant vender, floating above their heads.

He bought her flowers, too, every day, from other itinerant venders, for they found these humble merchants stationed at almost every street-corner, at every park and circle; Anne had always a small bunch to stick in her belt, a larger one on the plush-covered table in the center of their room. They walked up and down Pennsylvania Avenue, looking in the windows of the small, cheap shops which disfigure its fine length, purchasing "views" and other inexpensive souvenirs for themselves and their families; and when they had walked until they could walk no longer, Neil hired an open victoria by the hour, a sagging vehicle sadly drawn by a sagging horse, guided by a sleepy negro, in shabby livery that had seen better days; and in it they drove about the city. Last of all, marveling at their temerity, they went to the White House. It seemed almost too much to believe that they could actually walk inside those strong iron gates, unquestioned, and into that shining mansion. Yet no one stopped them. The uniformed attendant at the entrance regarded them kindly. He was used to bridal couples and this pair was an unusually attractive example of the species. He smiled. Neal and Anne smiled back. Then they found themselves in the dim cool basement corridor where the portraits of the Presidents' wives are hung, ladies smiling still, in their pictured satins, as they did in bygone days; next in the small square room where the china used in each administration, neatly ranged behind glass doors set them "choosing" the sets each liked best. From another smiling attendant they found that they were allowed to go upstairs; and there a guide awaited them. The day was torrid, and there were only a few other sightseers—some skinny, shabby school-teachers, a prosperous-looking merchant from California—as he himself proclaimed—an elderly man and his wife "doing" Washington in two days—none, except themselves, Neal and Anne instinctively felt, atune to the simple beauty and serene dignity that surrounded them—the marble-floored hall, the high-paneled dining-room, the Red Room with its glimpses of the garden and lawns beyond, the tall windows, the empty, circular, blue room, the homelike, dainty Green Room with its white mantel, the dazzling chandeliers and mirrorlike parquetry of the East Room. They left in such a state of exaltation that Neal felt the day called for some special celebration to mark it. . . .

"Let's go and have dinner at the Shoreham tonight. That's the swell hotel here, I've heard. Shall we? Next time we come we'll be staying there."

Anne agreed, joyfully, and deciding to wear her wedding-gown to their little feast. The dark blue silk, which had seemed so glorious a garment when she purchased it, was, she had already discovered, suitable only for sightseeing. Even in the unostentatious dining-room of the Hotel Hamilton, where they were staying, it was not just "right" for evening wear; but having no other dress, except her white muslin, which she could not wash out herself here, and her wedding-dress, which she wanted so much to save, she had tried to make it "do," even though this meant she could not change, when she came in, hot and dusty, at the end of the day. It was much too warm to wear her suit, unless she took off the coat, and that, she had discovered wasn't "right" either. Ladies wore their coats, just as men did, when they were in tailored attire. Yes, certainly she would have to wear the wedding-dress tonight. Then Neal, with that uncanny faculty of his for guessing what was in her mind suggested something else.

"But let's go shopping first. I want to have the fun of buying you a dress myself to *prove* I've got a right to."

"Neal, I don't need one, really—"

"Nonsense, of course you do. A pink dress. You had on a pink dress the first time I saw you."

"That hideous thing!"

"Well, this isn't going to be hideous, you'll see!"

It was not. It was frilly with ruffles, frothy with lace, a fairy frock. The saleswoman who waited on her outdid her own professional enthusiasm when she saw how Anne looked in it. And she showed the price ticket to Neal surreptitiously, that Anne's happiness might not be checked by the figures printed on it. It was, the saleswoman shrewdly suspected, far more expensive a dress than they had expected to buy. Neal noticed her strategy, but he paid for the dress unflinchingly, producing his billfold without an instant's hesitation, and drawing out quantities of crisp, clean notes as carelessly as if there were thousands more where those had come from. When the saleswoman saw this, she made a suggestion.

"Wouldn't Madam like a wrap to go with the dress? I have just the thing, marked very low, because it's so late in the season. The new fall goods are beginning to come in already. But this is just exactly as stylish, and such a bargain." Almost instantly she flung around Anne's shoulders a moss-green cloak, of soft-embroidered wool, satin-lined in a paler shade of the same color. The bride stood reflected in the tall glass before them like a rose surrounded by its leaves.

"Neal, you *mustn't*."

"Why, don't you *like* it?"

"Don't I *like* it?"

"Then I must." He counted out more clean, crisp bills carelessly. "Send that, with the dress, to Mrs. Neal Conrad, Hotel Hamilton, please," he said to the saleswoman, "right away. Be sure it gets there in time for dinner."

"Wouldn't you like to open a charge account here?" inquired the capable person addressed, grasping the bills with one firm hand as she wrote "Rush" across the address with the other. "It could be arranged in an instant, I'm sure, at the office. Then any time Mrs. Conrad came in . . . or if you live in another city, I could send things on approval. She would only have to write. Mrs. Maple, my name is, and I'd be only too glad. It would be a real convenience to her, I'm sure."

"A very good idea—where is the office?"

Anne was still protesting when they finally left the smart little establishment into which they had unwittingly wandered—the outside had not "looked expensive." A little fur neckpiece to wear with the blue blue suit on cool days, and slippers and stockings to match the new frock had been added to the other purchases.

"Neal, you know we ought not to open charge accounts and do wild things like that. You told me yourself we must 'begin small.' And then you go to work and spend more on clothes for me in one hour than I've spent in nearly twenty years."

"I want you to have pretty clothes. You're so darned pretty yourself, and sweet, and good." It was all he could do to keep from kissing her on the street. "That client of mine up in the mountains—"

"Well?"

"Well, his next bill will be bigger than I meant to make it, that's all."

The little dinner began with a surprise. They were hardly seated in the rose and cream dining-room, at the Shoreham—the only hotel dining-room in Washington with real atmosphere, even when swathed in the linen covers of the off-season—when a very sleek-looking young man sprang up from a near-by table and hailed Neal with genuine, if correctly tempered enthusiasm.

"Neal Conrad! my dear fellow! where did you come from—and when—and why—at this time of the year? Not that it matters, so long as you've arrived!"

Explanations were immediately in order. Clarence Hathaway, a former classmate of Neal's at Harvard, had entered the diplomatic service immediately after his graduation. He had spent much of his boyhood in Europe, and this had fitted him admirably for his future work. He was already third secretary of legation at Madrid. Home now on leave, he was receiving certain important instructions from the State Department before sailing to resume his post. Hence his presence in Washington. Neal sought to congratulate him upon his success.

"Nonsense! What about yours! Making money hand over fist, so I hear, and causing hibernating Hinsboro all sorts of spasms with your political prowess; Governor or something, aren't you?"

"No," said Neal, laughing, "sit down and have dinner with us, won't you? This is Anne . . . my wife," he added, with a shade of difference in his voice, as Hathaway swung around, apologizing for his intrusion, swiftly solicitous.

"A bridal party! My dear Mrs. Conrad, what must you have thought of me, charging in on your exquisite solitude *à deux* like that? But I was so glad to see Neal in this God-forsaken place, and I hadn't heard . . . Did you send me cards? They would have missed me anyway, if you had, no doubt, I've been tearing around so. Newport, the Adirondacks, the North Shore . . . But you will let me be host, of course! . . . What kind of cocktails do you like, Mrs. Conrad?"

Fortunately, he did not wait for her to answer. Anne, blushing with bewilderment was looking to Neal for help, and he had not caught her signal.

"A clover-leaf, of course, and Neal and I will have martinis. Then some jellied bouillon, salmon mayonnaise, with cucumbers—birds—a Waldorf salad—baked Alaska pudding—champagne to celebrate this glad occasion, some liqueurs with the coffee. After dinner we'll go to the theater —not that there's much to see, but we'll see what there is. —It's pretty dull, too, after Madrid—a wonderful city. I can hardly wait to get back there. Have you ever been to Spain, Mrs. Conrad? Well, you and Neal must run over soon—an enchanting country!"

Madrid! He suggested it as casually as George used to speak of driving her into Hamstead. But Neal took it calmly enough, or at least appeared to do so, and Anne steadied herself. She mustn't betray her nervousness, her provincialism, and embarrass Neal—Neal who was really twice as wonderful as this attractive stranger. Mr. Hathaway did not, after all, make many conversational demands upon her—it was only necessary that she should follow his dashing lead. And this, inwardly stumbling, but outwardly sure-footed she managed to do.

"I know a woman—a famous hostess here in Washington—who says that when she's one man short for a dinner she comes to the Shoreham for lunch, and invariably finds just the right person with whom to fill in, eating here. She says it saves a great drain upon her nervous resources. I'm in for a little of her luck, evidently."

"And so are we."

"That's sweet of you, Mrs. Conrad, sweet,—and very neat, too, wasn't it, Neal? Of course there's not much of any one here now. Over in the corner, all alone, is Madame Del Garde, the wife of the Portuguese Minister. They have a lovely summer place on the East Coast of Maryland. I spent my last week-end there. She must be in town for a few days' shopping. Stunning, isn't she?"

"Complete," murmured Anne, taking in the finished perfection of the dark, handsome woman's black satin evening dress, high comb, and white lace scarf.

"Complete, yes, that's the word exactly, complete! I must tell Madame Del Garde herself sometime, she'd like to hear that." His eyes wandered towards the diplomat's wife again, and he half rose, bowing in response to her smile of recognition. "And opposite the last window on the left, talking very hard together are the President's secretary, Mr. Taylor, and Senator Harriman of Nevada."

"The sheep-man?" asked Neal with interest.

"Yes— I wonder what ewe-lamb is going to be slaughtered now—but we mustn't talk scandal, must we, Mrs. Conrad?"

"No," said Anne serenely.

Hathaway glanced at her, in swift appraisement. She really meant it. Well, then—

"And opposite them, further on, are Shimera, the naval *attaché* of Japan, and his daughter. They're absolutely inseparable."

"It's so kind of you," murmured Anne, eating salmon for the first time in her life, "to tell us about all those interesting people. Isn't it, Neal?"

"You bet," said Neal enthusiastically. "Say, Hathaway —do you think the democrats mean to push Nerton in the next campaign?"

The two men plunged into politics; Neal was talking very frankly. He was thinking seriously, he said, of running for mayor, but it took so much money, and he wasn't sure the machine was friendly.

"Pshaw," said Hathaway. The salad was being served, and he produced a gold cigarette case, tendered it to Anne. She had been watching Madame Del Garde, and was prepared for this—nevertheless, she had made up her mind to decline.

"We don't, much, where I come from," she said easily.

"Of course not—please excuse a very stupid mistake!" He actually thought it was! Anne's heart beat high as the cultured, sophisticated voice trailed on, "I'm hoping to be made Minister, rather early in life, as such things go— that's the way my ambition lies. Confirm my appointment without a vulgar row, won't you, Neal, when you get to the Senate, which ought to be about the same time."

"Sure," said Neal heartily, and they all laughed again.

Later, while they were getting their hats before starting for the theater, he and Hathaway had a moment alone. And Hathaway asked a question.

"Where did you find her, Neal?"

"In a place called West Hamstead, Vermont, about two months ago. She taught the district school. She's the daughter of the village ne'er-do-weel."

"Are you in earnest?"

"Never more so."

Clarence Hathaway whistled softly. "Any more like her left behind?"

"There's no one," said Neal. "like her in the whole world."

Clarence whistled again. "I'm inclined to think you're right," he remarked. "However, I'm glad there's one. She'll do very well, as you said, in the Governor's mansion."

"I didn't say," protested Neal.

"Well, you better. *Allons, mon cher.*"

Still later, lying in the curve of Neal's arm, Anne

thought it all over—the strange meeting, the stranger visions of new worlds to conquer which followed it. How many worlds were there, yet to be revealed to her? She had already glimpsed so many of which she had never dreamed, these last weeks. And now it was their last night in Washington, the last night of their honeymoon, and in the morning they would be going back to Hinsboro, to the little four-room apartment, to hard work and everyday existence. It was fun to joke, of course, about embassies and executive mansions, but, after all, it was only a joke—at least for the present. Yet, there seemed something about this encounter with Clarence Hathaway that was pregnant with meaning—with promise, with prophecy.

On the squat, substantial chair that stood by the tall window draped, correct hotel-fashion, in lace curtains and crimson velvet over-draperies, lay her moss-green cloak and her frilly pink dress, the long silk stockings fallen beside the little satin slippers that matched it. The rest of their baggage was packed, but these new treasures she had decided to leave out until morning, in order to be able to look at them once more in daylight. The latest bouquet that Neal had bought her—great warm, top-heavy roses—scented the silent room. He was asleep, or nearly so; and yet, asleep or awake, he encompassed her with his thoughtfulness, his solicitude, his love, of which the dress and the flowers were but the visible tokens. That—not future fame, but present happiness, was, after all, what counted.

He stirred slightly, kissed her drowsily, drew her more closely to him. Instantly, thrilling to his touch, she responded with an ardor that surpassed his own. So he had not been asleep after all. He wanted her. He needed her. He was all hers. She was as essential to him as he was to her. These were the glad thoughts which surged through her senses. Yet, before they really slept, he spoke to her again of Clarence Hathaway, whom she, in her rapture, had entirely forgotten.

"Attractive, isn't he, darling? And brilliant! I believe he'll prove a great diplomat, one of the greatest we have."

Anne resented, ever so slightly, this mental intrusion,

just as she had resented—though she must be careful not to let Neal guess it—Hathaway's physical intrusion at dinner. "If only," she said gently, "he did not look quite so much as if he had been stroked."

CHAPTER VIII

It was a long time before she thought of Clarence Hathaway again; or Washington, except as a honeymoon memory.

When they reached Hinsboro, they had to begin, right away, to economize. They had spent more money than they expected. But that, Neal said with a laugh, was, of course, to be expected! And Anne laughed too, when he said it. But after he had gone to his office, she sat still, with a pencil and a piece of paper in her hand, and did sad little sums, before she even washed the breakfast dishes or made the bed.

It had sounded *huge,* the amount they could count on for housekeeping, when Neal first told her about it; and here it was melting away to nothing, in her careful hands, . . . just as those great blocks that the iceman brought melted away in her immaculate little refrigerator, so that she had to buy more—and more—and more. The steaks and the chops that reposed so juicily on that same ice melted away likewise—in Neal's mouth, the instant he got home at night, starving hungry.

"My but you're a good cook, honey—another helping please, and lots of butter gravy—just floods of it, all around the baked potato. And stick a piece of bread in it too—'fish in the pan' we used to call that when I was a kid."

Two pounds of steak—porterhouse, Neal would listen to nothing less—four chops, one small fowl for boiling, one thick slice of ham—in less than a week he had devoured all this, with comparatively little help from her,

95

though she had a healthy appetite. He drank two great cups of coffee, every morning, thick with double cream, ate cream on his cereal, whipped cream on the molded jellies and blancmanges that formed many of their week-day desserts, ice cream, which Anne made and froze herself, every Sunday. So there was the milkman to be reckoned with to no small tune, as well as the iceman and the butcher. Then Neal liked iced orange juice, the very first thing in the morning, before he sat down at the table. She took it into the bathroom, and he sipped it while he tubbed and shaved. The friendly Italian at the fruit-stall, just around the corner, found in her a steady and not too unremunerative a customer.—And all the butter it took for "fish in the pan," gravies and white sauces, for crisp toast and light muffins, for the deep, hot, juicy pies which alternated with the molded jellies for dessert, for fresh vegetables— Neal, it seemed, expected her to buy string beans and spinach straight through the winter! The grocery bill was heavy, too. He asked her eagerly if it were too late in the fall for preserving, and answering eagerly that it was not, Anne made apple jelly and grape jelly and quince marmalade; sugar, sugar, sugar, white mountains of it, cool and high like the Alps, dissolved into the big kettles filled with sizzling, wine-colored juice, ranged closely together on her neat little gas stove.

Neal did not complain about the bills; and he praised her cooking, as he praised everything else she did. But once he drew money from the savings bank, where his account was already much depleted by her engagement and wedding presents from him, by the engraved invitations to their marriage and by their trip to Washington with all its delightful "extras," and once the bills were not paid when those of the following month came in, and then, were ugly little words—"account rendered"—at the top of the statements. It was then that Anne commenced to do her sad little sums.

She roused herself from them at last and began her day's work, for the first time, without joyousness. It was, as Neal had foretold, child's play for her after her long, hard drudgery at the farm, as far as actual labor was concerned. She did all the washing and ironing, including Neal's shirts and the sheets, all her own cleaning. And still, by eleven o'clock in the morning, earlier than that sometimes, her work was finished for the day until it was time to prepare supper. Neal did not come home to dinner, taking a light lunch, which she put up, to his office with him, and she easily fell into the way of eating a very light lunch herself, which did not take her five minutes to prepare—a cup of tea, a slice of bread and butter, applesauce or prunes; then she changed her dress, and did the mending. She slipped out of bed in the morning while Neal was still asleep, put the clothes to soak, swept and dusted, chilled his orange juice, steamed his cereal, percolated his coffee. At first he remonstrated with her; he liked to find her there beside him to kiss when he woke up —besides there was no need of it. But gradually the mental satisfaction and deep physical comfort of rising in a warm, tidy house, to a waiting breakfast perfectly cooked and served, overcame his remonstrances. In the evening he came home to the same shining order, the same complete refreshment. There was never a towel out of place, or a crumpled one, in the tiny tiled bathroom, which Anne scrubbed every day. There was never cool soup or lukewarm salad; and half an hour after they had finished supper, the dishes had been put away, the gas stove was cold, the kitchen dark, and she was curled up against his shoulder in the big Morris chair that was so hideous, but which held them both so luxuriously.

"One thing I'll never fling in your face," Neal chuckled more than once when they were thus comfortably settled, "'the bread that mother used to make.' Why, you can give mother cards and spades in housekeeping right now!"

It was true. Neither Mrs. Conrad nor Harriet excelled in the domestic arts, which they considered beneath them. The "flat wash" went out to a little steam laundry, whence it returned grimy and torn; the more personal things were entrusted to a lady of color who lived in an adjacent alley, and who had the habit of procrastinating and pilfering.

She also came in once a week to do a little alleged cleaning, which never seemed to reach the back stairs or the more remote corners. Nominally, the elder Conrads also kept a "general maid"; actually, they were oftener without one; and during the intervals, they "managed." This management was nothing to brag about. At first, it had been suggested that Neal and Anne should dine with them every Sunday after church; but during one of the periods of "management," Anne asked her family-in-law if they would not like to reverse this arrangement, for once, and they accepted, with condescending reluctance. The dinner which she set before them was neither elaborate nor original—tomato bisque soup; roast chicken, mashed potatoes, onions and string beans, accompanied by light rolls, and her new grape jelly; fruit salad; vanilla ice cream with chocolate sauce, sponge cake, and coffee; but it was a better one than she had ever eaten, as to seasoning and serving, in her mother-in-law's house, and both were well aware of the fact. The temporary reversal of plan became a permanent one. Then the Thanksgiving feast took place at the younger Conrads', and it was a feast, for Anne outdid herself. It looked as if the Christmas one might take place there too. Then they began to ask in Neal's friends, young lawyers and their wives who had been swift to offer hospitality to the bride and groom; the mayor and his sister, the minister and his two married daughters. This meant shaded candles on the table, salted nuts, chilled celery and olives, more elaborate courses. It meant extra work, too. Still the labor was nothing, absolutely nothing. Anne laughed at that.

But those bills! The figures began to dance before her eyes. Anne, who was never sick, began to realize that their horrible cavorting, their sinister leaping, were giving her a headache. She continued, mechanically, until she had finished everything she needed to do, then she lay down on the davenport in the living-room so as not to rumple the clean white spread on the brass bed, and thought matters over. That night, when supper was over, instead of curling up in Neal's arms, she faced him with grave determination.

"Neal," she said soberly, "I've been thinking things over. Our expenses. We've got to make them less."

"Can't," replied Neal comfortably. "Come here."

"We've got to. It makes me unhappy not to have bills paid promptly."

"All right. I'll draw some more money out of the bank."

"That makes me unhappy, too."

"Goodness, Anne! You're probably the unhappiest woman in Hinsboro."

"Besides," she continued relentlessly, and without noticing his levity, "you can't keep on, much longer, drawing money out of the bank, can you? I mean, there isn't such an awful lot left."

"Look here, Anne, what's set you worrying about money? I earn it, don't I? I earn more and more all the time. And I haven't kicked at its going. I'm just as proud as I can be—"

"I want to pay cash for everything. I have plenty of time to go out and get things myself instead of having them delivered. The 'cash and carry' shops are much cheaper than the ones we're dealing with now; and Hamburg steaks, and stews, and roast pork are cheaper than porterhouse, and chicken and chops, and just as nourishing. It's possible even to have nice suppers without any meat at all—I've been studying food values. Macaroni and cheese and cocoa and grapefruit make a very nourishing meal."

"Good Lord!" exclaimed Neal.

"Besides," went on Anne, "we're feeding too many people. I never saw any one with such an appetite as Arthur. That Sunday dinner for your family costs as much as everything we eat, the entire week, by ourselves. And if we must 'pay back' every time your friends ask us to their houses, we'll have to stop going."

"Why, Anne! I never guessed you were so inhospitable."

"I'm not inhospitable, but I'm honest. It isn't honest to feed one group of people with food for which we haven't paid another group of people."

Neal did not answer.

"I want you," said Anne, "to give me thirty dollars, the first of every month, the rest of this winter. I'll do the best I can with it. If I can save out of it in one month, we'll have company the next. If I can't, we won't. In the spring, if you've earned enough to put back all you've taken out of the bank, and have enough left over to increase my allowance say to forty dollars, we can have company every week, if you want to—first your family, then some of your friends. But of every increase you give me, I want you to put the same amount back into the bank."

"Anne, I've been mistaken in your character. I see you're a cold, calculating woman."

"Oh, Neal, *darling!* Don't say that, even in fun!"

"How can I help it, when you propose to starve me?"

"I don't propose to starve you. You'll hardly know the difference."

The tears were very near her lashes, her lips were trembling; but she stood her ground, even through Neal's onslaught.

"It's a good investment for me to appear prosperous. Instead of talking about economizing, we ought to be talking about new clothes, and a new car and a new house. I need all that, building up my future."

"We can have all that in the future, if we're careful now. But your future won't amount to much, if you found it on debt."

Finally, without having given her a definite answer, he absolutely refused to discuss the question any further. She could see that he, as well as herself, was hurt. He was generous to a fault, and he could not bear to see his generosity curtailed. Besides, what right had she to call him over-confident or question his judgment, when his self-confidence and his judgment had always been justified? Perhaps she was making a mistake. She was nothing but an ignorant, inexperienced little country girl, presuming to dictate to him. Perhaps she was making a mistake. Yet instinctively she felt, though she did not know, that she was right.

The next morning, without comment, Neal gathered up

the offending bills, and a day later, they came back to her, receipted. On Friday evening he asked her, casually, if she had telephoned his mother asking her for Sunday dinner.

"I telephoned her that we couldn't have any Sunday dinners for the present because I've accepted an offer to sing in the choir of the First Congregational Church," said Anne calmly. "I'll have to sing twice on Sunday and go to at least one rehearsal during the week. Mrs. Simmons told me while we were hanging out our clothes that a soprano was needed badly. So I went and offered. The minister is awfully grateful to me; he thinks the favor is all on my side. I'm going to be paid two dollars a week."

Mrs. Simmons was their landlady, who lived on the ground floor of the little story-and-a-half house.

"She told me about a little boy, too," Anne went on, inwardly quaking but outwardly collected, "Jimmie Scott. He's been sick and fell behind in school work. His mother's been trying to find someone who would come to him late every morning for an hour and tutor him. I went to see Mrs. Scott this morning, and she was lovely to me. And Jimmie is a darling—eight years old, but he doesn't look it. I'm going to begin teaching him on Monday. Mrs. Scott says, if he does well with me, and is happy, she may not put him back in school at all this winter. He's going to do well. And he's going to be happy. And I'm going to get a dollar a day. You said you didn't want me to teach *school,* but you never said anything about *one* child, and I thought perhaps . . ."

"That was quite a wash you hung out, wasn't it?" Neal asked dryly.

He was angry, terribly angry, she was sure of it. She, who would gladly have let herself be chopped to pieces—small pieces—to save him a pain in his little finger, had made him angry. It was almost too much to endure. Almost, but not quite. The streak of hardness in Anne saved her now. She faced him, somehow, without flinching. And then, suddenly, his expression changed, and he pulled her towards him, joyously, laughingly, wrapping his long, lean arms about her in a bear hug.

"You precious kid! You got the better of me after all, didn't you? Well, go to it! But stick your money in the bank. I'll give you the thirty dollars for housekeeping the first of every month."

CHAPTER IX

NOVEMBER, December, January, February, March, April, May— Twenty-five dollars a month for food, another thirty for incidentals—ice, telephone, gasoline, contributions in church, cigarettes for Neal, a new pair of shoes for Anne, small dentist's bills for both of them. They were spending no more, on all their living expenses, than Neal was giving his family, and yet how much more they got for the money! Though they would have been perfectly contented to stay at home, occasionally they attended a concert, or the movies, and there were frequent subscription dances in Hinsboro, at moderate cost, to which they went, Anne wearing alternately the pink frilly dress and the white *crêpe de chine* in which she had been married—there was, after all, no chance to "save" it, she found with smothered regret. At Mrs. Simmons' instigation they joined a small musical club, the Bach and Beethoven Society, to which she and her sons, Fred and Frank, belonged. This club met on alternate Saturday evenings at the homes of its various members, when a short "program," also supplied by the members, was followed by light refreshments. Several of the same young women who belonged to this club played bridge together every Wednesday afternoon, and Anne, without much difficulty, mastered the rudiments of the game, and the art of serving tea after it. And, gaining courage, when her mother-in-law entertained the Hinsboro Chapter of the Daughters of the American Revolution, Anne offered her services for the day.

"It's very kind of you, my dear. I should have asked you of course, in any case, but I thought you might feel it embarrassing to attend, when you are not eligible to the organization."

"I am eligible," said Anne carelessly. "Mother has belonged for years, though she seldom goes to the meetings —we don't think much of it at home, because we're all descended from Revolutionary heroes there. Hamstead has a Chapter that's been active for years. Mother joined through the Colonial Governor, Ephraim Wadsworth, afterwards General Wadsworth. And my father's great-grandfather, Moses Chamberlain, who was one of the first settlers in the upper Connecticut Valley, was a Lieutenant Colonel in the Revolution. I could of course go in through both those men, and I believe several others, but I've never bothered."

Anne was continually taking the wind out of her mother-in-law's sails. Mrs. Conrad had difficulty in suppressing her righteous indignation.

"Neal never told me you belonged to *those* Chamberlains—"

"I don't believe Neal knows it. We've never discussed it."

"And the Wadsworth—why, Anne, you could belong to the Colonial Dames too—as far as your ancestry is concerned. But of course you have to be formally invited to that."

"I *have* been formally invited," said Anne, still carelessly, "Mrs. Scott, Jimmie's mother, asked me. But I'm considering whether I can afford the dues."

"I should be delighted to pay your dues."

Anne, who by this time was well aware of Neal's contribution to the Conrad family, felt that this offer had its humorous aspect. But she did not say so. She dipped her white *crêpe de chine* carefully in gasoline, hung it on the clothes-line which she shared with Mrs. Simmons to dry, and made individual golden cakes frosted with White Mountain cream for her mother-in-law's party.

When spring came, Neal took out the horseless carriage, which had been stored in Mrs. Simmons' shed through the colder winter months, and every Sunday afternoon they went out for a drive. Sometimes Neal reached home early enough for one on a week day, too; but he was staying later and later at his office, as the volume of his work steadily increased. When Jimmie Scott went away to the seashore, and the soprano whose place Anne had filled at the First Congregational Church returned, Neal tried to extract a promise from his wife that she would embark on no more wage-earning ventures without consulting him.

"We're really ahead of the game now. Everything's back in the savings bank that we took out, and more too; and if I don't take any vacation this summer, not even for a few days, but plug right ahead——"

"Oh, of course, that's what you ought to do——"

"But wouldn't *you* like to go home for a little while?"

"This is home."

"I meant to Hamstead. It gets terribly hot in Hinsboro."

"And leave you?"

She would not hear of it. She insisted that she did not mind the heat at all, that the outings which they would take together in the horseless carriage would furnish her with all the fresh air she needed. Those, and working in the little garden which she had planted in Mrs. Simmons' back yard. That garden was going to save them a great deal, in vegetables.

She did mind the heat, however, much more than she had expected, much more than she ever confessed. The low-ceilinged rooms, close up under the eaves, which had been so cozy and comfortable in winter were hideously hot by the first of July. At the end of September they were still hideously hot. Neal was out of them from half-past eight in the morning until six in the evening; then, after a supper served on the tiny back porch—iced tea, crisp salad, cold meat sliced thin, a light cake—he was out in the horseless carriage until bedtime. Sometimes he took Anne with him; sometimes he did not; there were "men to see"—"certain matters had come up——" He was gone more and more, became more and more preoccupied—and more and more he prospered. He bought her an electric fan, and then another. She put them in the bedroom which she kept closed and dark all day, and when he entered at night, he never found it unendurably warm. But her work never seemed to give her any respite from the heat. If she went into the garden early, she had to wash and bake in the middle of the day. If she did her household tasks first, the noonday sun was streaming down on her plants and vines by the time she was bending over them. She "put up" quarts and quarts of string beans, peas, corn, tomatoes—all they could possibly need through the following winter. The vegetables simmered and boiled on the little gas stove, the thermometer in the kitchen mounted higher and higher. But so did that account in the savings bank, which she had seen at first almost destroyed and then restored, bit by bit. Neal bought her a sewing machine, the best on the market, and paid cash for it. With this in her possession, she began to replenish their wardrobes, which were both becoming depleted. Materials were marked down, in the summer sales, and she bought remnants and mill-ends for a song that went into neatly tailored pajamas and shirts for Neal, dresses and aprons and underwear for herself. The bureau drawers, which had been growing empty, were re-filled with fresh piles of clothing.

Suddenly the heat broke, there was an unseasonable "cold snap." Anne, who had gone out in the horseless carriage for a short ride without a wrap, came home chilled to the marrow of her bones. The next morning she was too ill to get up.

She did get up, nevertheless, her head throbbing, her limbs alternately quivering with cold and burning with fever. She ached all over. Her feet felt like lumps of lead, which, however heavy, she must drag after her. Neal, reading the morning paper, drinking his coffee, eating his cereal, noticed nothing the matter with her. When he had gone for the day, she lay down on the unmade bed, her breakfast dishes unwashed, her bread unbaked. Towards noon she roused herself, telephoned for the supplies which she could not go out and get, and forced herself to put the flat in order before she succumbed again. Mrs. Simmons had "gone to the beach" for a vacation, with Fred and Frank, who had arranged to get "time off" together by going late, or she would have appealed to her kindly landlady to help her. At five in the afternoon she staggered to her feet, having eaten nothing all day, made herself a cup of strong tea, peeled potatoes and dropped them in cold water, opened a jar of string beans, molded Hamburg steak into little balls. Just before six the telephone rang. It was Neal.

"Hello, honey. How are you?"

"All right."

"Would you mind very much if I didn't come home to supper? There's a Mr. Dawson, of Belford, here, who wants to go over some matters with me, and he's asked me to take dinner with him in the hotel. I think I better, perhaps—"

"Why, of course, Neal—"

"I won't be late. Good-by."

But he was late. Anne put the half-prepared food into the refrigerator, and crept supperless back to bed. She lay there for hours, too miserably uncomfortable to sleep, too stupid and dizzy to read, counting the moments until he should come and comfort her. At last she heard his key turning in the latch. He bounded into the bedroom and sat down beside her, bubbling over with excitement.

"Anne—Anne—are you asleep? What do you think has happened? Mr. Dawson and a few other men have been talking to me, and they want me to run for state legislator. The candidate from this district—Mr. Sooker, you know —has died, and they think I'd never have a better chance to try my luck. There are only three weeks before election, and of course that means a whirlwind campaign, but I bet I can make it, though of course I'd have to be gone from home a lot. But you wouldn't mind that, would you? It's what we've both hoped for, come sooner than we dared to hope. And, thanks to you, there's plenty of money saved up for the necessary expenses. Oh, Anne, do say you're glad!"

She said so, of course, dizzily, her voice sounding a long way off to her. She *was* glad—thankful—overjoyed. Only —why didn't she feel so? Why did she merely feel wretchedly ill, dreadfully lonely, and so much like a tired child who wanted to cry out her troubles against some kind, strong shoulder, instead of like a woman sharing exultantly in her husband's triumph. And why—oh, why—couldn't Neal—Neal, who had always been so thoughtful, so solicitous before, in the light of this new conquest, even see, how sick she was without being told?

CHAPTER X

HE had not seen, the next morning when, earlier than usual, he left for his office. He still had not seen, three weeks later, when the duly registered voters of the district signified at the polls their willingness to have him represent them in the legislature at Belford that winter, and he came home, in the gray dawn following election day, to tell her so.

During the intervening time, struggling, striving to keep on her feet, and do her work, Anne had waited, at first hopefully, then despairingly, for the confidences which she had expected he would pour into her ear, the advice which he would seek from her "womanly intuition." She was sure there must be principles at stake, great principles by which he must either stand or fall. Instead, she heard, when he had time to talk to her at all, about rallies, about advertising space in newspapers, about quantities of cigars and dozens of bottles of whiskey. He was constantly telephoning that he wouldn't be home for supper, that he was in an awful rush just at that moment, but later he would tell her all about how things were going—pretty well, on the whole, he thought, though the only time to guess was after the votes were counted! And then later, when he did get home, someone would telephone him, and he would dash out again, without having exchanged a dozen words with her. He bought a new automobile—a "motor car" he called it now—a lower built model, with a top and windshield and acetylene lights, "turning in" the horseless carriage without a pang, though Anne watched it as it was being backed out of the shed for the last time with quivering lips. He bought a new overcoat, two new suits, quantities of new ties. Anne had hoped for a silk dress that fall, for she had patched and mended her navy-blue taffeta until it cracked away from her careful fingers with every stitch she took; but that, she knew, would be out of the question now. Sick as she felt, she longed to have him ask her to go with him to some of the public meetings, but he never did. Harriet went, making disturbances at several with her raucous pleas of "Votes for Women" and Neal was very angry. He spoke his opinion loudly about women who "meddled in things they didn't understand and never would," and Anne saw that it would only annoy him if she expressed an interest even dimly resembling Harriet's in the affairs of the nation. He had a secretary at his office now, Miss Lillie Letts, who chewed gum and wore transparent, flesh-colored shirtwaists; but she was efficient, she did everything for Neal that Anne had pictured herself doing some day. His mail went to the office, not to the little flat; Miss Letts opened it, answered it, filed it. He received his political visitors at the office, ushered in by Miss Letts. He rented an extra room, and invested in an Axminster rug, and a new center-table, mahogany veneered. Miss Letts selected them. He had no time for the Bach and Beethoven Society, for church, or the movies. Anne sat at home, coughing her head off—for her cold had settled in her chest—and aching all over, mentally as well as physically. There were no evenings together in the Morris chair, her head on his shoulder, his arms about her. She tried to wait up for him, night after night, but she was so tired, and he was so late—nearly always after midnight. She read the newspaper, cutting out every reference made to Neal, disregarding all mention of such minor candidates as Governor and Senator, then she went to bed. She was never asleep when he came in, but whether he hesitated to risk disturbing her, or whether he was too tired himself to crave for her companionship—Anne never knew which it was—he tumbled into bed beside her without a sign that he was aware of her presence. In the morning he never wakened until she shook him gently, telling him that he had overslept, or the telephone bell jangled across his blurred senses. Then he bolted his breakfast, and was gone.

Then finally he came to her and told her that he had won. . . .

So that was what a campaign was like.

The Legislature met in January, still two months away. In the meantime, Neal felt that he must, as far as possible, catch up with his neglected profession. It had been neglected, of course; but it had not suffered. He had gained prestige as a successful candidate, and new cases poured in upon him. He decided to keep the extra room, and Miss Letts. He really needed both. At last, he talked to Anne about his plans for going to Belford.

"I shall have to be there at least from Monday to Thursday every week. Sometimes from Monday to Friday, though I hope not often, for it's going to be hard, managing the office work with only two days here. I'll have to keep it open Saturday afternoon, and maybe sometimes Sundays. Miss Letts is willing. Of course I've raised her salary."

There seemed to be no answer expected of Anne. She made none.

"So I'll be going back and forth, all the time. And it seems to me that it would be better for you to stay right on here. You're comfortably settled, and it would be a nuisance for you to pull up stakes just for two or three months—the sessions will be over in April. Of course it isn't as if you were in a house all alone. I know Mrs. Simmons is right here, and you can call on her, if you need anything."

This time, had any reply been expected of her, Anne could not have made it. He meant to leave her behind! The idea had never occurred to her, and here it was all mapped out, in orderly fashion, in his mind. He would miss her so little, with his new interests, that he could face with resignation—with approval—the thought of being separated from her more than half the time for several months. And she would not have left him, for any known bribe, to spend a few days during the torrid summer among the mountains that were so dear to her. She had

111

slaved for his comfort, for his well being, and she had insured both, at the cost of her own radiant health, for try as she might, she could not seem to pull herself up physically. But the rest, the change, the excitement to which she had been looking forward would, she had not had the slightest doubt, do that. And now she was to have no rest, no change, no excitement.

"It'll be much cheaper that way, too," Neal was saying. "Of course the rent here has got to go on, for office and flat both, and I can get a single room, without a bath, for two dollars a day at the Talmage Tavern. A double room is at least a dollar more, and the food would be twice of course what it would for me alone. I spent a good deal of money during those three weeks of the campaign. Concentrating that way, it cost more. I know you'll get all those debts cleaned up quickly."

Mercifully, she did not doubt either his love or his sincerity, as indeed, she had no reason to do. He was looking at the situation in the reasonable, logical way, the way he always looked at everything, the way that enabled him to get ahead so fast. When the arrangement became known, everyone seemed to regard it as eminently sensible and suitable. Mrs. Conrad thought so; Mrs. Simmons thought so; Miss Letts thought so. Anne was ashamed at not sharing their enthusiasm more wholeheartedly, but at least she did not let them guess that she did not do so. She longed to suggest having Sol and Sam spend the winter months with her, going to school in Hinsboro; but she recalled the size of their appetites, the expense that would be entailed in food and suitable clothing, if she had them both; and either one would be lonely without the other, lonelier than she would be all by herself. She gave up the idea without even mentioning it. Neal, she supposed, would hardly object if she occupied herself by taking a pupil or two, provided she could find any. Jimmie Scott had, inconsiderately, recovered. But she did not feel well enough to attempt the undertaking.

In the flush of his victory, Neal's dormant passion for her awakened again and burned more hotly than ever before. But it had a different quality. If it was more intense,

112

it was less tender. He seemed suddenly aware, not that he had neglected her, but that he had been deprived of her; and, looking ahead, was aware that his impending absence would deprive him of her still further. He sought to possess her the more completely in the present because the past had dispossessed him, and because the future was about to do so, fiercely resentful of a condition for which he had only himself to blame. There was a lack of spontaneity, a weariness, in Anne's response, which changed it from an answering flame to a mere affectionate and dutiful acquiescence; still, she never failed to respond. And Neal noticed the change in her far less than she noticed the change in him.

The holidays brought a flash of gayety. Neal had whipped his affairs into shape, and was ready enough to join in a few festivities before his departure. They entertained the Bach and Beethoven Society, went to a subscription dance at Odd Fellows' Hall, to an oyster supper at the First Congregational Church and to Sunday dinner at the Mayor's. Somewhat tardily, he became aware that Anne's trousseau had grown very shabby, and that neither she—nor he—had suggested that she might like to have some new clothes. Penitently, he bethought himself of the long-forgotten Mrs. Maple, and dictated a note for Miss Letts to send to her. The plump and prosperous modiste responded with a boxful of the latest fashions; but this time Anne caught sight of the price-tickets, and resolutely sent everything back. Neal gave her two dress-lengths—a black satin and a green voile—instead, and she made them up herself, on the superior sewing-machine, and insisted that they would do just as well. He knew they would not; and, after he reached Boston bought a long, fur-trimmed coat, with hat to match, at an excellent department store directly opposite the State House—where he could not very well help seeing it—and sent them to her.

He never knew how seldom she wore them. His days in Hinsboro, which dwindled to one, or at the most two, a week, were spent in feverish activities at the office. He gave up all pretense of getting home to supper, not even telephoning any more to say that he could not do so.

113

From Belford he wrote her hurried little notes on scratch paper every day—well, nearly every day. "1 A.M. Tues. Dearest: Just home from the leg. dead tired, stormy session but very interesting. Tell you all about it when I see you. Neal." . . . "8 A.M. Thurs. Am just rushing out to breakfast with Dawson, darling Anne, as this is my only chance of seeing him today, so excuse a brief line. Yrs. ever, N." (Undated) "Afraid the Gov. is going to veto the tax bill. Have an appointment to see him at 11, in haste, N." It did not surprise him that her letters were not much longer, and not much more communicative than his own. He did not dream that day after day when he was not at home— and indeed often when, nominally, he was, she did not get up at all, or very little. The cold had vanished at last, leaving her weak and listless; but uncontrollable nausea had taken its place.

She hated the very smell of food, she could not bear the sight of it. All day long she revolted against the thought of it, and then, at night, dreamed of it. Resolutely she tried one form of nourishment after another, in the hope of finding something which she could retain, but one thing after another became loathsome to her. Milk—coffee —tea—dry toast—gruel—fruit juice—Mrs. Conrad and Mrs. Simmons both came to see her and offered advice. Unfortunately, their advice was not the same, and only puzzled their victim.

"You should lie very still, not make the slightest effort —the quieter you keep, until you get over the nausea, the better. I'll dust and carpet-sweep and wipe up the bathroom for you —nonsense, I'm glad to do it. If you'll promise me you won't stir. And take something *hot*. A cup of beef extract. I believe you'll find that very tasty."

"Exercise, my dear Anne, exercise is the main thing. Even if you don't feel like it, move about. I'd offer to come over and do your housework for you—not that I'm *accustomed* to doing anything of the sort—if I didn't know how much better it was for you to do it yourself. And try a little solid food. Often that sets better than liquids. No, don't say you can't, because of course you *can*."

Anne did not say she couldn't. Bewildered, but willing,

she tried to do as she was told,—and grew steadily worse, while the tiny flat in which she had taken such pride and which she had kept so sweet and shining was left to neglect and disorder. And still Neal didn't guess, didn't notice— Of course he loved her, loved her dearly, but—was he *blind?*

March came in like a lion, roaring lustily. Anne lay in bed, listening to the wind howling, to the icy tapping of sleet against the window panes. It was nearly dark by four in the afternoon. She had not tried to get up at all, since it made her faint with dizziness even to cross the room to her bureau, and, after all, what was there to get up for? She had not brushed her hair, or washed her face, or made her bed. She wondered, vaguely, if she would ever feel like doing any of those things again, and drew the tumbled sheet up about her head to shut out the sound of the storm. As she did so, the doorbell rang.

At first she paid no attention. It rang once more, insistently. It rang again and again, the sound reverberating through the gloomy little rooms. At last she staggered to her feet, thrust them into her bed-slippers, and threw her soiled kimono about her shoulders. When she reached the front door, someone was pounding on it.

Leaning against the wall, she turned the lock. Before her stood Mr. Goldenburg, his kind, round face beaming with joy at the surprise he had given her. She sprang towards him with a cry of happiness. The next instant she had fainted away.

CHAPTER XI

"Now, my tear lidel frient, tell old Abie all apoud it."

"Oh, Mr. Goldenburg, *I am* so glad to see you! I never was so glad to see any one in all my life."

"Vel, vel—you must yust lie still a minute, an' holt my hant. I ain't goner run away. You'll feel petter bretty soon, *hein?*"

He had carried her back to bed, still unconscious, put a hot-water bottle at her feet, and dashed cold water over her white face. When she came to herself, she was crying bitterly, and clinging to him as if she would never let him go.

"Hey, listen, Anne—haf you any aromatic ammonia?"

"No—but it wouldn't matter if I had. I—I throw up everything I swallow, even water."

"So—so. Where is Neal?"

"In Belford. From Monday to Friday every week. And from Friday to Monday he's in his office."

"So—so."

"He doesn't know. He hasn't noticed. Oh, Mr. Goldenburg, I've read in books about young wives whispering 'their sweet secret' to their husbands blushing divinely, and both rejoicing, and the husbands surrounding the wives with 'the tenderest care.' And all that. I never read a word about this awful nausea, and feeling as if you'd rather die than live, and being lonely and forlorn. If I did tell Neal he'd probably just say, 'Oh—I'm in an awful hurry just now, but I'll be glad to hear about it next time I come home.'"

"Now den, Anne. You know dat ain't fair to Neal."

"Well, has he been fair to *me* I'd like to know?—I

116

wouldn't have known myself what *was* the matter with me, if Mrs. Conrad hadn't told me. She told me in such a dreadful way—I'll never forget it or forgive her— She acts as if it were all my fault—you'd think Neal had nothing to do with it at all—and as if it were some dreadful crime. She had three children herself, didn't she? 'Don't you realize, Anne,' she said severely, 'that you can't *afford* to have a baby?' And then she said something about self-control. Self-control—she never talked to her son about self-control! And we could afford a baby every year on the money Neal turns over to her! And she won't come and take care of me because she thinks I ought to get up and take exercise! Exercise!"

"Now, den, Anne, you know it ain't respectful to speak so of your moder-in-law. I'm sure she's a very nice lady." Mr. Goldenburg tried to speak firmly, but the tones of his voice did not carry conviction, which was hardly surprising, considering that, at the moment, he was thinking boiling in oil too good for the elder Mrs. Conrad. "Vere is your landlady? She lives downstairs, hein?"

"Yes, but she won't come because when she had told me to lie still I got up and made some biscuits for Neal's supper. She doesn't believe in exercise."

"Haf you seen a doctor?"

"No, Mrs. Conrad said that wasn't necessary. She said it would be a 'needless expense.' That this—this awful feeling had to 'run its course' no matter what you did. So I thought—"

Mr. Goldenburg, disengaging his hand, walked over to the telephone. "There *is* a doctor in Hinsboro, I suppose, *hein?*" he asked sarcastically. "Dr. Pratt? So—led me see vat is his number—seven-thirty-five— Yes, yes."

Dr. Pratt was in, he would be over, he said, right away. And, in the scant half hour that elapsed before his appearance, Mr. Goldenburg proceeded to "tidy things up" with a dexterity and a swiftness remarkable in so plump and placid a person. He found a rag and a can of Dutch Cleanser, and scrubbed the bathroom basin; he hung clean towels beside it. He changed Anne's pillow cases and bureau scarf, and laid her tumbled toilet articles in a neat row

117

—hairbrush, mirror, nail-file, buttonhook. He ran the carpet-sweeper over the Axminster rug in the living-room, and dusted the flat surfaces of the mission furniture, wound the clock, watered the plants, threw away the rubbishy collection of old newspapers and magazines, lighted the gas stove and put the kettle on to boil. Then with complete composure he admitted the surprised physician, still wearing one of Anne's aprons firmly tied about his waist.

Dr. Pratt was not long in rendering his verdict. There must be regular care and skilled treatment without delay. Anne's condition was not dangerous, but he could not venture to describe it as otherwise than serious. She was very weak, had apparently been badly run down before—yes, yes, a heavy bronchial cold, also neglected. Well, would she rather be moved to a hospital, or have a nurse and maid installed? And of course her husband must be advised at once. It was useless for Anne to protest; Dr. Pratt spoke, brusquely, about the danger to the baby when she tried to do so. Appealingly, she turned to Mr. Goldenburg.

"Do you suppose, if you telegraphed Mabel, she would come and stay with me? I wouldn't know where to get a maid, or what to do with her afterwards. But Mabel—Mabel is my best friend," she explained to the doctor, "except Mr. and Mrs. Goldenburg. We've often planned that she should come and visit me, but somehow—"

"Why not telephone? Then she could get here sooner."

Mr. Goldenburg was already in action again. Without much difficulty, he located Mabel, and Mabel said that she would be delighted to come, that she would be there in the morning. The doctor departed, promising to send around a nurse at once; and, within an hour, the nurse materialized. And leaving her to bathe the patient and make her bed, Mr. Goldenburg sought out first Mrs. Simmons, next Mrs. Conrad, and finally—catching the last train to Belford—Neal.

Anne never knew exactly what he said to any of them; she was, in fact, too ill to inquire, or to care, for several weeks. But, as those weeks dragged their slow course through, she became vaguely and comfortably conscious, sick as she was, that she was happier than she had been in a long, long time. Mabel arrived, and barely allowing time to change from her travel dress to an all-enveloping apron, scrubbed and scoured the flat from end to end, and kept it, from then on, in a state of matchless cleanliness. Miss Keep, the nurse, waited on her by inches. Her hair was not tangled and matted any more, there was ice at the back of her neck, a hot-water bottle at her feet, she was gently rubbed—her back, her arms, her forehead—with bay rum. If it was given to her when she was drowsy, she soon found that she could retain a little food—only a spoonful or so, at first, and it had to be either very hot or very cold, but gradually the temperature did not matter so much, and she could take more and more. Neal came home looking very much cowed, badly frightened—all the gay self-confidence, the driving energy, wiped from his face. He brought her flowers—the first he had given her since her honeymoon, and sat down beside her on the bed, his shoulders sagging, and tried to talk to her, but couldn't because his voice shook so. At first, that is—afterwards he collected himself and spoke better. But not until she had seen how shaken he was, how sorry and, forgiving him, forgot there was anything to forgive.

By the first of April, Anne was sufficiently better so that Miss Keep could leave, Mabel caring for her—since now she did not need so much care—and doing the housework, too. By the first of May she was up for a little while each day. The session of the legislature was over, and Neal was home again for good, home, that is, until another election at least—he had decided to run for office again then, this time for the State Senate. He was very kind to her, very thoughtful, and though he was very busy, and usually brought work home with him, he seldom stayed in the office during evening or on Sundays—once in a while, of course, but not very often. Soon she was able to play for him on the new piano with which he had surprised her, the first time she walked out to the living-room, and to go for short, easy rides with him in the automobile. The first of June, Mabel went home, leaving them alone again, and they were very happy. They were grateful to Mabel, grateful beyond expression, but they would only have a few

119

more months alone. Anne did quantities of sewing, sitting on the little porch; she trimmed a bassinet with pink silk and white dotted muslin and lace which the Goldenburgs sent her, she lined a little wicker chest of drawers with scented pads, she feather-stitched tiny flannel petticoats and hemstitched tiny muslin dresses. Mrs. Simmons did her washing and ironing and the cleaning, and Neal took care of the garden; but except for this help, Anne did her own work again. Dr. Pratt made no objection to her working now that she felt all right, provided she did not overdo. In fact, it was much better that she should, he said, since she had always been used to activity, and idleness would be bad for her. When he delivered himself of this opinion, Mrs. Conrad announced with satisfaction, that this was what she had kept saying, right along.

Anne's baby was born in the Hinsboro hospital on a torrid night near the end of August. She was in labor for thirty-six hours, and, at the end of that time, the child was taken from her with instruments. At first she fought her hard battle uncomplainingly and bravely, submitting to everything she was told to do, and everything that was done to her, calmly and patiently. But as the agony increased and became unbearable, quite suddenly, she lost her self-control, shrieking and sobbing for mercy. When the doctor began to give her whiffs of ether to take off the sharp edge of the pains, Neal, who had stayed with her up to that time, became deathly sick from the smell of it, and left her. She felt herself abandoned to a bottomless pit of torture. When Dr. Pratt finally held the ether cone to her face, telling her to breathe as much as she wanted of it, she snatched it from him, and pulled it down over her mouth and nose, tightly, tightly, oblivion the only mercy she sought—if it could last forever, if it only could, her last conscious prayer.

Her consciousness returned in waves. She babbled, telling secrets she did not mean to divulge, and yet unable to be silent. She felt bruised and beaten, she longed to be left to die in peace—and still they kept doing things to her, things that disturbed her, things that hurt her. If they would only go away! She cried, weakly, the tears dropping

120

down from her cheeks to the pillow, and yet she could not move to wipe them off, and no one else seemed to notice them.

Then suddenly, Neal was there beside her, kissing the tears away; and between them on the bed, lay their little son.

CHAPTER XII

IN the next eight years, Neal built up his law practice, which continued to grow, not indeed by leaps and bounds, but steadily and satisfactorily. He also served four terms in the state legislature, the third as Speaker of the House, the fourth as chairman of the most important committee in the Senate; and, during all this time, he commuted back and forth between Belford and Hinsboro, bringing his laundry with him to save expense, and occupying his two-dollar room at the Talmage Tavern.

During the same eight years, Anne, smothering again and again her disappointment at taking no tangible part in her husband's campaigns, and at being left behind when he went to Belford, washed, cooked, cleaned, sewed, and took care of Junior; presented that husky youngster, when he was three years old, with a little sister, Nancy; took care of them both; washed, cooked, cleaned and sewed some more.

When the second baby was imminent, it became apparent that the little flat, in which they had continued to live up to this time, would not suffice for the family needs any longer. They had not saved up enough money to carry out their treasured plan of building, unless they built a house which would be merely another temporary makeshift. So they moved to a six-room cottage, which they were able to rent cheaply, and which was sorely in need of paint, paper, and plumbing. By degrees they persuaded a reluctant landlord to make it more comfortable and attractive. With two more rooms in their possession than they had had since their marriage, they converted one into a nursery, and one into a den, and the wide, though dilapidated veranda which encircled the house, usually much cluttered with a sand box, a kiddy coop, a never-emptied basket of mending, and a miscellaneous collection of shabby toys, gave them, in mild weather, an extra living-room; while the large yard provided the children with a space in which to range, and Anne a space in which to plant and cultivate both a flower and a vegetable garden.

But, though they were glad to be free of Mrs. Simmons' flat, they missed Mrs. Simmons herself. She had been willing enough to help with the heavier housework and to "listen" for the baby when Neal and Anne went out together as long as they remained under her roof, but she felt it beneath her to "hire out"—the "out" being taken literally. Mabel came and spent a month with them when Anne left the hospital after Nancy's birth, a complacent Mabel, engaged to George, who had become more and more prosperous and who now had the largest farm and the finest barns in Hamstead. She was most helpful and kind; but she was unwilling to prolong her visit, as she had done before. After she left, Anne was unable to go motoring with Neal, or attend the meetings of the Bach and Beethoven Society, or entertain her little bridge club. Worse than this, her close confinement to the house, and the never-ending drudgery of her work began to tell on her heavily. She not only grew very thin herself, but the baby stopped gaining, became fretful, and turned blue under her eyes. Alarmed, Anne consulted Dr. Pratt, and he told her that unless she had regular help and equally regular recreation, she would have to wean Nancy.

"And that," he added, meaningly, "you should not, of course, consider in this warm weather."

Anne's dread of the "servant problem" rose from a deeper source than the horrible stories she had heard from her mother-in-law about the depravity of all domestic workers, and the fact that she felt she could ill-afford to feed and pay a maid; it rose also from her very sincere sense of her own probable incompetence in directing, rather than doing, work, and her unwillingness to entrust the care of the children to any one else. But to her infinite surprise and relief, Dora King, the first applicant in response to the advertisement which Anne inserted in the *Hinsboro Times,* came when she said she would, contentedly took possession of the attic, and seemed perfectly satisfied to remain. She was not a skilled servant; indeed, she had never had a "place" before. She was, like Anne herself, a farmer's daughter, who had drifted to a little city, and who had not enjoyed "clerking" as much as she expected. She was willing to learn; and Anne, far from resenting her ignorance, marveled at the quickness with which she overcame it.

But, even with Dora's help, her working hours were long and hard, and though she managed to nurse the baby through the summer, she was obliged to wean her with the coming of cool weather, a process which proved trying for them both. Indeed, as time went on, Anne became more and more appalled at the number of things that could happen to children, normal, reasonably healthy children. They had croup, and kept her awake all night; they had colic, and kept her distracted all day; they had measles and mumps and whooping-cough and chicken pox; they had nasty little sniffling colds, and deep frightening coughs and after a certain number of these, Dr. Pratt insisted that they must have their tonsils and adenoids removed. Junior fell out of a tree and broke his leg; Nancy upset a kettle of hot water on herself and scalded her arm. They outgrew their rompers as fast as Anne could make them; tore them as fast as she could mend them; soiled them as fast as she could change and wash them. Their faces were continually becoming smeared with mud or egg. They clamored for drinks of water after they had gone to bed, for sugar cookies as soon as they had been sent outdoors to play. They swarmed over her the minute she put on a fresh dress, and they scattered disreputable toys all over the living-room ten minutes after she had whipped it into perfect order.

But they adored her. She was to them far more important, far more precious than their father. They loved him, of course; but he did not figure largely in their field of life, not nearly as largely as she did, not even as largely as Dora. He was away from home a great deal, and they learned to take this as a matter of course. They were glad to see him when he returned, but they did not miss him when he was away. They were not dependent on him—in a manner which they recognized—for food and comfort. Neither did he read them stories at night, or sing gay little songs with them in the morning, sitting down with them at the piano directly after breakfast to do so. He did not dress dolls, or stuff depleted teddy-bears, or cause limping railroad trains to leap forward again, or build cathedrals out of stone blocks. He was BUSY.

So, in the adoration of her children and of Dora—for she attained that also—Anne found, for a long time, all the beauty and romance which her life contained. She was not unhappy; she felt fewer and fewer pangs because Neal seemed to need her so little, in her overwhelming consciousness that Junior and Nancy needed her so much. If she had no talents towards directing political destiny, she at least had undeniable gifts as a homemaker. The dingy little cottage became gradually more and more lovely. She experimented with hangings, with rugs, with furniture, reading omnivorously and far into the night every authority she could find on such subjects, buying cautiously and cannily, on her rare trips to Belford, where she studied the shops as carefully as if they had been equations in algebra, and on her rarer trips to Hamstead where antiques were still to be found in sheltered attics. And her housekeeping became so locally renowned that the elder Mrs. Conrad was much annoyed. She "put up" more fruits and vegetables than any woman in Hinsboro. She kept hens, and supplied not only her own family and her mother-in-law's with eggs and poultry, but sold some of both besides, until Neal put a stop to that; then canned her extra chickens, and stowed away her extra eggs in waterglass. Her angel cakes, her lemon pies, her Parker House rolls were in demand for every church supper and harvest festival. She continued to make all her own clothes, to make Neal's shirts and pajamas; she began to make the children's clothes, too, and Dora's.

And so the seasons sped past, filled to overflowing, with hardly a landmark to show their passing. She had been married five years, six, seven; Junior was five years old and starting in Kindergarten; she had been married eight years, nine, ten; Nancy was five years old and starting in Kindergarten. She was not so busy any more, and the house was empty, terribly so. Then war was declared, and suddenly, she was busier than ever. She knitted innumerable sweaters, she joined a class in surgical dressings, she sold Liberty bonds from house to house, she fed her family on "substitutes" so successfully that they saw "meatless, sweetless, and wheatless" days go by without a murmur. She was spurred to supreme efforts in "conservation" because Neal had been appointed Food Administrator for the state. He filled the position with the greatest brilliance and thoroughness. He organized and promoted his department with consummate success; he went into every county, making patriotic speeches, presiding at rallies, attending conferences. Twice he was actually "called to Washington" by wire, and on one of these occasions, he went to the White House and talked earnestly to the President for five minutes. His picture surmounted the charts of instructions which conscious housewives—not only of Hinsboro and Belford, where he was well known already, but of the entire state, where he was less well known— hung in their kitchens. The press of the state, which, up to this time, had paid him scant attention, began first to notice and then to "feature" him. It was rumored that the governor, a rather shy, retiring man, was jealous of him. He gave substantial contributions to all patriotic causes—a thousand dollars here, two thousand dollars there. He did not consult Anne beforehand in making these donations and when she heard them publicly announced, she could hardly believe her ears.

"How can you give a thousand dollars to the Fund for French Wounded when you haven't *got* it?" she demanded aghast.

"I've *got* to have it . . . well, if you must know, I've borrowed a little . . . I meant to suggest that you should come to Washington with me the next time I get a wire— the President intimated he would want to see me again be-

126

fore long—but I guess, from the way you talk you wouldn't think the expense of the trip was justified—"

"No, I wouldn't," she answered quietly. She was terribly wounded at the sarcasm with which he had spoken, terribly hurt by her renewed consciousness of her own unimportance. She rose, half blinded with tears, and going out to the kitchen, began to put together a cake-batter which contained neither butter nor white flour and only one egg. Mixed with melted chocolate, and eaten very fresh, it was not really bad at all. As she stirred, she lifted her eyes to the chart surmounted by Neal's picture and read, for the hundredth time, his stirring proclamation. Slowly her vision cleared, and she felt serene and proud once more.

By the time the Armistice was signed, there was no doubt that Neal had become the most conspicuous figure in his state. Emboldened by this progress, he ran the following fall for Lieutenant-Governor. He had been confident, glowingly confident, of victory. And, by one of those strange turns of fortune which make gambling a safe and sure sport compared to politics, he had been overwhelmingly defeated. The blow was the more bitter because Low, the man running for Governor on the same ticket, was elected by a substantial majority.

Neal was not a good loser; he had been silent in his success—that is, at home—seldom discussing his progress with Anne; now he became complainingly loquacious.

"Low sold me out; it was money that defeated me, money and crooked politics."

"You have always spent quite a little yourself, in your campaigns."

"Are you accusing me of being a crook?" he almost shouted at her.

"Of course not; quite the contrary. I'm saying that I don't believe your opponent was either, or Mr. Low. It stands to reason that Mr. Low would rather have you for Lieutenant-Governor than a man of the opposite party."

She did not again fall into the error of expressing such an opinion. Neal could not bear to have her, or any one else, think that he himself was to blame for his defeat. He actually swore at her, he was so angry. He apologized, after a time, for his language, but in the meanwhile he went sullenly about the house, or shut himself up in his office, declining to come home to his meals. This was not the worst of it; sometimes when Anne telephoned the office he did not answer, and she had no idea where to find him. She had hard work to keep from crying—then hard work to keep him from seeing that she had been crying. If his political success had been difficult for her to bear, his political failure was doubly so. Through her tears she saw in remembrance the man she had married—so gay, so kind, so loving and tender. Through her tears she saw too, in reality, the man to whom she was married—somber, selfish, indifferent, curt. If she had loved him less, it would have been easier for her. But to her he was still as he had been on the day when he first held her in his arms, the most wonderful being in the world.

She had the wisdom, greater than might reasonably be expected, to neither reproach nor nag him; and, after a few weeks, he pulled himself together, and flung himself into his law-practice with renewed vigor. He was making money now, real money, and if he kept his nose to the grindstone, and closed his ears to the humming of the political bee for all time, he could become—well, very comfortably fixed financially. On Christmas day he gave Anne the deeds for a large lot on the outskirts of the city which she had long admired, and suggested to her, a little gruffly, that he thought the time had come when they could build if she would still like to, and that he would tell an architect who was said to know his business to start drawing plans whenever she said the word. They could amuse themselves going over blueprints, these long winter evenings. By the time the ground had thawed out enough to start excavating, they could probably have decided what they wanted. She knew that this was his way of seeking to make amends, and responded with delight. With the plans spread out before them, their heads touching, they came closer together, mentally and spiritually as well as physically, than they had been in a long time; and, with the coming of spring they spent every spare moment in supervising the building. This took longer than they had expected—almost a year—which annoyed Neal; and it cost more than they expected—by several thousands—which troubled Anne. But they had found a common interest, a common enthusiasm again, and both were happy.

The new house, when it was finally done, was extremely comfortable, and very attractive. It was white-painted and green-shuttered, a "simple Colonial model" with a flower garden in front, a vegetable garden behind, a neat garage at one side, and a glassed-in sun parlor at the other, wide lawns all about it. Downstairs there were a broad hall, a large living-room with a big, friendly fireplace, a small den for Neal, a good-sized dining-room and a kitchen with light on two sides, and every possible appliance to make cooking easy and pleasant. Upstairs were a sewing-room and five bedrooms, one for Neal and Anne, one for Junior, one for Nancy, one for Dora, and a spare-room; and three bathrooms. Overall there was a spacious attic, and under all a spacious cellar. The most modern type of furnace was installed; so were all imaginable electrical devices—a vacuum cleaner, a washing machine, a mangle, a stove. And there was Colonial furniture upstairs and down, Persian rugs on the ground floor, simple ornaments scattered here and there, open bookcases well filled, a few good prints and water colors. They bought no new car that year, though theirs was several seasons old already, and Anne pared her housekeeping expenses almost as closely as in the first days of her marriage. But no reasonable expense was spared on the house, and it stood in her name, unmortgaged and fully paid for. They had built for all time, and built well.

CHAPTER XIII

THEIR first guest, after they were duly installed in the new house, was Clarence Hathaway.

He appeared in the wake of a telegram stating that he was passing through Hinsboro on his way back to Washington after a vacation in Canada, and would like to "spend the week-end if they could put him up." And Anne felt a stirred excitement, even greater than Neal's surprise, when the message reached them.

"Good old Clare—he doesn't forget his friends, does he? He's first Secretary now, you know, in Paris—getting on the way he planned all right, and look at me—"

"You're getting on all right too, aren't you? *I* think so! Oh, Neal—what shall I wear?"

Neal burst out laughing. "That's the first question any woman asks, under any circumstances, I guess," he jeered gently. Then after a moment's silence, he added, "I suppose it does matter. Couldn't you run up to Belford and get something?"

"There isn't time."

"Well, you look all right to me whatever Hathaway may think, and that ought to go as big with you as it does with me when you say *you* think I'm getting on all right whatever—"

"It *does* go big with me, darling. Only—"

She realized how big the "only" was with the first casual glance which Hathaway cast in her direction after the mutual greetings had been exchanged. The house was quite all right; Anne felt sure of that; she hoped especially that he had noticed the guest-towels and bed linen in his room, which she had embroidered herself. And Dora was all right. She carried off her unaccustomed but wholly correct black uniform and spotless frilly apron with pleased pride, and served tea without a visible tremor. The tea was brought into the living-room on a silver tray, steaming in a silver pot, flanked with thick cream and hot water in smaller silver pots and lemon sliced thin on a little crystal dish, and fragile flowered teacups; and it was accompanied by lettuce sandwiches, and hot biscuits stuffed with marmalade, and frosted cakes set out on a mahogany muffin-stand. The children were all right too. They came in for just the proper moment, Nancy, in smocked China silk, curtseying, Junior, in a blue serge coat and white trousers, shaking hands, neither shy nor forward, neither silent nor chattering. Anne saw them go out of the room, her heart swelling with satisfaction. And of course Neal was all right; his old charm, his old buoyancy, had come to the surface and bubbled over again at the sight of his friend. Hathaway himself, for all his elegance, had no more distinction, no more magnetism. But she—

There had been so much else to do in preparation for the great visit that she had found herself with only fifteen minutes left in which to dress; so she had washed hastily, and hastily twisted her curls into a knot on the top of her head. Neither her hair nor her skin had ever had any care, and beautiful as they still were, they had begun to suffer from neglect; she had not been to the dentist's since Nancy was a baby—at Dr. Pratt's insistence she had gone then; while her hands, inevitably, had suffered most of all. They were rough, enlarged, reddened. Her "best dress" was nearly a year old, and she had made it herself, as she did all her dresses; it was a brown taffeta, many seasons behind the style, too long, too full, overtrimmed. She had thought it pretty once; now she hated it. And when Hathaway gave her that casual look, she felt that she could gladly tear it off and throw it into the scrap-basket.

That was, indeed, exactly what she did do with it, several hours later, when, the perfect dinner served, the children in bed and asleep, she left the two men to "talk over old times together" and went to her room. Exhausted, from emotion as much as fatigue, she flung herself down

on her bed without undressing. Then, jerking herself upright
with a swift, ungraceful movement, she ripped the offending
garment from neckband to hem, and stamped on it.

"No wonder he thought you were a perfect fright," she
sobbed aloud, "I'll never own another dress like that as
long as I live. I'll take the first train to New York after he
goes and buy myself some clothes. No, I won't either; I'll
go to that nice Mrs. Maple in Washington. I guess I can
go there and shop, if I can't go for—for any other reason!
I can leave the children with Dora perfectly well, and I
don't need to scrimp and save any more. Why have I been
such an awful fool as to keep on doing it, and on, and on!
I'll have my hands taken care of too; they're as rough as
nutmeg graters! And my face massaged and my hair
treated. I—I am probably the most hideous looking
woman in all the world."

Meanwhile, downstairs, the conversation had taken a
turn which she was very far from guessing.

The discussion of "old times" did not last long, and the
"dear old college days" supposed to form the sole topic of
conversation between classmates meeting after a long separation, received no more than a passing mention. Hathaway talked of himself for a while, of his satisfactory
advancement, his delightful post in Paris, his hopes for an
even more notable appointment; easily and quietly, without arrogance, without even a too apparent complacence.
And it was he who finally began to talk of Neal.

"But you'll get terribly fed up if I go on like this— How
about yourself? Doing well, aren't you?"

"Financially, yes. It was hard sledding at first, but this
year I've earned close to fifteen thousand. I give both
Anne's family and mine a regular allowance, and she has
two brothers whom I'm helping to educate. But even so,
we'll be pretty comfortable, if I can keep on going ahead,
and I think I can. I've never run into debt, or even spent
all my income—Anne's seen to that," he added ungrudg-
ingly. "I have a few good investments, and I carry life insurance. We all have savings bank accounts—the children
too. And of course now we have this house."

"Not startling, but pretty solid, I should say. But why do you stress the word 'financially'? Don't you feel you're doing well every way?"

"I was thinking that I hadn't done as well politically as I'd hoped."

"Because of one trivial defeat!"

"It didn't seem trivial to me. I expected to be Governor of this state by now."

"Well, yes. I rather thought that was your plan. But after all—"

Hathaway tapped the arm of his chair with his fingers, gazing into the open fire as he did so. Then he asked a most astonishing question.

"How about your wife? Was she interested in politics too?"

"Anne?" Neal's surprise was apparent in his voice. "Why, Anne would be interested, I guess, in anything I wanted to do. She—she's devoted to me."

"Yes, of course, I saw that. But I mean—has she been helping you actively and directly as well as passively and indirectly?"

"She's gone without everything," Neal answered, coming swiftly to Anne's defense, under the impression that she was being attacked. "Good times, and pretty clothes, and trips and friends. I never would have been able to go into politics if she hadn't. And she's been a perfect wife and mother. The children adore her, and so do I, though I guess I don't show it as much as I might. I've got a devilish one-track mind, and when I get started on a lawsuit or a campaign, I almost forget I have a family—sometimes. Just the way I forgot everything else in the world when I saw Anne, and made up my mind I'd got to have her. It would be hell if I didn't know she was still there, in the background, too. Once I thought I was going to lose her— I'd neglected her terribly, and she was going to have a baby, which made it all the worst—and I nearly went wild when I realized what I'd done."

"But after you'd had a chance to forget about that bad time, you neglected her again?"

"I suppose I did—do. But—there's never been another woman."

"Good God! I should say not! What do you want—the Capitoline Venus?"

"No," roared Neal, angrily, "what are you driving at, anyway?"

"My dear fellow, please don't think I'm venturing to criticize your conduct. And as for criticizing your wife— well, I thought ten years ago she was one of the loveliest, as well as one of the most remarkable girls, I'd ever met in my life. I've remembered her, pretty vividly, all this time. That's a little unusual for me. And I confess that seeing her tonight has been an acute disappointment."

"Well, I'm not disappointed in her. She suits me."

"Just wait a minute, can't you? I still think she's beautiful—and remarkable. Even more remarkable than I'd guessed. But I think she's tragic."

"Tragic!"

"Yes. How old is she? Under thirty? I thought so. Well, she looks over forty. She has a good mind, hasn't she? Taught school before you married her, was awfully keen on educating herself better? How long is it since she's read anything but nursery rhymes? She's stagnating, mentally as well as physically. Kept in the background! I should think she had! She's submerged herself in your personality, and your career and your children until she's nothing but a washed-out drudge without a particle of individuality left. She's done it voluntarily, because she loved you—loves you. But she must know, even if you don't know, that she was capable of something a good deal bigger. And she must have passed some pretty bitter hours when she first realized you didn't intend to give her a chance to fulfill her destiny. For God's sake, why haven't you tried putting her in the *foreground?* With her looks, and her mind, and her natural gifts as a hostess— Neal, you utter fool."

"Even if you are my guest, and an old friend, I think you've gone about far enough in discussing my wife."

"Then suppose we discuss mine for a change."

"Yours! I didn't know you were married!"

"I'm not. But I was."

"You mean you lost her? Clare—I'm darned sorry, I hadn't heard—"

"Yes, I lost her. But she didn't die. She found out she cared for someone else more than she did for me. I found it out, too."

"Oh—"

"Yes. Exactly. She was a poor girl when I married her, almost as poor as Anne. And she came from a home that wasn't much better. But she was pretty, devilishly pretty and ambitious—for herself. I was much the best bet that her hand had ever held. I fell for her, hard—and fast. I ought to have known better— Lord knows I've had experience enough—but I married her. She began by almost ruining me financially. There was absolutely no limit to what she wanted. And she ended by almost ruining me diplomatically. Cæsar's wife had nothing on that of a rising young secretary. I left that post in Rome, which I enjoyed so much, because I was given an indefinite leave of absence. When I went to Paris, I went without her."

Slangily, casually, without a trace of his usual careful elegance, Hathaway had told his story. But Neal found himself clearing his throat, more moved than he could have imagined. And not only moved—enlightened. Clare —had made no comparisons—aloud. But Neal saw those that he had made mentally, as clearly as if they had been engraved in flaming letters. Saw, too, how he had injured Anne; and since he could, perhaps, never be entirely selfless, how he had, in injuring her, injured himself as well. Before he succeeded in framing an answer, Hathaway spoke again.

"So that's that. And seeing Anne—you don't mind if I call her Anne, do you?—here tonight brought it all back to me—because she's—she's so different. And you're so lucky—and playing against your luck!"

"What," Neal managed to ask, "would you do, if you were I?"

Hathaway balanced the question. "Would anything very dreadful happen," he asked at length, "if you left those two corking kids with that pretty maid—she'd look after them all right, wouldn't she?—and took Anne on a vacation? You could do with a little change yourself—you'd find that one-track mind of yours developing into a transcontinental trunk-line when you got back. You're stale, man! I'm sailing next week on the *France*—why don't you see if you could get a stateroom on the same boat? And—and spend the summer in Paris—and let me help give you both a good time!"

CHAPTER XIV

Neal had come down with a heavy cold which kept him confined to the hotel, but he insisted, since he was not really sick, and since there was so little time left, that Anne should not stay in with him, but should go, as they had both planned to do, and have tea with Clare at the Château de Madrid.

She did not answer at once when he made this suggestion, or even turn towards him. She was standing by one of the long windows of their *salon*, looking out on the courtyard of the hotel,—the green grass plot, the tall feathery tree that shaded their bedroom, the prim little iron chairs standing stiffly about. The open doors of the dining-room beyond revealed it to be empty, as befitted the time half-way between luncheon and dinner. But there were bright crowded nosegays on the white-covered table, and, beyond, the cheerful clatter of silver and glass being put away. Now and then an aproned *garçon* flicking a napkin, passed into view and disappeared again.

It was very warm, for Paris, and Anne's beautifully dressed hair, shining like burnished gold, escaped from its net about the white nape of her neck and her white brow, and curled in little soft moist tendrils. She was flushed, too, with the heat, a little languid; her cheeks were very pink, and her long lashes drooped over them as if it were an effort for her to keep her eyes open. Her diaphanous *négligé*, pale orchid-color, had slipped away from one white, rounded shoulder, and she raised a slim white hand and pulled it into place. The *négligé* was cut in a deep V, and when she had adjusted it over her shoulder, she also

137

tightened the ribbon on the sheer lace-edged slip beneath it, to raise it over her breast.

"I shan't be disappointed," she said at length, "if I don't go. There are some letters I ought to write and—"

"Nonsense!"

"And I shall have to dress."

"Since when," teased Neal, "has that been a burden to you? . . . though I must say you look very nice the way you are."

She flushed, deliciously. "I meant—it is so very warm."

"That new powder-blue crêpe has just come in from Lucien Lelong."

"Yes—I know—and the powder-blue hat from Camille . . . I suppose that Clare might think it unappreciative if we both went back on him."

She disappeared, into the bedroom, and a moment later Neal heard the sound of running water from the bathroom beyond. He smiled. There would be scented salts in that bath, he knew, and scented powder, showered from a great ball-like puff, after it, and just a touch of liquid scent besides, *jasmine de corse* that cost four dollars for a tiny bottle and came from a famous perfumer. Then fresh lingerie pulled from a deep drawer, another lace-edged slip, silk stockings as fine as gossamer. Last of all, that powder-blue frock, as perfect of cut as it was of color, with a wide hat and narrow slippers to match the frock. Then Anne would reappear, smiling almost shyly, waiting for his exclamation of approval.

How happy she had been all summer! It was nearly four months now since they had stood beside the gangplank, watching it lifted, waving good-by to Dora and Junior and Nancy, to Mr. and Mrs. Goldenburg and George and Mabel, who had all come to see them off, for it was a great day for these old friends as well as for themselves when Neal and Anne actually "went to Europe." Neither of them was seasick a single minute, and every inch of the ship, from their own tiny cabin, to the great *salon* where they played bridge and danced, and drank strange new refreshing drinks, was a source of delight to them. Then came the landing at Havre, with the choppy blue waves beneath them and the scarless blue sky above them, and the hurrying porters in their blue blouses chattering French, and the funny train with seats facing each other across the car in the little compartment. Then the garden-like country side, the stone cottages, red tiled roofs, high walls, smug fields; and finally—Paris, the lights streaming in the Place de la Concorde as they crossed it for the first time, the quaint hotel on the Rue St. Honoré where Clare had engaged rooms for them, and the Bois de Boulogne beckoning them for their first evening drive.

The very morning after their arrival, while they were still laughing over their breakfast of *café au lait* and long hard rolls, served in their little *salon,* and wondering how they were ever to "hold out" until lunch time on such meager fare, Clare, who had not left them until nearly midnight, reappeared, and mapped out their program. Before they did a single thing, before they even went to see the Louvre and Notre Dame, before they had lunch at Ciro's or dinner at the Café de la Paix, Anne must be re-clothed. He would accompany them to a dressmaker's—a *petite maison* not too expensive but very *recherchée,* and worthy of being entrusted with this task.

"And I expect," he said frankly, "that the job will have to be done from the skin up. You don't look to me as if you had on the right things underneath. Nobody has waist-lines any more; on the contrary, everyone has legs."

"You don't expect *me* to go with Anne to the dressmak-er's?" protested Neal, aghast.

"Of course. Both of us. Husband and interested friend. They'd think she didn't have any male relatives to pay the bills if she went alone."

And Clare was right about this as he was about every-thing else—Neal found himself welcomed with open arms at the *petite maison,* and in course of time at several *grandes maisons* as well. He actually enjoyed the welcome —at the first three or four establishments—then it began to pall on him, and he suggested that Clare and Anne should go without him, while he went around to the

139

American Express to see if, by any chance, any one from Belford had registered there. But he paid the bills without a murmur, in a glow of satisfaction, as he saw Anne transformed, almost before his eyes. This was not entirely due to the dressmakers. There also was a *coiffeur*, Antoine, in whom Clare had great and well-deserved confidence; and under his direction a course in beauty culture was begun which in a few weeks produced astonishing results. Presently Anne looked no more than her age again; then she began to look a good deal less than her age. Clare dropped in occasionally, to watch Antoine's skillful ministrations, to suggest that the shining hair which glittered like gold when it had just been washed, should be massed a little higher on the erect little head, that the small pink nails followed the shape of the fingers better when they were curved than when they were pointed, that not even a suggestion of rouge should be dusted over cheeks so softly rosy. The color deepened in Anne's face at the tribute implied. It was still deep when, immaculate and demure, she went back to Neal.

As soon as she had the proper toilette, Anne, still acting under the direction of Clare, who had spoken a word for his friends to his chief, left her own card and Neal's at the Embassy. And shortly after these cards had been returned, Clare gave a luncheon in his apartment to which the Ambassador and the Ambassadress came as "honor guests," though it was really in honor of Neal and Anne. Thus launched, they found themselves approaching the *Grande Semaine* with a new circle of delightful acquaintances. They went to the races, Neal showing himself, from the very beginning, to have a real *flair* for betting. He won a great deal of money, which Anne tried hard to feel was not ethical; but when he announced that they could prolong their holiday on the strength of his ill-gotten gains, she forgot all about their source; and her costume for the Opera Ball, which Clare designed and Neal paid for, took a prize.

Left to their own devices, they would probably have fallen into the error common to their country folk, of trying to see all Europe in this one brief visit; but when Clare caught them looking at circulars and timetables, he drew these away, and laughingly threw them into the scrapbasket. Enough to see Paris, this time, he insisted. There was more there than they could discover in three years, let alone three months. And how was Anne to keep up with her French lessons with the shabby but brilliant little old *professeur* if they went dashing off to Switzerland or Italy? He relented, later on, to the extent of advising them to accept certain very attractive week-end invitations to big French country houses, which were the result of the *entrée* he had secured for them—invitations in which he also was always included. And, in August, when *monsieur le professeur* took his meager *vacances,* they toured the château country and the battlefields in his motor car, and went, after that, to Chartres and Rouen in the same conveyance. But, for the most part, they limited their excursions to day-trips on the Seine boats, or long afternoons in the forest of Fontainebleau and the gardens of Versailles. Anne learned to ride—Clare had two horses so there was always one at her disposal. She learned to drive Clare's Mercedes. Neal had never thought she "would be able to manage" the Dodge, but now he saw that he had been mistaken. Watching her development, he realized that Clare had not said half what might be said about her possibilities. Well, he would never make the old mistakes again. They were going home now, very soon, and when they did . . .

Anne came into the room, dressed as he had foreseen, waiting for his praise. A violent fit of sneezing interrupted him as he tried to express it.

"I don't dare kiss you, darling," he mumbled, behind his enveloping handkerchief. "Sure to give this darned cold to you.—Clare's sent up word he's waiting for you. Have a good time."

She found Clare leaning against the boxlike desk of the *concierge,* chatting with that functionary. The *ménage* was devoted to him.

"Neal has a cold," she said as they shook hands, "he
141

couldn't risk going out, of course. But he insisted that I should come, just the same."

"Naturally. I should never have forgiven you if you hadn't. But how on earth could he catch a cold in such weather?"

"Absurd, isn't it? *Mais le voilà, tout de même!*"

"My word, Anne, how you are coming along! You ripple that off as if you'd lived here all your life. What are you reading now?"

"Balzac—trying to anyway. '*La Femme de Trente Ans.*'"

"A wonderful story, and a wonderful study in psychology. You ought to find it especially interesting."

"Why?"

"You're just turning thirty yourself, aren't you?"

Something in the way he asked the question made her flush. They were skimming out towards the Champs-Elysées now and Clare was driving himself—it was a long time, Anne realized, since she had seen his discreet little chauffeur.

"I'm not in the least like Julie," she protested.

"No? Well, don't be discouraged. You're progressing wonderfully."

"I didn't mean it that way. Of course I don't *wish* to be in the least like Julie."

"Why not? She's immortal, you know."

Slightly troubled at his tone, she did not answer. He changed the subject swiftly.

"And so—you're really leaving Tuesday?"

"I suppose so."

"You sound as if you were sorry."

"Oh, Clare—how could anyone help being sorry to leave Paris for Hinsboro?"

There was real grief in her voice; but the next instant she tried to catch back the words.

"Of course I'm counting the days until I see Junior and Nancy. If I could only have had them here too, it would have been quite perfect."

"Like most women, you like to have your cake and eat it too, don't you, Anne? . . . Well, I can understand that the sort of existence you were leading when I came to your house last spring might pall a good deal now."

"And if it hadn't been for you," she said with eager gratitude, "I never would have had a glimpse, perhaps, of any other kind of existence! The minute you looked at me, I saw how shabby and provincial I really was. I went upstairs—and—and cried, Clare. And all the time I was crying, you were persuading Neal to give me this wonderful chance. I can't ever thank you enough."

"Don't try," he said lightly, "it hasn't been a dull summer for me either you know. Riding with you at dawn, driving with you at dusk, lunching with you at Neuilly, dining with you at Chartres, and then that afternoon at Reims, those week-ends in the country. Ah—here we are."

He helped her out of the motor, and they passed through the arched entrance of the Château de Madrid. In the court-yard the little multicolored lights were already twinkling, and their table which they had occupied so many times before, was reserved for them, the solicitous headwaiter pulling out their seats. In a moment, a *garçon* who had waited on them before, and whose flashing smile gave them welcome, began bringing in tea and little cakes. The orchestra was playing, most unusually, a slow and ancient waltz. Clare rose, pushed back his chair, and bowed. He had never, Anne thought, looked handsomer, his slim elegance set off by his perfect clothes, his smile entrancing, his manner even more charming than usual.

"Shall we dance?" he asked.

She nodded, and rising, laid her arm lightly on his sleeve, as they walked over to the parquet. Then she slipped into his arms. He was a remarkably fine dancer, and, closely held, she followed his sure and graceful lead for a few moments without speaking. Then suddenly, she raised her head.

"Isn't that 'The Beautiful Blue Danube' they're playing?"

"Yes. The best waltz ever written, probably."

"Would—would you mind very much if we didn't finish it? If—if we didn't finish our tea?"

"Aren't you well, Anne?"

"Yes. But I—I feel a little faint. I think I had better go home."

"Too bad—but never mind! I'll drive you back through the Bois. You'll feel better moving about in the air. It *is* frightfully hot. And heat always seems so much worse, out of season."

He made no objections, expressed no surprise. In fact, he said nothing at all until they had reached the little lake where so many happy bourgeois lovers hire boats and row placidly about. Then he stopped the car.

"We may as well have this out now, Anne," he said, quietly. "I'd prefer to take you to my apartment, but of course you'd refuse to go. We can sit on that bank. None of those people will notice us. They're all too much occupied with their own affairs."

He spread out a light wrap she had brought with her, and motioned to her to sit down. It was characteristic, that even in as tense a moment as this, he did not forget to protect the Lucien Lelong frock.

"Well," he questioned, still lightly, when looking a protest but uttering none, she had settled herself, "have you actually realized at last that I am in love with you?"

She nodded, her eyes filling with tears.

"Don't cry, Anne. There'll be nothing to cry about, you'll see. . . . And you feel sure Neal doesn't suspect at all?"

"How could he?" she asked simply.

"You mean, it would never occur to him that his best friend would try to approach—his wife?"

A more meaning word had been on the tip of his tongue. He had softened it just in time.

"Of course it wouldn't occur to him. He would never do such a thing himself."

"You're probably right. Neal, with all his faults, is intrinsically honest. Also, he is not oversexed. Which makes it the easier for him to be honest."

"You shan't speak of Neal like that!" flashed Anne, "as if it were ridiculous to be honest and—and decent!"

"It isn't ridiculous. But it's sometimes inadequate."

"Listen, Anne," he went on, as she stared at him, apparently too stunned to answer, "I must ask you to believe that I haven't gone about this—with malice and forethought, so to speak. When I came to your house last spring I pitied you, and admired you, and I wanted you to have a good time. That was the reason I persuaded Neal to bring you here, and the only reason. I hope very, very much that you will believe this."

"I do believe it," said Anne.

"But I was very lonely. I'd been through a dreadful domestic experience—"

"And now you want me to do the same thing to Neal that your wife did to you?"

She had scored. But, after a moment's hesitation, he went on, still speaking calmly. "Since you put it so crudely, I suppose I do now. But I never dreamed it was going to come to that. You had haunted me, in a way, ever since that dinner at the Shoreham so long ago, and I knew you'd interest me, and amuse me. But, to be perfectly frank, I didn't think you had it in you to attract me, in the sense of making me—want you. Well, I was mistaken. But even so, I don't believe matters would have gone as far as this if I hadn't begun to see that—I attracted you, too."

"You don't," cried Anne. "Oh, how can you say such dreadful things! I never loved any one but Neal, never in all my life! Why, I wouldn't even finish that dance with you because I suddenly remembered that the 'Beautiful Blue Danube' was the very first waltz Neal and I ever had together. . . . I *hated* your talking that way about 'The Woman of Thirty'—insinuating that you—that I . . . I very nearly didn't come out with you today at all. I hesitated a long time. If Neal hadn't insisted . . ."

"Exactly. If you weren't in love with me you wouldn't be self-conscious about motoring with me or joking with me, or having me close to you in a dance. You wouldn't give it a second thought. What's more, you wouldn't be here *listening to me now*. Anne . . ."

In the deepening twilight he leaned suddenly towards her, and flung his arms about her. Then, abandoning all restraint, he kissed her, over and over again, on the mouth. The passion and violence of the embrace, without preliminary caress, struck her like a blow. But with a sickening sense of self-horror she realized that she had made no determined effort to escape from it; that she had, for a moment, actually responded to it; realized also that Clare, still holding her, was speaking to her in a voice vibrant with triumph.

"You see,"—he whispered. "Anne, darling, won't you admit—for you do see that you love me. You wouldn't have kissed back if you didn't. I'll make everything very easy for you, about the children and all that. Neal wouldn't take them from you. He'll either find, when he gets home, that he's dead politically once and for all, as I rather suspect, or he'll throw himself into his career again, and forget about you, as he's done before. In either case, you'll be left to face that awful isolation and drudgery, and you know you can't do that. You know you want to stay here with me, in this beautiful, bright city, where you've really begun to live for the first time. We'd have to be careful for awhile, of course, to avoid scandal. But once we were married, everyone would forget about it, if we behaved ourselves. Why, the ambassadress has been divorced herself."

Somehow Anne wrenched herself free. She was trembling now, violently, but her eyes were quite dry. Indeed, she felt as if she would never know the healing of tears again. She could hardly speak. Her lips were shaking, as well as her body; nevertheless there was an inner force about her which compelled him to listen to her.

"I don't love you," she reiterated, brokenly but persistently. "I've been grateful to you and I always shall be, in —in spite of what's happened. I believe someday you'll be as sorry that it happened as I am. And you're right. I have been—been attracted by you. Perhaps that's what made me—for the moment—kiss back—something restless and reckless and primitive. Women are primitive sometimes as well as men. I wish more people would recognize that. But I don't love you. It's Neal I love. I'd rather go back to Hinsboro, to all that drudgery and isolation as you call it

—to being neglected and forgotten by him as you've hinted, as *long as I can be with him than to stay here* in Paris—and all that it means—with you. Not just because I never could look the children in the face again if I didn't; not just because I'd give his family the chance they've always been looking for to prove how unworthy I'd been of him if I did; not just because I'd be an unchaste woman, seduced—seduced—" she brought out clearly the word over which he had stumbled—"by a dishonorable man. But because I love him. Because I know he belongs to me, no matter what he does or doesn't do. Because I belong to him. If he fails, I'm willing to fail with him. And if he succeeds, in the end, I'm going to be there to see it, even if I can't share it." She stopped, overwhelmed by her own vehemence—that, by itself, would have counted for nothing with Clare; but he quailed before the depth and beauty of her sincerity. For one vibrant moment of silence they faced each other—then he bent his head, stricken by the consciousness that he had been very close to violating a shrine—

"From the bottom of my heart," he said, "I ask your forgiveness."

. . . . . .

Groping her way down the dark, winding little corridor that led to her rooms, Anne was suddenly confronted with a large lozenge of light. Neal had heard her approaching footsteps,—he must have been listening for them—and had flung the door of their little *salon,* with its welcoming radiance, wide open. And dashing out to meet her, he almost smothered her in a bear hug.

"Oh, Anne, where have you been so long? I thought you'd never come! Do hurry! You can't imagine what's happened. Anne—Anne—read that cablegram—"

She snatched at the flimsy bit of blue paper which he was waving in her face. She had barely regained her composure; and now, glimpsing the typewritten message, she began to tremble again.

It was signed by Low, the Governor of their state. And it read:

"SHELTON, JUNIOR SENATOR, DIED THIS MORNING. HOPE YOU WILL ACCEPT APPOINTMENT FROM ME HIS SEAT UNITED STATES SENATE."

PART THREE

Weaving the Pattern

CHAPTER XV

To the day of her death Anne Conrad will remember her first winter in Washington as a Senator's wife with driving insistence.

She and Neal discussed the question of a temporary home all the way over on the boat coming back from Paris, and finally decided, on account of the children, that a small house would be preferable to an apartment. Dora brought Nancy and Junior to meet them in New York; and after a brief and unsatisfactory glimpse of her small son and daughter, for whom she had begun to actually hunger, Anne sent them back to Hinsboro in care of the faithful maid, who could be trusted with the preliminaries of closing the house there—the house into which she had put so much loving effort, so much Spartan self-sacrifice, and which she would now hardly see for years to come. She herself went on at once to Washington with Neal to begin her search for a dwelling-place.

She began it confidently. It should not, she thought, be very hard to find exactly what they wanted—their needs were not extensive nor their standards exacting; and she urged Neal to follow his impatient desire to begin "getting settled" in his quarters at the Senate Office Building. These certainly left nothing to be desired. Though he was a newcomer, and therefore not entitled to the most convenient and luxurious apartments, his large private office, handsomely furnished in mahogany, and opening from the smaller room which his private secretary, stenographers and page were to occupy, seemed to both him and Anne the last word in distinction and elegance. Neal felt himself swelling with national importance from the first moment that he sat down in front of the blank polished surface of his enormous desk, the warm autumn sunshine falling full across it from the high window near by, and pushed the little bell which summoned Miss Letts to come and take dictation from him. A cable had informed Miss Letts of the impending change in her sphere of usefulness, and she had preceded the Conrads to Washington. By way of preparation for her rising fortunes, she had attained a bob and a permanent wave, and a complexion as brilliantly hued as her varied wardrobe. Anne, secure now in her own simple and correct elegance, thought that the little secretary's skirts were too short and her blouses too sheer, and she knew that there was very little underneath them; but she had the wisdom to do her thinking silently. She recognized the competence of Miss Letts and was grateful for it, because it made everything so much easier for Neal. The offices had been cleaned, and the framed pictures of the Mayor of Hinsboro with his council—when Neal had been a member of it—and the grouped legislature—all the years that Neal had been a member of it—his diploma from Harvard College and the Harvard law school and the "enlargement" of Anne with the children were already hanging on the walls. They had been transferred without trouble to Neal from his office in Hinsboro. The ormolu clock on the mantelpiece was going, and it was correct to a second; there were fresh yellow candles in the "side-pieces" that matched the clock. Laid out where he could not fail to see them instantly were a brand-new copy of the Congressional Directory, a seating-plan of the Senate Chamber, and numerous blocks of "scratch paper"—the large thin ones white, the small fat ones pink, with the heading—"United States Senate" imposingly printed upon them. His personal stationery had been tentatively ordered, and as soon as an impression of his signature had been obtained—for this would appear on every envelope he used, thus insuring the franking privilege—the order would go through. There was a scrap basket of ample proportions, there was a scrap book full of flattering comments about his appointment. And of course there was the appointment itself. Miss Letts had not had it framed, because she wanted to consult his taste, but she had samples of several suitable frames, waiting to submit to him, that he might make his choice between them.

So the beginning of Neal's "settling" was made comparatively easy for him, by Miss Letts, and soon there was a complete office force to make the continuance of it easier still. But Anne agreed with him perfectly when he told her that everything was in terrible confusion, and that he did not see how he was ever going to get straightened out and adjusted. So she went out to look for houses by herself. The real-estate agent to whom she had applied assured her enthusiastically that he had the very thing she wanted. He led her to several untenanted marble palaces, hung with mangy tapestries and furnished in rickety gilt, and to a long succession of tall narrow edifices made of bright red brick, with one tin bath, and gloomy "back-parlors." She regarded these docilely at first; then she began to object mildly.

"But this isn't at all the sort of house I described to you. You said you understood perfectly what I wanted."

"Indeed, Mrs. Conrad, I do. Nothing could be more suitable for a Senatorial establishment than these residences. You will wish to entertain extensively, of course. The Argentine Ambassador occupied this house we have just been in, for several years. His dinners were famous. You noticed, of course, the advantages of the dining-room."

"I noticed its disadvantages," replied Anne, the trace of hardness which was sometimes apparent coming in her voice; "it isn't on the same floor with the kitchen. And the pantry has no windows in it."

"But most houses, I assure you, are built that way. And the rent is so very reasonable—only six hundred dollars a month."

"Almost exactly my husband's entire monthly salary. Now will you please show me what I asked you for in the beginning: small houses, with about eight rooms, conveniently arranged, and at a reasonable rental. Unless it is clear to you now what I want, I think I had better go to another agent. Several have written and telephoned that they would be glad to show me houses."

The agent was grieved. It had not occurred to him that such a young, pretty, and gentle lady would be so unamenable to his blandishments. Allowing her to see that his feelings were hurt, first by coming for her in a dilapidated open car, instead of the stately limousine he had hitherto affected, and next by maintaining a lofty and dignified silence, he led her from one small dingy dwelling to another. They were all dirty beyond description, and in most of them both plumbing and heating plants were antiquated and inadequate; the maid's room, generally without a bath, was built in a dark corner of the basement. Anne went back to the Willard, late in the afternoon, dizzy with discouragement, and Neal expressed surprise at her lack of success.

"You don't mean to say you haven't found anything *yet?* I hate to keep talking about money, but it's darned expensive here, as you know, more for this one small room than our two big ones cost in Paris, while the restaurant charges are three times as high. Aren't you a little too fussy? We ought to be getting settled, you know, and having Dora and the children come down. They'll be late starting school as it is, and that's always a disadvantage. Surely you must be able to get *something*. I'd take a day off and help you hunt, but things are so terribly piled up at the office—"

"I know, Neal, I'll try again. But honestly, it's awfully hard. I think I'll write Dora to start the children in at school in Hinsboro."

"Good heavens! Is it as hopeless as *that?*"

"Well—I'm afraid it is."

But the next morning she began again. This time the houses she saw were somewhat newer and cleaner. But they were either built with basement entrances, which she knew would multiply the cares of housekeeping, on account of the number of stairs to be climbed, or else they were flimsily constructed in boxlike blocks on unattractive and inaccessible streets.

At last she dismissed the agent, declined the doubtfully useful services of several others, and started out by herself on foot, stopping before every house that displayed in its window a sign of "For sale or to let." The bewildering aspect of the city, in which a hovel and a palace often stand side by side, so that it is difficult for an outsider to recognize a "desirable" neighborhood, and the prevalence of "squares" and "circles" which constantly caused her to lose her way, made her task more difficult. But at last she discovered tucked away between two handsome brownstone "residences" a small house of yellow-painted brick. It was only two stories high; its location was excellent; and a notice so large that it completely filled the modest bay window in which this was placed, proclaimed that it was seeking a tenant. Tremblingly, Anne sought out the agent, one of whom she had not previously heard. He catered to so small and select a clientele that he never advertised, and considered solicitation beneath his standards; but he received her with condescending cordiality. Yes, he would be glad to show her the house, which had just come on the market—Mrs. Harrison, its owner, had suddenly decided to go to Europe, for the winter, perhaps for longer. It proved to contain a small but sunny drawing-room opening into a dark little dining-room whose one window overlooked a diminutive back yard, and a kitchen in the ell; on the second story two large bedrooms and one small one, and a bathroom; in the basement, under the drawing-room, a storeroom which might conceivably be used as a playroom. The furniture was shabby, and Anne was amazed that any woman could leave her house so far from clean. But she felt, at last, that she had found something which offered possibilities, at least. She asked the amount of the rent.

"Two hundred and fifty dollars a month, without heat or light, linen and silver, of course. Very reasonable. And the telephone hasn't been disconnected. You won't have the inconvenience and delay of waiting to have one installed."

Anne was aghast. But she was also desperate.

"I'll let you know tomorrow. I think probably I'll take it."

"I'm sure you couldn't do better, Mrs. Conrad."

It was because Anne was so miserably sure of this herself that she painted the little house in brighter colors than it deserved to Neal that evening. And, even with this effort at *couleur-de-rose* he was not enthusiastic.

"That's a terrible price. Why, we wouldn't have any more room than we did in the cottage—not as much, really—and you know what that cost! There's no family living-room except the one that will have to be a parlor, too, no place for me to work. Dora would have to use the same bathroom we did—imagine, all five of us, mornings—and Nancy would have to sleep with her. And there's no garage."

"I know all that. But we *could* manage. And it's the first place I've seen where we could."

It was on the tip of her tongue to urge him to go out and hunt himself if he felt he could do better. But she managed to restrain herself remarking only, "I wish you'd come and look at it in the morning."

"I really ought to get to the office in good season. You see—"

"Yes, I know; but it will take only a few minutes."

Somewhat grudgingly, Neal consented to accompany her; and equally grudgingly he signed the lease a few days later, conveying the impression, though he did not actually say so, that he could have done much better himself if the affairs of the nation had not weighed so heavily upon him. Then Anne, with a regretful look at her pretty hands, which she had hoped were to be kept looking that way always now, bought herself some cheap gingham dresses, a supply of scrubbing brushes, cleansing powders and soft cloths, and began the process of cleaning house from top to bottom.

It was backbreaking work; and her muscles were soft after her summer of physical inactivity. But she did not know where to seek for a scrubwoman; and she already saw, very plainly, that she would have to begin to save pennies again. She left the Willard directly after breakfast, carrying a cold lunch with her, and worked until dinner time. By evening she was so tired that once she actually went to sleep while Neal was telling her about the exciting events of his day, and he was offended.

She did not even have the satisfaction of doing her housecleaning in uninterrupted peace. The telephone rang constantly; she began to feel that the "inconvenience and delay of having it installed" might have had its advantages. At first she answered it conscientiously, believing that its peals might portend tidings of importance to Neal. It usually proved, however, to be a photographer, who had —miraculously, as it seemed to her—discovered that she was in town, and wished her to have her picture taken. She would not have guessed that a city the size of Washington could contain so many photographers, or that a new Senator's wife could seem so desirable a victim to any of them. She answered their suggestions with increasing vagueness and decreasing courtesy. No, she was afraid she couldn't set a time for an appointment just yet; no, really, it wouldn't do any good to mail her a card reminding her that she would be in the studio at noon on Monday; no, she couldn't say that she would prefer home portraiture. When the same firm called her three times in twenty-four hours she hung up the receiver with a bang, and answered the telephone no more. Then, of course, a magnate from Belford who had only a day in the city called and received the report that "they didn't answer." It did not seem to occur to him that he could call up the Senate Office Building. He went home to Belford and wrote Neal an indignant letter, and spread the news among his neighbors that "Conrad was getting a swelled head already." Neal was very angry about it, and Anne felt that he had a right to be.

At the hands of the newspapers she fared even worse. The society editors, like the photographers, had telephoned her; like the photographers, she had put them off. She could not bear the thought of giving interviews. But if a man is known by the company he keeps, so is the journalist known by the interviews which he—or she—secures. Miss Sharp, of the *Evening Inquirer* decided to present herself at the new Senator's residence, and take her chances on being rebuffed, even though she went without an appointment. Her ring at the doorbell remained unanswered; and she turned for help to a young woman, her head enveloped in a mobcap, who was vigorously washing windows.

"Can you tell me whether Mrs. Conrad is at home?" she asked.

The window-washer wrung out her cloth from the pail of steaming suds by her side, and turned her head halfway around.

"I am Mrs. Conrad," she replied calmly, and went on washing windows.

Miss Sharp fled; but as she fled, she thought, and thought rapidly. There are some things, of course, which it is not proper for the society department to cover, but there is nothing in its code of ethics to prevent it from helping some other department to cover the same things. Before the sun had gone down, Anne had been surreptitiously photographed in the act of washing her last window; and the following evening, this distorted likeness of herself, together with the heavy headline, "SENATOR'S WIFE ACTS AS OWN SCRUBWOMAN" surmounted two columns, more conspicuous for their imagination than their accuracy, on the front page of the *Inquirer*. This was such good "copy" that it was, of course, copied—from one end of the United States to the other. Reporters were sent to Hamstead and to Hinsboro, to dig up forgotten or unknown facts or fancies about the new Senator's wife. Photographs of "Pupper and Mummer" with Sol and Sam on the front porch between them adorned the Sunday supplements, with the schoolhouse where Anne had taught in a "circle" above at the left, and the little house with a cross marking "the honey-moon flat" in a "box" below at the right. Anne was delineated bending over the washtub and milking the family cow. Had Neal been a candidate for the presidency no sort of publicity could have been more helpful; since he was instead an appointee to the Senate, none could have been more disastrous. Anne knew it, without his comments on the subject, and without her

mother-in-law's letters. Nevertheless, she was spared neither of these.

By the time the nine days' excitement had subsided
somewhat, the housecleaning was finished, groceries and
coal had been installed, and Anne had gone to Hinsboro
to help Dora finish closing the house there, and bring the
maid and the children back with her to Washington. The
beauty and comfort of her own home, even in its disman-
tled state, affected her poignantly; and as she walked
through her little garden, set in stark order for the winter,
she was very close to crying. A cold autumn wind was
blowing through the bare branches, and she tried to persuade herself that it was this which brought the quick
color to her cheeks and the tears to her eyes. But that
night, on the train, in the drawing-room which she had
taken in an unusual fit of extravagance, she told her troubles to Dora and wept on that comfortable shoulder, as
they sat side by side on the hard little sofa that was to be
Dora's bed, after Junior had been tucked away in the
upper berth, and Nancy in the lower berth which she was
to share with her mother.

"A shame I call it!" Dora kept saying, patting Anne's
shoulder gently. "A lovely lady like you! Inventing such
stories!"

"But they're not invented—not all of them," sobbed
Anne. "You know I never had any one to work for me
before you came. I *did* teach school and do the washing
—though I never milked a cow! And that house in Washington was so dirty. I couldn't bring the children into it
until it was cleaned—they'd have caught typhoid fever or
whatever it is you do catch when things are dirty."

"I ought to have been there to help you," began Dora
regretfully, but Anne interrupted her.

"How could you? There was the other house on your
hands, wasn't there? And the children? Did Mrs. Conrad
offer to help you at all? No, of course not!"

"Well, anyway, we'll manage better from now on."

But the managing when they reached Washington, did
not prove to be any too easy. After an early breakfast,
Anne walked over to the garage—the nearest one they had

been able to find was several blocks away—and got the car, while Neal read the morning paper, for it was, of course, important that he should keep himself thoroughly informed about current events. By the time she had taken the children to school he was, however, ready to have her take him to the Senate Office Building; and after she had left him there, she did the marketing, for the "cash and carry" stores were much cheaper than the ones that "delivered." Back at the little brick house, the chamberwork awaited her, for Dora had agreed to take care of the furnace if Anne would do this; and the maid, in addition to looking after the fires, with the trips back and forth to the basement which this involved, had also cooked, served and cleared away breakfast, cleaned the living-room, and answered the doorbell and telephone. She struggled through the heavy washings, too, with none of the conveniences or space that had made these comparatively easy for her in Hinsboro; and Anne helped with the ironing and did the mending. In no time, the hands of the clock were pointing to the hour at which she must go and get the children; steer them through their luncheon, plan for their afternoon outing. She usually took them with her when she went to get their father, his labors for the day over, and they skipped home on either side of her after she had left the car at the garage for the night. Then there were the simple home lessons with which they needed help, preparation for Sunday-school on Saturday night, dancing-school to dress them for and take them to Saturday morning. There was supper to get for all of them on Dora's night out—a hearty supper, for Neal had quickly fallen into the way of taking a very light lunch, and came home hungry.

"Just a piece of pie and a bit of cheese," he assured her, "or cracker and milk. That's all most of the men take at noon—plenty, too, when you're getting no exercise.— Yes, another piece of steak, please, dear, a thick one, with lots of gravy." (Neal's senatorial importance had not cured him of his taste for "fish in the pan.") "What have you got for dessert?"

Anne found herself standing beside her bed at night

158

pressing her hands against her throbbing temples, as if by this pressure she could push back the pressing duties which drove her forward. She was tired all the time, tired as she had not been since the days when Nancy was a delicate baby and Junior an exacting three-year-old and she had been obliged, at the doctor's orders, to engage Cora and cease doing all her own work. She began to dust every other day, instead of every day, to overlook the smaller holes and less important buttons when she did her mending, to shorten the bedtime stories and songs which had always given her the most precious hours of association with her children. But still she was continually hurried and hurried; her driving weariness threatened to annihilate her. For, as she soon discovered, the demands made upon her time and strength by her home and family were as nothing compared to the outside demands made upon her in her official position as a Senator's wife.

CHAPTER XVI

ANNE'S experiences with photographers and reporters should have given her a glimmering of what lay before her, should have brought home to her the fact that she was no longer a private individual whose life, however full, was at least her own, to regulate and arrange as she chose. But the first task of finding and fitting and running her home had been so heavy, that she had allowed herself to overlook this fact. The oversight was, however, of short duration.

She had settled herself with an overflowing mending-basket before the living-room fire one rainy afternoon, comfortably conscious that she had an hour or more to herself before it would be time to go for Neal—though after that there would still be supper to get, for this was Dora's day out. The children were playing contentedly enough in the basement nursery. (Was it going to be too damp for them down there? She must assure herself that it wasn't, and yet, if it *was*—good heavens, where else *could* they play?) She had on a rather shabby little serge house-dress, because she found it easier, with running the car so much, to slip a big coat over such a dress, than to keep changing all the time to her smart Parisian *tailleur*. She knew, of course she knew, that she ought to put on something more suitable for afternoon, but it hardly seemed worth while, when she must go out again so soon in that driving rain. The side curtains of the car leaked, and she suspected that the top was not above reproach. Decidedly, it was not worth while . . . Her shoes, too, she realized, glancing down at them, were getting shabby with all this driving, and she hadn't blacked them the night before, she had been so terribly tired. She mustn't let herself get careless, get shoddy again, after all she had learned in Paris. But—oh, well—she picked up her fourth sock.

The doorbell rang. She started up, dropping the contents of her basket on the floor as she did so. Before she could restore thimble, scissors, spools and stockings to their proper place, it rang again, more insistently. She ran to the front door and flung it open.

Two very elegant ladies confronted her. They had on dark velvet dresses, rich furs and white gloves, and their satin slippers were smooth and narrow. Behind them, at the curb, stood a shiny limousine with a man in livery at the wheel.

"Is Mrs. Conrad receiving today?" they asked simultaneously, in shrill, high voices. And as they did so, they each extended three cards, two little ones and one large one, neatly folded into triangles at the upper right hand corner.

Mechanically, Anne reached behind her for the silver card tray that reposed on the hall table, and set it down again, the cards fluttering over its edge, before she answered. Then, in spite of her bewilderment, she spoke cordially.

"Won't you come in? I'm Mrs. Conrad. . . . I think you'll find these chairs, here by the fire, comfortable."

"Oh, *thank you*. We didn't know whether you'd have begun your Thursdays yet or not, it's so *early* in the season. And it's early in the afternoon, too, of course we *know* that. But we're going to the concert—we *never* miss it—so we have to start early. If we don't get started on our calls we *never* could get around, it's such a *problem*, isn't it? But perhaps you weren't quite *ready* to begin receiving, Mrs. Conrad? You must excuse us, but we've been so *anxious* to meet the new Senator's wife. I'm Mrs. Roper and this is my friend Mrs. Ranger. We always make our calls together, we're such *friends*."

Anne's head was whirling. Her Thursdays? Mrs. Roper and Mrs. Ranger? She groped towards a light which she could not find, and her visitors were instantly aware of the fact.

"Of course you *knew*, Mrs. Conrad, that Senators' wives receive on Thursdays? The Supreme Court ladies on Mondays, the Congressional ladies on Tuesdays, the Cabinet ladies on Wednesdays, the Senatorial ladies on Thursdays, the Diplomatic ladies on Fridays—that leaves Saturdays and Sundays for the resident society, the *cave-dwellers*, you know. But *of course* I don't need to tell you all this! How are you getting on with your own visits?"

"My own visits?" gasped Anne, thinking of the windows she had washed and the floors she had scrubbed and all the other pushing, daily duties which made her press her hands against her temples at night, they harried her so. Visits indeed!

"*Of course* you've called promptly on all your superiors in rank—it's so important to do that *at once*. It creates quite a wrong impression if you don't. And if you don't *return* the calls we poor *inferiors* make upon you, we'll think you're *snobbish*, you know. So many Senators' wives *are*. Well, next week we shall expect to see you, dear Mrs. Conrad. We always receive together, we're such *friends*. Of course you've heard how *intimate* we are."

They rose, shook hands, and hurried away with staccato exclamations about ten more calls to make before "the" concert began. The front door closed behind them, but Anne could hear them talking as they went down the steps.

"My dear, did you *ever*? I do believe all those stories about the cow and the washtub and everything are true, don't *you*? No tea and no one to open the door, and those shabby clothes, what did she do in Paris, do you suppose, go to *art-galleries*? And it's evident she doesn't know a *thing* about what's expected of her. Where do you think we better go *next*? What do you say to Mrs. Stone's, everything is so *lovely* there, and she and the huge crowd she always has on her Thursdays will so enjoy hearing all about this *freak* . . . Oh, Madame Estavi, are you coming to call on Mrs. Conrad, too? Yes, we've just *been*. Yes, she's *in*."

Another caller was coming up the steps, and it was plain that those who were leaving were refraining with difficulty from telling her how inadequate her reception was going to be. Anne saw, with relief, that the new visitor was of a different type—was indeed herself timid and ill at ease, in spite of her pretty clothes and air of unmistakable good breeding. But this relief was short-lived. Madame Estavi, the wife of the Third Secretary of the Peruvian Embassy, was herself a newcomer embarking on her first round of calls, and finding it an ordeal to explain her identity and purpose in a foreign language with which her acquaintance was of the slightest, and amidst strange surroundings which still appalled and bewildered her. She accepted the place by the fire so recently vacated, and sat holding herself very erect, with painful pauses, which Anne did not know how to fill in, between her civil, stilted little sentences. In the midst of one of these pauses, a fearful shriek rent the air; and an instant later, Nancy, with Junior in hot pursuit, tore wildly into the room, tripped over the rug, and fell sprawling on the floor between the two ladies.

"He hit me."—"I didn't either."—"Well, he took my rabbit, and said he was going to vi-vi-sect it, and the stuffing all came out, and so I knocked him over the head with my shovel."—"And then you bet I hit her. Wouldn't you?"

The last remark was addressed to the astonished caller by Junior, who had picked himself up, and was confronting her accusingly. She rose, looking very much startled. Anne had visions of little Peruvian children, beautifully behaved always, in charge of a competent and devoted nursery governess who never, under any circumstances, left their side.

"I'm dreadfully sorry," she said wretchedly. "Really, they don't often act like this. Junior, go upstairs and wash that—that—whatever it is—off your face and hands. And stay there until I send for you." The "send" was sheer bravado. Anne had, as she realized all too well, no one to send. "Please, Madame Estavi"—But Madame Estavi had quietly and effectively vanished, and there were more callers coming up the steps. Before the riotous and untidy children could be eliminated, these callers were upon Anne. One of them was a bluff and hearty naval officer who sat down in an antique chair which promptly broke beneath him. (Anne had already discovered that much of the furniture in her furnished house was not reliable, but this was the first disaster she had faced because of it.)

The naval officer, who had lumbago, as he explained in detail to her, appeared less bluff and hearty after his accident, and tried to signal to his wife that his back hurt him, and that he felt they had better move along. But his wife was stone deaf and she did not catch his meaning. She thought he was trying to call her attention to the picture over the mantelpiece.

The dreadful afternoon wore on. Anne, nervously keeping her eyes from the clock, was nevertheless aware that Neal would be expecting her, would be waiting for her, and yet she could not escape and go to him. At last the telephone rang sharply.

"Neal, dear," she whispered into the transmitter, "I can't come for you, I'm sorry. No, I can't speak any louder, there are people here, they'll hear me. No, I can't explain. No, I'm not sick. No, the children aren't either."

She returned to the drawing-room certain that she had been overheard. Well, that was bad enough, but at least it meant that these intruding strangers would go—would leave her in peace. But it did not. Sensing that something was amiss, and eager to know what it was, they lingered to find out.

Neal let himself in with his latchkey, banging the door after him, and shouted to her from the hall.

"Why didn't you *tell* me you were going to have company?" he roared, "I waited, and waited . . ."

Neither of them ever referred again to the next few minutes. He strode into the little parlor, halted, and became dumb. Introductions were mumbled, but afterwards the silence deepened. One by one, disappointed, the callers departed. As the last one vanished from sight and hearing, Anne turned on her husband with a rage such as he had seldom seen her display.

"Don't you ever dare speak to me that way again!" she cried. "You ought to have realized I was in some difficulty and helped me out instead of making things ten times worse than they were already! You ought to have known

164

that Senators' wives have to receive on Thursdays and make hundreds and thousands of calls themselves other days, dropping little dog-eared cards from one end of Washington to the other. Tomorrow I'm going to get all this straightened out by some one who *does* know and will tell me all about it. I'll find out what I've got to do, and do it well. But in the meantime, I'm going upstairs and I'm going to bed. You can get your own supper and the children's and hear their home work and see that they take their baths. If any of you come near me this evening, I warn you that I'll have hysterics."

"Why, Anne," said Neal gently, "I'm awfully worry. I didn't think . . ." His own annoyance had vanished into thin air at the sight of her distress, which he did not minimize. He spoke with unaccustomed and unexpected tenderness. "Darling, it's all right. You'll get the hang of all this in no time. Anne—don't cry."

CHAPTER XVII

AT nine o'clock the next morning, Anne called up the Vice-President's house, and asked for Mrs. Hammel.

She thought that the man who answered her gasped slightly. But she was not sure. He only said, "I will connect you with Mrs. Hammel's secretary, Madam," and after a short succession of clicks she heard a smooth, purring voice that sounded somehow, in spite of its smoothness, as if it might, upon occasion, grow dreadfully hard. "Miss Butters speaking."

"This is Mrs. Neal Conrad, Senator Conrad's wife. I asked for Mrs. Hammel."

"Oh—but you see Mrs. Hammel never goes to the telephone, Mrs. Conrad. Couldn't you give me the message? I am her secretary, you know. I take all her messages. Everyone who wishes to get in touch with Mrs. Hammel does so through me."

Again reproved, again convicted of ignorance! Anne felt herself flushing, alone in the little dark entry where her telephone hung. But she gritted her teeth.

"I wonder if she would let me come and see her? Today?"

"Today? Really, Mrs. Conrad, I doubt whether that would be possible. Mrs. Hammel would be delighted to see you of course, but she is very much engaged. Perhaps next week I could give you an appointment."

"Won't you *ask* her whether she would see me? It's really urgent."

"In that case . . . What is your telephone number, Mrs. Conrad? I will try to call you back a little later. But of course I can't promise. Mrs. Hammel always gives up her mornings to her correspondence, we try not to let anything disturb her. There are so many demands upon her, you see."

Anne hung up the receiver, already regretting her sudden impulse to appeal to the Vice-President's wife. As she lay in bed the evening before, miserably wakeful, she had remembered a "feature story" that she had read about Mrs. Hammel in the *Inquirer* the Sunday before. This article had praised the "Second Lady of the Land" in no uncertain terms, her tact, her sweetness, her sympathetic graciousness. It was accompanied by a picture of her huge white marble residence, that looked like a great block of vanilla ice-cream, ornamented with whipped cream that had been forced through a tube into all kinds of festoons; also by a picture of the lady herself, smiling, plump, bejeweled and bewaved. But there was a look of real human kindness in the gentle eyes and soft mouth, and withal a look of mild shrewdness, which even the artificial pose of the photographer could not destroy; and there was a paragraph in the article which had arrested Anne's attention especially, and which seemed burned on her memory.

"Mrs. Hammel before her marriage was a Miss Sarah Gown, a school teacher in the great Western state which her distinguished husband has so rapidly 'put on the map.' When they first met he was a cattle herder. The early days of their marriage were spent on a ranch, sixty miles from the nearest village. Mrs. Hammel of course did all her own work, and, in the evenings, taught her husband, who had had fewer educational opportunities than herself, from the shabby text books which she had taken away with her from the mountain schools. She lost her first baby, a little daughter, and came near losing her own life, because no doctor could penetrate to the ranch through the snow drifts which covered the rough trails to the ranch in winter. Mrs. Hammel's second daughter is now the Duchess of Nebalini, her husband being the cousin of the King of Italy."

There were other paragraphs after that, describing the rise in the Hammel fortunes, both political and financial. But they did not matter so much. What mattered was that

Mrs. Hammel had once been a little country school-teacher, like Anne herself, had suffered far more in her bridal days, and she had married a man who possessed far fewer advantages, of every kind, than Neal. And she had won through. She lived in an ice-cream palace, she had an English butler and a private secretary, and that dreadful Miss Sharp wrote complimentary articles about her. She was so remote that no one could speak to her on the telephone, and of course she always, always, did the right thing—now. But she must have had to learn, too; and perhaps, perhaps, she remembered how bitterly hard that learning was. . . .

The telephone rang. Miss Butters was speaking again, her voice even smoother and more purring than before.

"Oh, Mrs. Conrad . . . I gave Mrs. Hammel your message, and she will be pleased to see you at eleven. She is of course very much pressed, very much occupied, so I am sure you will understand and make your call brief. At eleven then—"

"It was Miss Butters," Anne said to herself as she buttoned on her little blue *tailleur* and jammed her small, perky blue hat down over her curls, "who made up the last part of that message. Mrs. Hammel never said it at all. If she hadn't meant to be kind, she wouldn't have said she'd see me."

Anne was right. Mrs. Hammel did mean to be kind. She looked to the bewildered newcomer like a comfortable, middle-aged angel, her wings concealed by her perfect Worth gown of gray *crêpe de chine*, but her halo almost distinguishable above the smooth ripples of her permanent wave. A single string of beautiful creamy pearls quivered slightly over the ample bosom which was so trimly confined by the smoothly fitting undergarment that lay beneath the insidiously simple, costly gown, a single great emerald glittered on her plump right hand, three great diamonds above the narrow platinum band on her left. There were steel buckles on the gray suède shoes. But there was something very homey about her, in spite of the fact that she might have served as the personification of "What the Well-Dressed Woman (with unlimited means) Will

168

Wear"; she almost patted Anne's hand as she shook it; and an uncanny degree of intelligence shone from the beams of her kindly eyes.

"So you're the wife of the new appointee to the Senate? Bless me, how young you look—I shouldn't wonder if you're the Senatorial baby. And pretty as a picture. I always tell women when I think they're pretty, and I never apologize for it, either. I know they really like it. Your husband's young, too, isn't he? Mr. Hammel's been watching his career with interest—he believes there's a big future ahead of him yet. And ahead of you, too, of course. I'm pleased you wanted to run in and see me like this. Was there something special—? Tell me while we have some nice hot chocolate with lots of whipped cream on top—terribly fattening, but you don't need to worry about that, and I'm past worrying—now then—"

Anne went straight to the point. She told her story quickly, and she told it well. In a few brief sentences she had outlined her background, upbringing, and previous experience. Then, with slightly more detail, she related the events of the afternoon before. Mrs. Hammel listened attentively, drinking cup after cup of hot chocolate, each one sweetened with three lumps of sugar and smothered with whipped cream. Once or twice the corners of her mouth twitched, and when Anne had finished she coughed a little behind a fine cambric handkerchief which she extracted from a small silver mesh bag. There was an agreeable aroma of French perfume about the handkerchief.

"Well, well," she said, "I don't know when I've been so much interested. And you thought of coming straight to me—which I'm very glad you did—on account of that article in the *Inquirer*. Are you on good terms with the press yourself?"

"I'm afraid not. You see—" Anne plunged into that story too. This time Mrs. Hammel laughed outright.

"Yes, I've read some of these articles, and of course I realized they weren't overaccurate, but I didn't know just what lay behind them. Well, my dear, the first thing for you to do is to get a picture taken of yourself that does you justice—several of them—and then ring up Miss

Sharp and ask her to come and have tea and a little chat with you."

Mrs. Hammel stirred her fourth cup of chocolate reminiscently.

"When I first came here," she said, "I thought I didn't want to have anything to do with the newspaper women. Miss Sharp wrote *me* and asked me for an interview and I declined to give it to her. Her reply, which she sent me by special delivery, was a masterpiece. I've kept it ever since —someday I'll show it to you. She told me that her bread and butter depended on getting something about me, but that, after all, was beyond the point. If her newspaper couldn't secure a real interview with me, it would fake one. If she didn't write that article—false or true—someone else would. If I would coöperate with the newspaper women, give them what they had a recognized right to ask of me as Vice-President's wife, I'd never regret it. If I told them anything in confidence, that confidence would be respected. If I admitted that I was going to a certain place, or was on the point of doing a certain thing, but that for reasons of my own I wished this kept quiet, no word about it would ever appear in print. In short, that they were prepared to help me in every way they could if I would only let them. If I wouldn't, all sorts of false and sensational reports would inevitably appear about me. I sent for Miss Sharp and had a frank talk with her. We've been the best of friends ever since. And she's kept her word—absolutely."

"Oh, thanks," began Anne, "I'll—" Mrs. Hammel interrupted.

"She belongs to a rather interesting organization—the Woman's National Press Club. All the society editors do, besides a number of other reporters and advertisers and a few magazine writers. About forty of them in all. I'm going to one of their Monday luncheons—jolly, informal affairs—as guest of honor next week. I wonder—would you like to come with me? It could be very easily arranged. You'd have a good time, and—well, I think it would be a good plan all around."

Anne's quick gratitude was so real that Mrs. Hammel

was more touched than she betrayed. Her capacity for chocolate being at last exhausted, she began to turn the great emerald around on her carefully manicured finger, not with any indication of nervousness, but as if she frankly enjoyed its gleaming gorgeousness.

"And of course you must start right in making calls. Today. Diplomatic day. Ordinarily the wife of the senior senator from your state would go with you, to help you at the beginning. But Senator Brown hasn't any wife. He's a widower. Many of them are. You won't wonder at that, when you've lived here a little while—it's a killing pace for a woman in official life. Many a poor lady should be buried with the inscription, 'She died of making too many calls.' And other Senators are bachelors. That's not to be wondered at either. They pay attention—marked attention—to a girl for a season or two, and she's flattered and all that, but she gets to thinking it over, how many Senators are widowers I mean, and she decides— You'll find them all labeled in the Congressional Directory. 'The star designates those whose wives accompany them; the parallel lines designate those having other ladies with them.' Well, the first time I saw that, I wondered who those 'other ladies' were. It sounded suspiciously vague, as if—ahem! But, bless you, Senators don't have any time for little diversions like that. Those parallel lines only mean that a wife having perished, or not having been attained at all, because the hours at hard labor look too long for her, a sister, or a mother or some one like that has been pressed into service."

Anne, shaking with laughter, had begun to realize that she was going to like Mrs. Hammel very, very much.

"But to get back to the calls you must make today. You'll find a list of the embassies in your copy of the Congressional Directory. If your husband hasn't brought yours up from the office he's been very remiss. Every Senator's wife has one, with her name stamped neatly in the lower right-hand corner. 'Mrs. Neal Conrad' will look very nice, you'll see. Only the Ambassadresses, remember. The Ministers' wives come first to you. They don't like it, because that distinction isn't made in other capitals, but it's

171

made here. And return Madame Estavi's call, of course. She's really a dear, though very shy. You don't need to be afraid of *her*. Then go through the cards that were left you yesterday, and return the calls of any 'cave dwellers' who may be receiving Saturday and Sunday. Monday go to all the Supreme Court ladies—there are only nine of those, you know; you can gallop right through them in an afternoon, easily. Tuesday of course you'll go to the Congressional ladies if any have called on you. No? Well, then, that's easy. Wednesday—now there's a moot question. Most of the Senators' wives feel that the Cabinet ladies should call first—the Senate confirms the appointment of Cabinet officers, you see. But the Cabinet officers and their wives always take precedence at dinners—I think, if I were you, I'd stretch a point, and go at least to see Mrs. Standish, the wife of the Secretary of State. She's a perfect dear, and you'll have such a good time at her house; you may not get much farther anyway. Then next Thursday, if I were you, I should receive again myself. And—er—do it right. After that, you ought to receive and make calls on alternate Thursdays, till you've been the rounds. But this time, I'd—er— Mrs. Roper and Mrs. Ranger will tell every one they see, of course, about yesterday, and next Thursday your house will be packed with people who've come to see if they were told the truth. And my, what a disappointment they'll get." Once more Mrs. Hammel gave vent to hearty laughter. "I'd like to be there myself, my dear, to see the fun. If I can possibly make it, I shall be."

She rose, gathered up her silver mesh bag and other small effects, and kissed Anne on the cheek.

"Run along now, and get to work, my dear," she said. "I've lots of confidence in you."

This confidence was not misplaced. Doggedly, even as she had scrubbed floors and taught school doggedly, Anne set to work to pay her official calls. She drove her own car, changing her gloves before entering a house, and again after she left it, and finding her own parking spaces. But Neal came home on the street cars from the Senate Office Building and the children walked home from school, so that she would not have to go for them. And Dora announced beforehand that she could not dream of going out the next Thursday, and by Tuesday had begun on even more substantial plans for helping Anne. It was barely half-past three when, as Mrs. Hammel had predicted, Anne's callers began to come. The polite Ambassadresses instantly returning their official visits. The Supreme Court ladies, whose program was not yet very full. Mrs. Standish, always sweet, efficient and poised, to whom, moreover, Mrs. Hammel had been able to murmur a few words about Anne, as they drove home together from the informal monthly tea to which the President's wife always invited the ladies of her "official family." The excitement eaters and curiosity seekers regaled by Mrs. Roper and Mrs. Ranger. Miss Sharp and several other members of the Woman's National Press Club, who had been most agreeably impressed by Anne when she had come, with Mrs. Hammel, to their Monday luncheon. The "professional callers" who are the bane of every woman in official life, and who go from house to house either because they are utterly idle, or because they are actually hungry, supplying themselves, in the latter case, with unlimited sandwiches and cakes. A large contingent from a girls' school, which made a point of advertising that its pupils would be "conducted to see the wives of the great men who are forming the destiny of our nation." Numerous young secretaries and *attachés*, who had heard rumors that Mrs. Conrad was—really—extremely pretty, and who thought it quite likely that she might often like to go to Charity Balls during the season when Neal would be either unwilling or unable to accompany her. A scattering of tourists' and government workers from the Conrads' own state. Ministers, Colonels, a judge or two, with their wives. In short, the kaleidoscopic fragment of Washington life which confronts the official hostess on her day at home.

The door was opened for these callers by a wholly correct butler from Rauschers' who was in great demand for "at homes"; near him, at the drawing-room door, stood a smiling little boy, his face very rosy and clean above his Eton collar, his hair slicked back from his moist part. The

173

fame which Junior's smile has since enjoyed, and which is well merited, may be traced from that day. It was frank, sweet, intelligent, and withal, just a shade wistful. It was arresting and disarming. Nine times out of ten, the callers' first remark to Anne was, "Is that *your* little boy who welcomed me so politely? What beautiful manners he has! And what a LOVELY SMILE." Anne smiled herself in appreciation of this greeting, and Anne too had a smile which was nothing to be ashamed of. She stood in front of a bright little fire, which glowed under a mantel banked with flowers, to receive her guests, her golden hair wound like a coronet above the curls which framed her rosy face, her slim figure supple and graceful under its sheath of rose-colored satin. Neal, scintillating with cordiality, sartorially perfect in gray trousers and cutaway, stood beside her. Stood beside her, that is, most of the time; now and then he wandered about a little, to chat with a group which seemed a trifle silent, or hasten the progress of a guest who looked a little hungry into the dining-room. Here an immaculate maid, the stiff, embroidered *bretelles* of her apron snowy against her black silk uniform, was hovering over a tea table, on which silver dishes containing tomato-jelly sandwiches, angel food, tiny frosted cakes, and tinier biscuits stuffed with chicken salad, were scattered over an embroidered tablecloth. The maid was being assisted by a beautiful little girl, whose angelic gaze as she held out a plate or a cup seemed to supplicate the further consumption of delicacies. ("I don't need to ask if that's your little girl," the callers said, nine times out of ten, as they took their departure. "She looks *exactly* like you! Why, she's perfectly *lovely!*") And, pouring the tea, bland, and benign above the silver service, sat Mrs. Hammel, dressed in mauve velvet, orchids fastened to her bodice, plumes nodding from her brocade toque . . .

The "leader" in the society section of the *Inquirer* on the following Sunday was written by Miss Sharp. A picture of Anne, with Junior and Nancy as they had appeared at her *second* At Home—smiling and seraphic as they gazed over their mother's shoulder—surmounted it. This picture left nothing to be desired; neither did the headline "Vice-President's wife pours for Mrs. Conrad." Neither did the text which accompanied these.

"Mrs. Neal Conrad, whose husband's recent appointment to the Senate has been a matter of national interest, made her bow to official society in Washington last Thursday, at a delightful reception which she gave in the charming residence on New Hampshire Avenue which she and Senator Conrad have leased for the winter. Mrs. Conrad was assisted in receiving by the Senator, who forsook the cares and responsibilities of office for the afternoon, and who, like his wife, will quite evidently be a great addition to the senatorial circle. Mrs. Conrad was charmingly gowned in a Lanvin confection of pink, one of the many beautiful dresses which she brought home with her from Paris, where she and Senator Conrad spent the summer as guests of Mr. Clarence Hathaway, First Secretary of the American Embassy, a close friend of Senator Conrad's ever since the days when they were classmates at Harvard. Mrs. Hammel, who has been one of the first to welcome Mrs. Conrad, with whom she has many tastes in common, to Washington, presided at the perfectly appointed tea table, coming directly from the luncheon given in her honor by Madame Marceau, the wife of the French Ambassador, who also called on Mrs. Conrad during the course of the afternoon. Among the many distinguished guests were noticed . . ."

There was more, a great deal more. But that was all that mattered. The first hard weeks had been lived through, the first dreadful mistakes lived down, the "features" about the washtub and the cow forgotten. Anne had begun to "arrive."

CHAPTER XVIII

"I DO solemnly swear that I will support and defend the Constitution of the United States against all enemies, foreign and domestic; that I will bear true faith and allegiance to the same; that I take this obligation freely, without any mental reservation or purpose of evasion; and that I will well and faithfully discharge the duties of the office in which I am about to enter—so help me God."

Neal, facing the Vice-President, with his back to the Senate Chamber, stood beside Senator Brown, repeating the words, a phrase at a time, after Mr. Hammel. Anne, sitting in the Senators' gallery, her cold hands clenched tightly in her lap, colder chills of excitement creeping up and down her spine and stabbing swiftly at her heart, looked down at him with misty eyes. The mist blurred her vision so that she could hardly see him as the Vice-President shook hands with him, and he turned, signed his name in the large book held open by a clerk, and walking with his head held high, to a desk at the rear of the room, slid sidewise into the chair behind the desk.

It was the opening day of Congress, and Neal had repeated the oath of office administered to a new Senator, and then, literally, had taken his seat.

Anne had not been to the Capitol since she had visited it, years before, on her honeymoon-journey to Washington. Driving down to it now, she found it surrounded by police; and a friendly officer helped her to locate a parking-space. Another policeman, standing beside the revolving door at the entrance to the Senate wing, noticed her hesitation as she paused between the crowded elevator on her left and the empty one at her right marked "For Senators Only."

"Does that mean their wives too?" she asked shyly, but smiling.

The policeman grinned and pushed the bell for her himself. "Sure does," he answered reassuringly. "Get right in, Mrs. Conrad. . . . I read that piece about you in last Sunday's paper, and reggernized you by the pickshur. You sure have got some cute kids.—Gallery floor, you want."

Elated by this evidence of her dawning prominence, Anne confronted the doorman of the Senators' gallery without qualms. But he apparently did not read the papers; and he was struggling with a persistent mob which was striving to get past him, and which even his massive bulk and grim manner could not entirely stem. He could hardly be expected to look with favor upon another contestant for space.

"Mrs. Conrad?" he snarled, peering at her with suspicious, bulging eyes. "Lord! why don't they give out cards to this opening?—No, you don't neither. Can't tell, but it's against the rules— Senator Conrad's wife? Say, that don't go down any more. He's got three wives in there already."

There was a titter of derision about her, and Anne felt her cheeks growing hot.

"I will try to get someone to identify me," she said with a composure which she was very far from feeling.

"That won't be very hard," a merry voice boomed behind her; and turning suddenly, she almost bumped into Mrs. Hammel. "Come and sit with me, my dear. Delighted to have you. You know Mrs. Hastings, don't you—the Speaker's wife?—You and Mrs. Standish are friends already, of course. Now then—right down there on the left —no, not in the front row. Those are the seats reserved for Mrs. Shaw. But the ones directly behind."

Panting, but placid, Mrs. Hammel wove her way into the gallery. Anne, with a withering glance at the now obsequious doorkeeper, squeezed behind her and her two distinguished companions, and edged down the crowded steps to the designated places. There was the slight, pleasant confusion of removing wraps. Mrs. Hastings dropped her white kid gloves, and Anne quickly bent and picked them up. Mrs. Standish's sable cape stuck a little at the shoulders, and Anne helped to pull it free from her velvet dress; then, murmuring her appreciation of her rescue, she loosened her own coat, and settled down to look about her.

The Senators' gallery was already packed to the last row, except for the unoccupied seats which were roped off for Mrs. Shaw, the President's wife. There was a shining brass plate on the balcony-railing, she noticed, requesting visitors not to lean their elbows or place small personal possessions upon it; and she wondered why so trivial a thing should have caught her attention. All the galleries were crowded, and the one above the clock back of the rostrum was seething. Mrs. Standish caught her questioning gaze at this, and answered her.

"The press-gallery," she said in a voice that was unusually distinct, in spite of its softness, "full today, of course, because this is the opening session. You'll learn to watch that gallery—it's always the best gauge of the importance of what's happening here. If it's empty, you'll know there's nothing special going on. If it's teeming, even if you haven't heard that there's anything afoot, don't leave your seat, for something *is* afoot." Then, as the journalists suddenly began to clap, she smiled and added, "They've caught sight of Mrs. Hammel. She's marvelously popular. Applause is forbidden in the Senate—though the House lives on it—but these sporadic outbursts will occur."

Mrs. Hammel rose, bowed, smiled; almost imperceptibly, she flicked her handkerchief. She could not actually be said to wave to her admirers, but the gesture almost amounted to that. They clapped with renewed vigor.

The Senate Chamber, Anne thought, as she resumed her contemplation of it, was strangely unimpressive for so important an apartment. It was drab, dingy, close. Certainly the Senators could not derive much inspiration from their surroundings, wherever else they might gather it. They were beginning to come in now—not very impressive, either! Anne was disappointed. She did not know exactly what she had expected, but certainly not this. Many of them were bald; nearly all of them were gray; some were very lean or badly overweight. Little pompous groups, clad in shabby morning-clothes, were greeting each other ceremoniously, as they met for the first time that season. Others, more rough and ready as to both dress and manner, reached out welcoming hands, and slapped their colleagues on the back. One Senator, tall, thin, and harassed of expression, sat adding up columns of figures, apparently oblivious of the confusion around him. Another, a broad expanse of white linen waistcoat covering the front of his ample person, seemed all ready to deliver a spell-binding speech, although nobody appeared ready to listen. A third, dressed with faultless informality, a dark carnation in his buttonhole, was, quite superfluously, striking attitudes. His roving eyes caught Anne's, and rested for a moment on her face; then he bowed slightly. She felt quite sure she had not met him, but she returned the salutation, angry at herself for blushing, and conscious that Mrs. Standish, whom nothing seemed to escape, was watching her.

"Senator Lassiter," this lady remarked, her sweet voice a trifle dry, "the Beau Brummell of the Senate. Also—ah —the Lovelace. I believe you know Clarence Hathaway? Well, something the same type."

Anne was grateful for the rap of the Vice-President's gavel. He had entered, on the stroke of twelve, so unobtrusively that she had not seen him. The Chaplain offered prayer—a very long and all-inclusive sort of a prayer. Senator Brown delivered a short eulogy on the late Senator Shelton, to which nobody paid much attention. There was, actually, more of a stir followed by a deeper silence when Brown, his address finished, turned towards Neal and waited for the younger man to join him. Neal had made a fine record in his own state, and there was genuine interest in his appointment. But Anne, watching him, was experiencing a deeper emotion than interest; she was remembering, poignantly, the day she had joined the church, the testimony to her faith that she had given before the assembled congregation in the bare little building with its slender spire pointing towards the green hills behind it. This oath that Neal was taking seemed to her no less solemn, no less sacred—did he, she wondered, feel the same way about it? She hoped, prayerfully, that he did.

At all events, he had not forgotten her in this great and pregnant moment of his life. He had hardly taken his seat when he turned, swept the gallery with his keen eyes, and smiled as he found her and saw the expresssion of love and emotion on her face. For a moment they looked full at each other; Anne felt her composure returning, her vision clearing. She was able to return his smile. Then, apparently satisfied, he nodded, and looked away again giving his undivided attention to the business of the day.

This did not last long. Several brief resolutions were submitted, considered by unanimous consent, and agreed to.—"Resolved, that a committee consisting of two Senators be appointed to join such committee as may be appointed by the House of Representatives to wait upon the President of the United States and inform him that a quorum of each House is assembled, and that the Congress is ready to receive any communication he may be pleased to make."—"Resolved, that the Secretary inform the House of Representatives that a quorum of the Senate is assembled and that the Senate is ready to proceed to business." —"Resolved, that the hour of daily meeting of the Senate be twelve o'clock meridian until otherwise ordered."—The Vice-President's gavel descended again. The crowd began to stream out. Anne was conscious that Mrs. Hammel was speaking to her.

"You'll come to the House, tomorrow, of course, and hear the President read his message?"

"Oh, of course! I wouldn't miss it for anything!"

As a matter of fact, she had not intended to do anything of the sort; her interest in public affairs was still bounded by Neal's participation in them; and Neal, who had been a figure of importance today, would have no part in the morrow's proceedings. Moreover, being extremely sensitive, she dreaded the possibility of another rebuff such as she had received at the hands of the ruthless doorman; no occasion, she felt, could be worth a repetition of that. But it was evident that Mrs. Hammel expected her to return to the Capitol the next day; and she had made the gallant resolve that Mrs. Hammel should never be disappointed in her.

Her determination was rewarded. When Neal came home that night, he gave her a beautifully engraved little card, upon the back of which she discovered the number, row and section of a reserved seat. Armed with this, she penetrated to the House of Representatives without difficulty; and, having found her appointed place, she saw that Mrs. Hammel, Mrs. Hastings, and several other women whom she knew were all near her, and all in welcoming mood; and when Mrs. Shaw, accompanied by a military aide, came in and sat down immediately in front of her, she experienced an unexpected thrill in being presented to the First Lady of the Land. And, after that, one thrill followed another in swift succession: The House, which had struck her at first as being as disorderly as the Senate was drab, subsided quietly on one side of the great hall, in order to make room for the members of the Diplomatic Corps, of the Supreme Court, of the Cabinet and of the Senate, who filed impressively down the aisle. The quiet Vice-President took his place beside the genial Speaker. The President, with his escort of Senators and Representatives, advanced slowly, and mounted the rostrum, dignity and power emanating from his presence. It was *all* thrilling, so thrilling that Anne caught her breath with excitement. When the President began to speak her sense of stimulation increased— She listened with rapt attention to his recommendations, even though she did not understand all of them very well. There were, it seemed, many matters to which he felt Congress should give immediate attention. Appropriations for the army, navy, farm relief, a ship subsidy, a maternity bill. Anne recognized her ignorance on these subjects, and resolved to study them, in order to be able to follow intelligently any action that might be taken on them as the season progressed.

Suddenly she realized that her attention had begun to wander, perhaps because she was hungry. The hands of the clock over the rostrum were pointing to one, and she was relieved when the President, now somewhat hoarse, stopped reading and inclined his head to acknowledge the applause of his listeners. Mrs. Shaw, bowing graciously in every direction, was preparing to leave the gallery; and Mrs. Hammel, touching Anne's arm, was asking her a question.

"You are coming over to the luncheon, of course?"

"The luncheon?"

"Yes—the Senate Ladies' luncheon. Don't tell me there is *another* thing you haven't heard about! Well, I will explain as we go over in the subway. We will say good-by to Mrs. Standish and Mrs. Hastings here. They don't come with us."

Breathlessly, Anne followed Mrs. Hammel through the crowd to the basement of the Capitol, around several corners, and into a small open electric car with seats running sideways and facing in both directions, which was waiting, drawn up beside a concrete platform. It was full already, but Mrs. Hammel, bowing right and left, was immediately afforded space for herself and Anne. A bell clanged, with a sharp, tiny report; then the little car leapt forward, and they bounded noisily away. By raising her voice, Mrs. Hammel succeeded in making Anne hear her above the clatter.

"Every Tuesday. Marble room in the Senate Office Building. Take turns acting as hostesses. Six at a time. Cold meat, salad, rolls, coffee, cake, no more allowed. Can't have competition in menus. Make feeling. I'm the President. Great fun. You'll see. Here we are. Get out."

The marble room, reached by marble stairs, draped with red velvet and glittering with chandeliers, proved a most imposing apartment. Down its wide length ran a long narrow table, covered with a white cloth. Thermos bottles, plates of rolls and jelly, and large heavily frosted cakes were placed upon this at regular intervals; and several well-dressed women were fluttering about it, pouring water and straightening silverware. Another group was clustered about a smaller table in a remote corner, almost concealing the platters of cold meat and salad with which they were occupied. Mrs. Hammel, interrupting herself with frequent greetings, continued her explanation to the still bewildered Anne.

"The waiters from the Senate restaurant come over and set the table for us and clear away afterwards. But the hostesses for the day act as waitresses. They are chosen in alphabetical order—your turn will come next time since your name begins with a 'C.' The chairman—whoever is chosen—will tell you what to bring. . . . Oh, good morning, Mrs. Churchill. How are you? Nice to see you back. . . . All Senators' hostesses are eligible for membership— you must sign your name and pay your dollar for yearly dues today. The rules are simple. . . . Hello, Mrs. Farnham! . . . But mind you never bring a guest with you who is a resident of Washington—that *will* get you into trouble! Mrs. Lee, I want you to take Mrs. Conrad under your wing today, and see that she meets everybody and has a good time."

Mrs. Lee, thus announced, shook hands with Anne and led her to a seat at the long table introducing her to the other women who had already taken their places near her. Then she sat down on Anne's left, and reached for a thermos bottle. It contained piping hot coffee, and she filled Anne's cup and her own before sending it down the line. The hostesses were already beginning to pass the great platters of cold meat and salad. There was a good deal of informal merriment—a much pleasanter medium for getting acquainted, Anne reflected, this luncheon, than those stiff brief calls. A few of the women she had met already, though not many, as only two Thursdays had elapsed since the memorable one when she had involuntarily held her first "At Home." Those she did know welcomed her cordially and presented her to others. When the rich, moist cakes had been eaten—from the same dishes on which the meat and salad had been served—Mrs. Hammel rose in her place at the end of the long table, and called the attention of the Ladies of the Senate to the fact that one of their members, Mrs. Long, was ill. It was voted to send her flowers. Then a note of appreciation which had come from Mrs. Sheldon was read acknowledging a letter of condolence which had been written by the secretary. Afterwards, as there was no further business Mrs. Hammel announced the names of the hostesses for the following week

183

—Mrs. Bean, Mrs. Brainard, Miss Bullard, Mrs. Clay, Mrs. Conrad—with Miss Bullard appointed as chairman. Anne found herself carried off for a conference. A salad, it was decided, was to be her contribution—and would she please plan to be a little early, the following Thursday, to help with preparations? The hostesses usually *did*.

The merry little party was already breaking up when the deliberations of the committee were finished. Mrs. Hammel had vanished. Anne found herself approaching the elevator with Mrs. Lee and Mrs. Stone—the same Mrs. Stone, she instinctively felt, to whom her first callers had gone from her house on that fatal Thursday to relate her short-comings. At all events, Mrs. Stone, a tall, grimly handsome woman, had seemed less cordial to her than to any of the others, and she now felt the chill of the elder woman's cold, critical gaze.

The elevator man slid open the door of his cage and the three ladies prepared to enter.

"Up or down?" he asked.

"Up," said Mrs. Lee who had an errand to do in her husband's office.

"Down," said Anne, who was intent on getting home to relate the exciting events of the day to Dora.

The elevator slid down. Unconscious of wrongdoing, Anne alighted, nodding good-by to Mrs. Lee as she ascended out of sight and turned to find Mrs. Stone standing balefully beside her.

"Don't you know any better than that?" she demanded angrily.

Anne cringed, inwardly but not outwardly. The fabric of her happiness was rent, but she did not allow this disturber of the peace to guess that she was hurt.

"Know any better than what?" she asked.

"Than to tell the elevator man to go down when Mrs. Lee had told him to go up. Her husband has been in the Senate for eighteen years. She takes precedence over *all* of us. And all of the rest of us take precedence over *you*."

"Oh," said Anne shortly, with no indication of being impressed. Mrs. Stone became more and more indignant.

"The matter of precedence is one of *extreme* importance," she declaimed, "and those who do not recognize this only show their ignorance and ill-breeding. A hostess who does not seat her guests according to rank offends irretrievably. I myself have *left* three luncheons because I was not properly placed."

"And was that," inquired Anne, "well-bred?"

Mrs. Stone, who was a very important person—especially in her own estimation—stared speechlessly. No one had ever been so impudent to her before. Ann gathered courage.

"People don't ask you to their homes to insult you," she said, in contemptuous tones. "I am sure the people in my state would think I had 'offended irretrievably' if I treated a hostess like that. And I am confident Mrs. Lee knew I didn't mean to be rude—she looks like a very understanding sort of person. But I won't forget," Anne added with significance, "about precedence—that *you* always take precedence over *me*."

She walked down the steps of the Senate Office Building without a backward glance, and over to the place where she had parked her car. She was conscious that she had scored a victory. She was also conscious that she had made an enemy.

CHAPTER XIX

THE morning after the Senate Ladies' Luncheon, Mrs. Lee called Anne on the telephone, and asked if she might not stop and take her to the Congressional Club reception on Friday.

"You have had an invitation to join, of course?"

"Yes—but you see I have been so busy making diplomatic calls—"

"I know—it is hard to wedge both the calls and the clubs in the same afternoon. But everything is over at the Club a little after five, and that leaves almost another hour for calls afterwards. If you are pretty well caught up couldn't you manage somehow?"

"I believe I could; especially as I would love to go to the club with you," Anne said frankly.

"I am so glad, for I would love to take you," responded Mrs. Lee cordially. "Promptly at 2:45 then."

In her eagerness to be prompt, Anne was standing on the steps of her house, watching the street in both directions, when Mrs. Lee drove up; and as she took her place beside the older lady in the big limousine, Mrs. Lee regarded her with covert but thorough approbation. Anne had on a dress and coat of sapphire blue velvet, with close-fitting collar and cuffs of ermine; and her sapphire blue velvet hat was faced with white satin. Nothing could have been more becoming; she had "matched her eyes" as the *grandes couturières* are so fond of charging their customers to do. Moreover, her white gloves, her suède shoes, and the beaded bag which she carried were all perfectly in keeping. More than one woman stopped to look at her, almost enviously, as she and Mrs. Lee were leaving their

186

wraps in the reception hall of the Congressional club, which was temporarily transformed into a cloak room.

"Wouldn't you like to come in and see the library where we hold our board meetings before we go upstairs?" Mrs. Lee asked, "being third vice-president, I have to spend every Wednesday morning there, and I would like to show it to you. The secretary's little cubby-hole is cunning too —but we won't delay too long. The reception has begun already."

Mrs. Lee steered Anne gently in the direction of the broad carved staircase, banked with ferns and palms, and separated half way up into two branches. It was crowded —as every place in Washington seemed to be crowded!— and because of the confusion they were obliged to stop for a moment beside the statue of the Winged Victory that stood on the landing.

"Usually we have a program on Friday afternoons," Mrs. Lee explained during this enforced pause, "a concert or a lecture, or something like that; then a short reception afterwards. But as this is our first gathering of the season, the afternoon is *entirely* given over to the reception—it is so pleasant, isn't it, to have this meeting place for seeing our friends! The Congressional Club fulfills a much wider purpose than the Ladies of the Senate, since the wives of both Houses of Congress are members, and daughters may come in too as associate members if they wish. There—I believe we can squeeze ahead an inch or two now!"

The crowd suddenly surged forward, bearing Mrs. Lee and Anne with it up the stairs, and into the great oval room at the top. This room was hung from end to end with feathery southern smilax, and above the smilax floated the flags of every state in the union. The wide white mantle was banked with pink flowers; and above it hung a fine oil painting beautifully illuminated. Near the pillars at the entrance, in front of a little alcove cushioned in green velvet, the president of the Club, Mrs. Gray, and the two first vice-presidents, Mrs. Gorham and Mrs. Bean were standing to receive the guests—Mrs. Gray in beige lace, Mrs. Gorham in mauve crêpe, Mrs. Bean in black satin. At the front end of the room, the Marine Band, gorgeous in the scarlet, gold and blue of full dress uniform, was playing. About a dozen ladies were "floating" through the crowd making themselves especially agreeable to newcomers or those who seemed to be alone; and in the little dining-room beyond, an enormous basket of American beauty roses towered between two silver candelabra, on a table spread with a lace cloth and covered with delicacies. Mrs. Hastings sat at one end pouring tea and Mrs. Lassiter at the other pouring coffee; they both greeted Anne cordially, and Mrs. Lassiter detained her for a moment.

"My son and I were sorry to miss you when we called yesterday," she said. "Of course you can't stay in every Thursday, but Blythe very seldom accompanies me on my rounds and he was really disappointed. Have you and Senator Conrad, by any miracle, a free evening next week or the week after? We would like so much to have you dine with us—"

"We would be glad to come any evening," said Anne with her accustomed frankness. "You are the first person who has asked us to dinner."

"What a neglect of opportunity!" murmured Mrs. Lassiter, "but it won't last long. Next winter we will have to speak for you months ahead. Meanwhile, I will get in touch with you again very shortly, Mrs. Conrad."

Mrs. Lee seemed as pleased as Anne herself at the invitation, and she told Anne something about the Lassiters as they drove away. Mrs. Lassiter was a very wealthy widow, it seemed, and acted as hostess for her son, who was unmarried, and the greatest "catch" in the "Senatorial Circle."—"Only, no one has been able to catch him yet," laughed Mrs. Lee; "he is elusive—and just a bit delusive —but he'll give you a good time. You made quite an impression on him at the opening of Congress. He asked who you were immediately after he saw you in the gallery, and has told several people he thought you were the prettiest woman there."

The promised dinner invitation was delivered by hand before Neal and Anne had finished their own supper that night. It was surmounted by a gold crest, over which was written in ink "In honor of the French Ambassador and

188

Madame Marceau." Underneath, partly engraved and partly written, appeared the words

> *Mrs. Lassiter*
> *requests the pleasure of*
> *Senator and Mrs. Conrad's*
> *company at dinner*
> *on Wednesday evening, December the 14th*
> *at eight o'clock.*

2141 Massachusetts Avenue.

"Less than a week off!" exclaimed Anne. "Oh, Neal, what shall I wear?"

Neal laughed. "What a question for a woman who has just got back from Paris! Your clothes are lovely, Anne, you know they are,—and you mustn't try to save them. When the ones you have now begin to get shabby you must have some more. I think that white velvet with the glittery trimming—rhinestone do you call it?—is about the best—and I guess you better *wear* the best." He turned the invitation over thoughtfully. "They must have been going to have this dinner anyway; they've added us to their other guests, or asked us in place of someone who couldn't accept. But that doesn't matter. It's really a compliment.— The card wasn't mailed; perhaps you better not mail your acceptance either."

"I can run over with it right after supper," Dora, who had been listening with shared excitement broke in eagerly, "it's just a step and I need a breath of air."

"Thanks, Dora—it is going to be hard, Neal, driving a car in evening clothes."

"I know—I do wish we could afford more help. Dora must stop doing the washing, that's certain. You must send it out, Anne, or get a woman to come in and help with it and to get supper the nights Dora goes out."

"We can't afford it," Anne objected. But her objection was rather weak. It was all too obvious that neither she nor Dora could continue to work as hard as they had been

189

doing without breaking down, if so many outside demands were to be made upon them.

"We have got to afford it," Neal retorted resolutely. "Thank goodness this is a short season! I'll be back in Hinsboro the fifth of March, digging away for dear life! No vacation for me this summer! My poor old clients will have to cough up enough for us to live on decently here, since the Government won't, and next winter we will be doing things *right*. In the meantime, we will have to find some kind of a temporary solution."

The solution presented itself in an unexpected, not to say startling, manner. When Anne returned from her round of calls the following afternoon ("Will I *ever*," she was saying to herself, "do anything in the afternoon again but call, *call*, CALL!") she drew back in alarm before a huddled figure which was crouched on her front steps, in an attitude of the deepest dejection. At her startled exclamation, the figure unfolded itself and stood up—a gaunt, unkempt man, young but haggard, dressed in a shabby uniform.

"Good-evenin', marm," he said awkwardly, taking off his frayed cap, "sorry if ah frightened you. Don't need a man, do you?"

"Good gracious," exclaimed Anne, "I don't know. What kind of a man? What do you mean?"

"Well, ah meant my kind of a man," the intruder explained hopefully. "Ah ben lookin' for work quite a spell. But ah can't seem to find none. 'Pears like the fellers that stayed to home while we-all was to war collared all the jobs. Leastwise ah can't find none. No, marm, not in Washington. Ah come up here to try to fix ma claim at the Veterans' Bureau and ah ain't got ma claim and ah ain't got no money to go home with neither. Ah'm plumb broke. And ah got so dead beat, walkin' the streets lookin' for somethin' to do, that ah finally set down here on your stoop. Your house ain't so grand as most. Ah thought maybe some one lived here wasn't real rich, mat be glad to get a few odd jobs done cheap. Ah ain't askin' for much . . . your hired girl wouldn't let me in. But she said ah could wait outside till you-all come home."

"Can you drive a car?" asked Anne without circumlocution. The haggard veteran grinned.

"Well, ah hain't had much experience with Rolls-Royces and them, lady, but a Dodge or the like of that—"

"It *is* a Dodge," said Anne with surprising suddenness. "Are you willing to wash windows and tend a furnace and put on a white coat and open the door?"

"Ah'm willing to do anythin'," said the man with pathetic eagerness.

"Are you—are you white? It is so dark I can't see. I've had my maid a long time and I don't know how she would feel about a colored man in the house," said Anne with slight confusion.

"That's all right, marm, ah don't mind you askin'. Yes, ah'm white all right. 'Pore white trash' you'd call me ah reckon. Ah come from the mountings, Kentucky—ah seen your hired girl. She's powerful pert lookin'. Ah'd be pleased to help her any ways ah could. Ah can cook a meal, too, real good."

"What's your name?" demanded Anne.

"Delancy."

"Good gracious," said Anne, for the second time, "is that your first name or last name?"

"Mah first name's Hod—Horace."

"Well, Horace Delancy, if I get you the clothes you need and feed you, will you come to me for—thirty dollars a month? Until you have proved you are worth more? There's a little bit of a dark room in the rear of the basement. I'm ashamed to ask any one to sleep in it, but if you—"

"Oh, marm," exclaimed Horace Delancy, "oh, lady!"

He pitched suddenly forward. Anne caught him, supported him, reached for the door-bell. Before Dora could answer it Neal swung suddenly into sight around the corner of the street and ran towards the house. Anne turned to him, cutting short his startled exclamation.

"This is our new chauffeur," said Anne calmly, "an answer to prayer. He just fainted away because, I expect —it's some time since he had a square meal; but he is going to be another household treasure just like Dora."

CHAPTER XX

HORACE DELANCY, warm, fed, bathed, shaved, and clad in neat whipcord, drove Anne and Neal to their dinner at the Lassiters the following Wednesday evening.

It was—of course—a crazy thing to take a man off the street like that into one's house. Both Anne and Neal admitted it. But somehow, neither of them hesitated to do the crazy thing just the same; and Dora's harsh and suspicious comments were nullified by her kind and charitable actions. She scrubbed, scoured, and set in order the little basement room; she placed heaped dishes of steaming food before the derelict at frequent and regular intervals; she lengthened the sleeves of the chauffeur's uniform and the white duck house coats that Anne bought. And she was repaid in kind. Horace Delancy had scarcely recovered from his faint when he assumed control of the furnace. The following morning he drove the children to school, Neal to the Senate Office Building, and Anne to the Central Market; and before evening he had washed every window in the house. It was not until Sunday, however, that his supreme opportunity came. Dora went out then, and he served his astonished benefactors, not the cold "pick-up" supper which is usually associated with a religious observance of the Sabbath, but a meal in which fried chicken, corn fritters, beaten biscuit, fruit salad, and Lady Baltimore cake were a few of the more substantial offerings. Afterwards Anne confronted him accusingly.

"I don't believe you are 'poor white trash' at all!" she remonstrated.

Horace Delancy grinned his disarming smile.

"Ah never said ah was. Ah said likely you'd *call* me

that. Mah maw's a good cook. She's got a right nice little place of her own. Widow woman. It was her learned me to cook when ah was a young 'un. Mis' Conrad, marm, Dora says you-all is figurin' on gettin' you a washlady. Ah kin wring out clothes real good and hang 'em up. Maw she learned me that too. Ah reckon me and Dora can handle that there wash between us *right*."

Her release from the pressure of domestic duties immediately gave Anne an increased freedom of both action and spirit. On the eventful evening of the dinner she sang as she put the studs in Neal's dress shirt and laid it on the bed beside the white velvet dress with the "glittery" trimming. When Neal came home she had already bathed and was sitting clad in her silk slip before her dressing table, her hair hanging like a cloud of gold about her.

"Lorelei!" he whispered, laughing, and rested his cheek, still cold from the December wind, against her smooth warm face. Then suddenly his arms slid down around her slim, pliant body, and tightened there. He lifted her up, and sat down himself, holding her closely to him. "Darling Anne! I do love you so! I don't say so often, I know, or show it as much as I might, and sometimes I know I seem preoccupied—indifferent—neglectful even but—" He did not try to go on. Indeed there was no necessity that he should. Anne understood, and made her understanding sweetly clear. When at last he set her on her feet again, he began to fumble a little weakly, a little shamefacedly, in his pocket.

"While we were discussing Horace the other night," he said, "you remarked that we needn't worry about his stealing, because there was nothing in the house he could possibly *want* to steal except your engagement ring and that you wore that all the time. Well—of course I don't want to put a premium on crime, but you set me thinking. It is a long time since I have given you a present—would this be pretty, do you think, with the 'glittery' dress?"

"This" when taken out of the satin box with a little spring that clicked, and unwound from layers of flat cotton and twisted tissue paper, proved to be a diamond pendant, hung on a slender platinum chain finished with a diamond clasp. Anne lifted it out breathlessly, starry eyed.

"Oh, Neal! Oh, how lovely! Oh—"

"You can't afford it!" finished Neal mockingly, "of course I can! A man can't afford *not* to give presents to his wife every now and then. Besides, you're not to worry, it is all paid for. I had an unexpected check today—an account long overdue paid up. I'd given up hope of realizing anything on it. But I attended to all our monthly bills, bang up, just like *that!* And still I had enough left over for this too!"

The pendant *was* pretty with the "glittery" dress. In fact it was perfect. And as Anne, followed by Neal, swept into the Lassiter drawing-room while the butler beside the silk portièred entrance announced, "Senator and Mrs. Conrad" in tones charged with suppressed importance, both were swiftly conscious of the fact that Anne was unsurpassed in elegance by any other woman present, though nearly a dozen, superbly dressed, were already gathered in the great apartment hung with tapestries and furnished with delicate chairs and sofas surmounted with the monogram of Marie Antoinette. Senator Lassiter, who was talking with the French Ambassadress, detached himself immediately from her side, and hastened forward; while his mother, with less *empressement* but with equal cordiality, turned to greet them also.

"We are so very happy to have you with us—now let me see. I wish to be sure you meet everyone here tonight —you know the Marceaus—and have you also met the Italian Ambassador and Donna Martinelli? Ah, I thought so, for I know you have been most punctilious about making your diplomatic calls! Madame Estavi is also a friend already, I am sure—the Speaker of the House and Mrs. Hastings, Senator and Mrs. Lee, Senator and Mrs. Stone."

The even, cultured voice flowed on. Two more servants in purple livery entered, bearing silver trays, laden with frosty cocktails, and tiny savory sandwiches. Senator Lassiter offered his arm to the Ambassadress, and advanced, with her beside him, at the head of the procession which wound its way to the strains of music from an unseen organ through a second great drawing-room, across a galleried hall, and into a long, paneled dining-room flanked with great carved sideboards. The table was covered with a lace cloth; golden vases filled with poinsettias alternated with golden *épergnes* filled with smooth, glowing fruit, down its stately length; at each place was a golden service plate, golden knives and forks, thin stemmed goblets of fine Venetian glass. The liveried men servants—six of them in evidence now—were offering caviar, resting in the carved hollows of great blocks of ice. This was followed by a clear green turtle soup, lobster Newburg in "horns of plenty" made of fluffy pastry, a saddle of mutton with multitudinous vegetables, a molded gelatine salad accompanied by cheese soufflé, white balls of ice cream, rolled in shredded cocoanut and resting on illuminated spun sugar, tiny candy-like cakes. There was sherry to drink, claret, sauterne and champagne, though Anne touched none of it, and after the ladies had returned to the drawing-room, there was coffee, dark brandy, colorless cointreau and emerald-colored crème de menthe poured slowly from bulky bottles into infinitesimal glasses.

Anne, feeling as if she had been suddenly transported to one of Monte Cristo's banquets, hoped that she was successfully concealing the swimming sensation which almost overcame her as she seated herself between Senator Stone and Señor Estavi at the very end of the table. To her, a "company dinner," achieved after hours of hard labor on the part of both Dora and herself, had consisted of fruit cocktail, tomato bisque soup, roast chicken, a sweet salad smothered in mayonnaise, vanilla ice cream with chocolate sauce, and angel cake. She must, it seemed, reorganize her ideas about entertaining as completely as she had reorganized them about dress. But she resolved to do so swiftly and competently; and rousing herself, she heard the small black-bearded man with indefinable charm and distinction who was placed at her left asking hopefully, *"Vous-parlez-français, Madame?"*

"Mais, oui," she answered breathlessly, her head clearing instantly, and launching into her newly acquired but fluent French she began to chatter pleasantly with the agreeable little Peruvian. He was delighted at this unex-

pected display of linguistic accomplishment. It was very rare, he explained, that he encountered *"une Americaine du Nord"* who could summon more than a few broken phrases of a foreign language to her command in an emergency; he would, of course, have learned English himself if he had had any idea that he might have the honor of being sent to Washington, but his appointment had been wholly unexpected. He had, however, a fair knowledge of French, German, Italian, and Portuguese besides his native Spanish; and in a month, if the pleasure of escorting her into dinner occurred again he would address her in her own tongue. (This promise, it may be noted in passing, he faithfully kept, astonishing her by the mastery of grammar, idiom and vocabulary which he acquired in so short a time.) So far, his positions had been in Central America and the Orient. Salvador—really a little Paris. Peking, the wonder city of the world. Anne, entranced, almost forgot the rather sullen, silent figure on her other side; then accusing herself mentally of being prejudiced against him for no better reason than because he was the husband of a woman who had been rude to her, she made a definite effort to seem sweet and gracious. Her attempts met with little response, however. Senator Stone seemed either unaware of conversational obligations or indifferent to them. He was brusque and biting in his speech; and Anne, feeling ill repaid for her pains, was tempted to turn again to Señor Estavi and the magic lands to which he had transported her in fancy. The streak of stubborness in her nature, however, rather than any social intuition, prevented her from following this path of least resistance; and she struggled bravely through course after course undeterred by sarcastic or monosyllabic replies and an attitude of critical indifference. In the end she had her reward. For Senator Lassiter, appearing at her side apparently from nowhere in an incredibly short time after she had finished her coffee, assured her that she would be much more comfortable on a deep brocaded sofa at the front end of the room than in the small high chair on which she was then sitting; and shepherded her suavely and inconspicuously to a place a little apart from the other guests.

"How I wish," he murmured, throwing his handsome head back a little and speaking through half-closed lips, "that once, just once, I could take a young and pretty woman out to dinner! But it is always my fate to have middle-aged, not to say elderly, Ambassadresses at my side—estimable ladies who have begun to put on weight and who hold their double chins high—it is unthinkable that any man should indulge in airy persiflage with dowagers of rank!"

"Because they would resent it as an impertinence? or because they offer no inducement to levity and indiscretion?" asked Anne, who was beginning to enjoy herself again.

"Both, my dear lady. You have no idea how virtuous I am when there is nothing about to tempt me. But in the presence of lovely young matrons with perfect complexions and a gift of repartee I sometimes forget myself."

"But they, I suppose, always jog your memory?" said Anne demurely.

"Oh, no—not always. Sometimes they are forgetful too—How's your memory?" he inquired with a slight drawl.

"Excellent," said Anne, with emphasis.

But Senator Lassiter did not seem to be daunted; and when a little later she told him that she thought perhaps she and Neal should be leaving, he informed her, with even more of a drawl, that they could not go until after the guests of honor had departed.

"But they will go," he said, "exactly on the tick of ten-thirty. That is the law of the Medes and Persians. Even if she were in the middle of a sentence, the Ambassadress would rise on the stroke of the clock, collect her husband with one well-directed glance, thank my mother and myself for the delightful evening we had given her, smile graciously upon the rest of you and disappear. The worst of it is, that after that you will be free to go too; you will no doubt take advantage of your freedom; and I do not feel at all sure when I shall see you again."

"Neal and I have been asked to another dinner," said Anne.

"Not really! Two in the same winter!" mocked Lassiter lightly.

"Yes, really. In honor of the Hammels. The Standishes are giving it. I think it is most awfully kind of them to invite us. But what I started to say was—perhaps you will be there and I might meet you then."

"I see," said Lassiter, suddenly grave. "Thank you. I shall be there."

Anne had the sudden, uncomfortable feeling that she had made an appointment with him. With his usual intuition he guessed this, and with his usual smooth skillfulness restored her composure.

"And at many other festivities which you will attend," he said casually. "We are certain to move in interlocking circles, if not actually the same one, as I rather suspect may be the case. I hope you dance? I shall permit myself to look for you at the Children's Hospital Ball."

He bowed slightly, in kind and superficial tribute. Near them a gilt clock, surmounted by Cupids, and standing on a high carved mantel between two vases filled with Annunciation lilies, chimed softly and struck the half hour. The Ambassadress, who was favoring Neal with a few formal remarks, instantly extended her hand in farewell, and sought the Ambassador with her eye.

"What did I tell you!" laughed Lassiter softly. "Good-by —dear Lady Delight."

CHAPTER XXI

LUNCHEONS, teas, dinners, calls. Official receptions, charity balls, evening musicals, calls. Tuesday noons at the Senate Office Building, Friday afternoons at the Congressional Club. Calls. Calls. Calls.

Anne had been swept breathlessly, into the swing of it, almost before she realized what had happened. In January came a week when she did not lunch at home, in February a week when she and Neal did not once dine at home, in early March a week when she was out for both luncheon and dinner every day. She grew very thin and she slept badly, feeling restless and "edgy" for some time after she went to bed, and tossing about so that she feared she might disturb Neal, and finally asked him, rather shyly, if he would not like to have her get twin beds for their room.

"No," he said shortly, "not at all." And laughed, drawing her to him. "Not trying to slip gradually away from me, with that as the first step, are you, Anne, now that you have all sorts of celebrities at your feet?"

"Of course not," she protested; and did not repeat her suggestion. Her beauty took on a slightly haggard quality, and there were dark circles under her eyes, fainter color in her cheeks; but what she lost in freshness she gained, subtly, in sophistication and distinction.

And she loved it all: the over-lapping engagements, the stiff, square, creased envelopes delivered by hand, the clanging telephone, the long cardboard flower boxes with their contents shrouded in moist oiled paper and tiny cards tucked in their corners, the cool home-comings when she left a heated ballroom just before dawn and felt the fresh breeze in her face as Horace drove her swiftly up New Hampshire Avenue, the warm, scented air of flower-decked drawing-rooms, the slamming of limousine doors, the little stir of welcome as she approached a group of friends, the merry approbation of Mrs. Hammel, the semi-serious attentions of Senator Lassiter, the evident pride with which Neal watched her rapid assent from rung to rung of the social ladder—

For Anne was progressing with a rapidity which was sufficiently rare to be remarkable even in that capacity where so many others have been tested, and have proven beyond any possible question the fine adaptability of the fine American woman.

Nothing perhaps was more indicative of her advance in *savoir-faire* than the difference in the degree of composure with which she approached the White House. When she first drove under its white-pillared *porte-cochère* to deposit her card and Neal's on the small silver salver extended to her by the manservant in livery who emerged from the imposing doorway before her car had actually come to a stop, her fingers trembled so that she could hardly lay down the neatly folded bits of cardboard. The deference which doth "hedge in a king" and which—deny it though we may—seems to many of us to hedge in a president also, rose before her in all its grandeur, terrifying her with its significance. It did not matter that the policeman on duty took her arrival calmly, and as a matter of course, that they actually motioned her on her way with a smile; and that the manservant closed the door of the motor, after he had taken her cards, with the manner of one who is proud to serve a welcomed and honored guest. Her sense of awe persisted all the afternoon; and when Mrs. Hammel told her she should follow up this ceremony of card leaving, after a little interval, with a note to Miss Hopkinson, Mrs. Shaw's secretary, requesting to be received by the President's wife, her reluctance to take this bold step was as evident in her face as it was in her voice.

"Why, Mrs. Hammel, I *couldn't!* Ask Mrs. Shaw to receive *me!* Surely I ought to wait for her to make the suggestion, if such a suggestion is ever to be made!"

"Certainly you ought not! Do you imagine that Mrs. Shaw spends her leisure moments glancing through the cards that are showered upon her and deciding whom to favor with an invitation? She never sees those cards. She *has* no leisure moments. But Miss Hopkinson, the grim old dragon—and a pretty good sort, too, when you get to know her!—has you all neatly docketed and knows whether you have done right by our Nell, and all that. So run along home, Goldilocks, and get your note written!"

Anne used up sheet after sheet of her new monogrammed paper before she achieved a letter that pleased her; but finally it was written and dispatched. When no answer was immediaely forthcoming she experienced a sensation of shame—surely she ought never to have written that note! She was being snubbed for her temerity! In the daytime she managed to forget the fancied reproof, but at night she cringed under the sheets at the thought of it. Then, when she had resolutely dismissed the matter from her mind, Dora came to her one morning, wreathed in smiles, and extended a small square envelope engraved on one corner with the magic words "The White House" in small gold block letters.

"This just came, Mis' Conrad. I thought mebbe you'd like it right away."

The flap crackled under Anne's eager hands. A neat card, surmounted by a gilt eagle was disclosed. Anne read:

Mrs. Shaw
will be glad to receive
Mrs. Conrad
on Wednesday, January seventh
at five o'clock.

"There!" said Dora triumphantly; for Dora had been told, of course, all about the note to Miss Hopkinson.

But Anne did not feel triumphant. She felt frightened. And when, at quarter before five on Wednesday, January seventh, she went down her front steps dressed in the sapphire velvet, she grew hot and cold by turns. But she walked steadily across the White House *porte-cochère*, bowed slightly and serenely to the man who opened the door for her, and regarded the tall formally dressed man whom she encountered just inside the entrance with composure.

"This is Mrs. Conrad, Senator Conrad's wife. I have an appointment to see Mrs. Shaw at five."

"Yes, Mrs. Conrad. Mrs. Shaw is expecting you. Would you like to leave your wraps here?—Now if you will come with me into the Blue Room Mrs. Shaw will be there in just a minute."

"How nice he is!" The tall figure had vanished and, relaxing a little, she looked about the circular apartment with its long draped windows giving glimpses of the garden beyond and the white flowers massed about the gilt clock on the mantel piece. The parquet floor shone like a mirror, and the stiffly beautiful chairs and sofa upholstered in smooth azure damask were grouped around the edges of the room.

"There must be some place more homelike than this where they can sit in the evening!" said Anne to herself, and thought with amusement of Neal's insistence that no man could be comfortable in a room that did not look as if he could put his feet up somewhere in it. She tried to visualize the President putting his feet on one of the blue damask sofas and failed. But the idea brought a smile to her lips. She was still smiling when the door at her left clicked and opened, and the tall spare formally dressed man came into the room again.

"Mrs. Shaw," he said in an impressive whisper.

Mrs. Shaw extended her hand. She sat down herself and asked Anne to do so; and then pleasantly, casually, and fluently she began to talk. Anne, answering at first almost in monosyllables, found herself, at the end of five minutes, talking pleasantly, casually, and fluently also. For the President's wife—amiable, composed, unpretentious, at once put her visitor completely at ease. Her flat crêpe dress of dull purple, with smooth, scalloped flounces and long, tight-fitting sleeves was simplicity itself; her dark hair touched with gray was skillfully but almost severely arranged; and she wore no ornaments except a glittering buckle which fastened the narrow, purple, velvet band around her throat and the glittering buckles on her narrow suède shoes. If she lacked something of Mrs. Hammel's merry charm she gave a greater sense of security and repose. Anne liked her, immediately and immensely. She forgot all about everything deferential. She remembered that this woman, sitting beside her—the First Lady of the Land—had in her youth worked her way through college, taught school, gone to Europe as the paid chaperon for a group of young "society girls," and married an impecunious young storekeeper whom she had endeavored to inculcate with her ideas of culture. Anne began to realize something of the struggle—both for him and his wife—that must have preceded his assent to the position of a prosperous cosmopolitan merchant—of a Cabinet member —of President of the United States. She visualized the grief—both for him and his wife—which must have bowed them to earth when both their children had died within a week of each other, of scarlet fever, and there had never been any more—

"Just a minute, Mr. Cooper," Mrs. Shaw was saying calmly. Anne turned and saw that the tall formally dressed figure was standing in the doorway bowing. "Mr. Cooper has come to let us know that our fifteen minutes together are over, Mrs. Conrad. I am so sorry. But I hope to see you very soon again. You will come to the Congressional reception, of course?"

Anne had not intended to do anything of the sort. She had been secretly relieved that Neal had had a sore throat on the night of the Diplomatic Reception, with which the official season had opened and that therefore they had not attended it. But now she answered eagerly.

"Yes, of course! I am looking forward to it ever so much!"

She found that she really meant this; and during the next week her view point did not change. There was no dread merged with her anticipation. The following Thursday she was athrill with excitement as she put on the "glittery" dress and her new pendant; she hummed a gay little air as she folded her evening coat around her, and she seized Neal's arm with an exclamation of pure rapture as their car marked with its "blue card" swung into the slow line of shining limousines advancing, a few feet at a time, down West Executive Avenue, and she caught sight of the effulgent globes of light glowing above the wings of the White House, like orange-colored flowers against the black velvet darkness. They passed through the grilled entrance gate with an easy turn, and stopped at the south entrance just behind Senator and Mrs. Lee. The two men lifted tall silk hats, and drew back for their wives to precede them through the revolving doors; then, as the ladies went into the cloak room to remove their wraps, Mrs. Lee linked her arm cordially inside Anne's elbow.

"Stay with us, won't you? We know the ropes, we'll show you just what to do and where to go so you will see the most—"

They went swiftly past a little room with its many paneled cupboards containing the china of former administrations, through the long corridor where the portraits of the wives of former presidents smiled serenely down from their golden frames, into the little elevator at the left. Then Mrs. Lee with a smothered exclamation that they were "just in time" led them part way across the great hall, and motioned them to take their places beside a tasseled silken cord which was placed across it. In the space beyond they could see the scarlet-coated Marine Band grouped near the front door. Suddenly the selection which the band was rendering came to an abrupt end, and there was a moment of poignant silence. Then the strains of "Hail to the Chief" rang out, and a brilliant procession turned from the broad stairway near the East Room and advanced slowly toward the center of the hall: six aides, gorgeous in gold-braided uniforms; two marines, one bearing the Stars and Stripes, the other the President's flag; the President with Mrs. Shaw on his arm—Mrs. Shaw carrying a small sparkling bag in her white-gloved hands, her long brocaded train flowing from her shoulders like a golden banner; the Secretary of State and Mrs. Standish, who was regal in purple velvet and rose point lace; the other Members of the Cabinet and their wives. Anne was so close to them that she could have touched them as they passed on into the Blue Room; and the Secretary of Commerce, a hearty, jovial sort of person, leaned across the silken rope and shook hands with her as he passed. Mr. Goldenburg greeting her after a long separation would have welcomed her in much the same manner—

But there was no time to stand still, making happy comparisons. The instant that the presidential party had disappeared Mrs. Lee whisked Neal and Anne away into the stately dining-room, where they took their places in line with members of both Houses and their wives who were already gathered there. Mrs. Roper and Mrs. Ranger with their submerged spouses were just ahead.

"This is your very *first* reception, isn't it?" exclaimed Mrs. Roper, thrusting her head back to speak to Anne. "We missed you so much the night of the Diplomats. But of course you did not realize that is the most *brilliant* of all! This is *tame* by comparison."

"It doesn't seem tame to me," said Anne with honest enthusiasm.

"Oh, well, of course! But when you have been here as long as we have, you will hardly ever bother to attend, will she, Mrs. Ranger? We wouldn't have come tonight if it hadn't been for the pleasure of coming *together*, we're such friends."

"Single file, please."

The crisp voice of the aide standing at the door of the Red Room suddenly hushed them. Neal stopped behind Anne, who watched the two great friends gushing as they paused before an unresponsive President. Then she gave her name and Neal's to the aide who bent to hear them.

"Senator and Mrs. Conrad." She was shaking hands with the President, whose tired face did not relax for an instant from its lines of dark fatigue. But there was something personal and cordial in Mrs. Shaw's welcome although she would be obliged, before the evening was over, to speak to hundreds of men and women.

"So you did come!" she said pleasantly to Anne, recognizing her instantly. "I am very glad."

"Is she always so nice?" Anne asked Mrs. Lee as, the

brief instant of contact over, they were swept along into the Green Room.

"Oh, always! She knows the President isn't well, that all this is an effort for him, and so she tries to make up for his unresponsiveness. She is naturally friendly, and she has a wonderful memory, which is a huge help to her of course! Shall we go inside 'behind the line' here and get back to the Blue Room where we can mingle with the Members of the Cabinet, or shall we join the *hoi polloi* in the East Room?"

"The Blue Room—no, I think the East Room—oh, I want to do both! I want to do everything!" Anne exclaimed joyously.

Neal teased her about it afterwards. He insisted that theirs was the very last motor to leave the White House that night; and though this was not strictly so, it was true that not until long after the presidential procession had wound its slow and stately way up the great stone stairs again would Anne hear of going home. No, she didn't mind the noise; no, she rather enjoyed the crowd; no, she didn't think they had seen everybody there was to see and done everything there was to do yet. She kept running into pleasant women with whom she was apparently on the best of terms and presenting Neal to them with an eagerness that revealed her immense pride in both her friends, and her husband. And when the dancing began, she was swept swiftly away from Neal by Senator Lassiter, who though he had not previously been in evidence, was discovered standing beside Anne before any one else could claim her, and who, though he surrendered her suavely to Senator Lee when his colleague had the temerity to cut in, hovered on the near horizon, and cut in himself soon and repeatedly.

"I didn't have a chance at you myself at all," Neal grumbled when at last they were on their way home again, and rolling slowly past the orange-colored globes of light.

"I know it! Wasn't it wonderful that I should be so— well, so really popular! It seems too good to be true."

He could not feel even a trifle resentful in the face of

her glowing happiness. He put his arm around her and drew her closer to him.

"It is wonderful perhaps but it isn't strange," he whispered. "I'm glad you've recovered from your stage fright about the White House. You fit in there wonderfully. You'd do just as well at the job as Mrs. Shaw herself!"

"Neal!" Anne exclaimed, "how can you?" But there was no reproach in her voice.

CHAPTER XXII

By early spring, Neal was frankly tired of the social strain and said so.

"Another dinner," he would exclaim, twitching open the envelope Anne offered him almost resentfully. Then he would read the invitation aloud, as if informing her of its contents for the first time. " 'In honor of the Secretary of State and Mrs. Standish—Mr. and Mrs. Brown request the pleasure of Senator and Mrs. Conrad's company'—well, I suppose you think we ought to go to that one."

"Yes," Anne would answer evenly. She always did think they ought to go to "that" one. And when the acceptance had been irrevocably sent she was apt to announce that there was a musical or reception the same evening to which they had better "go on afterwards."

"Well, you needn't stay long on my account," was Neal's invariable comment when they were on their way. "Should we have Horace come back at eleven-thirty, Anne? That will give us three-quarters of an hour."

"Not quite. It is nearly eleven now. So I really think midnight will be better. I know that there are to be singers from the Metropolitan and the program may be a long one."

"And after the 'program' there will be dancing and supper—when we have just had that enormous dinner—and then more dancing— Gosh! Midnight! I suppose I may as well face the fact that it will be nearly two before we get away."

"You might leave before I do. I could come home with friends."

"No, I'll stick it out," Neal would growl under his breath, "but next week isn't quite so full, is it?"

"Not quite," Anne always replied tactfully. But when the next week came, it was even fuller.

He had taken it for granted that they would all leave for Hinsboro immediately after the adjournment of Congress and had looked forward to their home-coming; but as Anne pointed out, the children had their school year to finish, and she could not very well leave them; besides, it would be almost impossible to open their own house, turning on the water and so on, until warmer weather came. There was no use in having delusions about Hinsboro weather in March.

"Well, what do you propose to do?" asked Neal almost angrily. "I can't sit around here until June twiddling my thumbs. I have got to get back and tend to my practice. It has been neglected too long already."

"Yes," said Anne tactfully. She looked very pretty sitting in the little bay window of their bedroom, wrapped in a rose-colored *négigé*, with the morning sunshine falling on her loosened hair. It was a Sunday morning and they had slept late; for with the arrival of Horace Delancy, he had insisted that "quality" ought not to be roused early every day in the week. With him to help, Dora could see the children through their breakfast and he would take Junior and Miss Nancy to Sunday School. But the Senator and Mrs. Conrad should have orange juice and percolated coffee with thick cream, and crisp toast made on an electric heater taken upstairs to them. Gladly acting upon his suggestion, Anne and Neal dozed half the morning, secure in the consciousness that the children were well cared for and happy, and, after breakfasting in bed, lounged comfortably about, reading the papers, talking with each other, and sometimes even settling down for another nap, until it was time for them to dress for their one-thirty dinner.

"I hardly dare say what I am going to," she ventured slowly, flashing a swift glance toward Neal to be sure that she had interpreted his mood correctly and that it was a propitious time to plunge, "when you don't take kindly to the idea of twin beds or even to the thought of having me stay on to a party without you. But I think we ought to—to be separated for a time, just as we had to be when you went to Belford."

"Just what do you mean?" inquired Neal grimly.

"I think I should stay on here through the spring with the children and I think you should go back to Hinsboro and earn all the money you can in your practice. Because we are going to need it. You can stay with Mrs. Simmons. I have written her and she will be glad to have you."

"Oh, so you have written Mrs. Simmons, already?" asked Neal without marked approval. "You seem to have this all figured out without consulting me at all! I think I might have something to say about it myself."

"I didn't, when you went to Belford without me," said Anne serenely.

"And why this sudden greed for filthy lucre?" asked Neal, deciding that it was perhaps well to change the subject. "You have always been terribly keen about saving, but I never knew you to make a point of spending money before!"

"Because, when the time came that we really *needed* to spend I wanted to be able to do it. And I think the time *has* come."

"I see," said Neal a little ironically. "Am I permitted to ask just how these vast sums are to be squandered, since I am to earn them?"

"Neal, darling, don't talk about it in that tone! You know how hard it was to find even this crowded little house that we could rent, and you know how uncomfortable we've been in it all winter! You know how difficult it is to entertain here, even in the simplest way. On my days at home, the walls fairly bulge, and it's impossible to squeeze more than eight persons into the dining-room for a meal. I want you to let me begin hunting now for a house that we can live in suitably—next winter—and buy it."

"In other words," he said dryly, "I suppose you have got your eye on one already!" And as Anne colored and gave a little laugh he laughed too and sat down beside her. "All right. I know you are right. Sorry if I was cross, dear. Tell me about it."

"It is in Georgetown," Anne breathed excitedly, "an old house, rather badly out of repair—"

"Georgetown!" interrupted Neal contemptuously. "Why that's full of shacks and niggers! What on earth do you want to go there for?"

"Because the best values in real-estate are there," said Anne proudly, "it used to be 'the court end of town' and was a metropolis before Washington even existed! Now the lovely colonial houses are being snapped up again and soon there won't be any left, people are moving out there so fast. This house I like is a big square brick one, on a corner lot, and it's a great bargain. Of course it needs a lot done to it, but—"

"But you could supervise the improvements this spring while I am leading a celibate life slaving away in Hinsboro —well—how much would it cost all told?"

"The house is only five thousand dollars, if we pay cash for it. I should have to spend at least that much more on repairs. And then of course I should have to furnish it."

"I see. You want at least fifteen thousand dollars then."

"I want more than that. I might as well tell you so, all at once."

"How much?"

"The clothes I bought in Paris are just about gone, they have had such hard wear this winter. I'll have to get new ones; I've made a list of what I need, and a thousand dollars is a conservative estimate of the cost. Then the Dodge is actually falling to pieces. We've got to have a new motor, and I think it ought to be a bigger one this time. More of a town car. And I want to put the children in private schools next fall—both of them—and meantime" —Anne drew her breath and went on—"I want to take them to Europe during their vacation. I'll have the work on the house all organized by then, and I'll be as careful about expenses as I possibly can. We don't need to go on a big expensive ship like the *France*. We can cross on a cabin boat, quite comfortably, and then we could go straight to Fontainebleau and stay there nearly all summer. The children can study French and I can go on with mine. And I want to take up my music again. I don't

211

think it's too late to get back the little I knew and have lost, and even learn some more. It—it means a lot to me —music—and I have—neglected it."

"I know you have, dear," said Neal.

"And I thought we might have some horses and ride in the forest. Of course if you could only come too it would be perfect. But I suppose you couldn't."

"No," said Neal steadily, "of course not. I'll have to work all summer. But I do want you and the children to go. I can see just how much it will mean to us—all of us —in the end if you do. Too bad Clare isn't in Paris any longer to smooth the path for you, that's all."

"I do not need any paths smoothed," said Anne crisply, "by any one but you. I think myself it was fine that Clarence got the appointment to Siam. He is very young to be a full-fledged Minister."

"And you think it is better to be first in a little Iberian village than second in Rome, do you?" quoted Neal gayly. "Well, perhaps you are right, though I imagine Clarence suffered some pretty bitter pangs when he left Paris behind him and started for the center of Asia."

"A few pangs won't hurt Clarence," said Anne still crisply. "He may get rid of that sleek look I have always hated in Siam— I'll book our passage right off, if you're willing, it's so hard to get reservations in late June, especially on the cheaper ships—and now about the house? Could you go with me this afternoon and look it over? It isn't occupied and I have the key."

They went, immediately after dinner.

The distance from the Capitol seemed to Neal a distinct disadvantage and the neighborhood so undesirable that he had to take Anne's word that it was not. Moreover, the fine old house was in a sad state of dilapidation. But he had discernment enough to see that it *was* fine, to notice the chaste elegance of the entrance, the exquisite carving on the mantels and above the windows, the grace of the curving stairway. The arrangement of the ground floor was adaptable both for family life and for entertaining—a long drawing-room on one side of the front door, a square library and a square dining-room on the other. All these rooms had fireplaces, and so did the four spacious chambers above; and though there was only one battered bathroom it was easy to see that others could be wedged in. The service quarters in the ell were adequate, with plenty of space not only for Dora and Horace, but for extra servants if they should eventually need them; the attic and cellar were both ample, and in the rear were wide long "galleries," while beyond the neglected lawns and gardens was a long stable. The house which he and Anne had built in Hinsboro was a comfortable, nondescript, middle-class home; this, properly repaired and furnished would become a residence of individual charm and distinction—the suitable setting for a rising statesman, the dignified background for his wife.

"Suppose we drive back and get the kids and Dora and Horace?" he suggested. "If they all like it as much as we do, I guess we may just as well consider the question settled."

CHAPTER XXIII

THE day after the adjournment of Congress Neal left alone for Hinsboro, facing the fact that as Anne had once stayed there without him, saving money that he might spend it, so he must now stay there without her, saving money that she might spend it. If he faced it rather grimly; if he found but little joy in his work; if his days at the office were monotonous, and his nights in the little room under the eaves in Mrs. Simmons's cottage, which had been his bridal chamber, were lonely; if he missed the variety and amusement of his political occupations, the crowded color of his life in Washington, the companionship of his wife and children almost unutterably; still, the fact remained that he accomplished what he set out to do, and more, that his reputation as a lawyer of national and international note dated from that summer. True, he already had wide experience and a large practice upon which to build; the foundations for his fame were laid; but it was only now that he began the brilliant super-structure which was to bring him fame and fortune. The money that Anne needed for her house and her trip was forthcoming before she asked for it, and in larger sums than she either expected or required; nor was this situation confined to the summer of their separation; never again were they confronted with "straitened circumstances." They were, quite definitely, on the way to wealth.

In June he permitted himself the brief luxury of going to Washington to see how the improvements on the house were advancing and to accompany his family from there to New York when they sailed on the *De Grasse*. He did not leave Hinsboro again until he returned to New York three months later, to welcome them back again. During the interval, since the little house on New Hampshire Avenue was closed when Anne left for Europe, he was able to live in his own home in Hinsboro; and Dora and Horace, whose wages had been raised, ministered capably and faithfully to his material needs. In the fall he returned uncomplainingly to Mrs. Simmons's cottage, the two servants accompanying Anne and Nancy and the new French maids to Georgetown. Junior, unbelievably changed, considering the brevity of his absence from his native shores —better mannered, better groomed, more mature—entered Groton, beginning his six years of preparation for Harvard. As Anne did not approve of boarding school for girls, there was no question of sending Nancy away. She was to go to Holton Arms in Washington.

Just before Congress opened again Neal rejoined his family. Anne had done her work well; and the place in Georgetown, in its completely repaired and renovated condition, surpassed his every expectation. It was comfortable, it was charming, it was distinguished. The uncrowded drawing-room with its two or three fine pictures, its crystal-shaded lights, its rose brocade hangings and upholstery, its carefully chosen antique furniture, was a real achievement in selective taste and arrangement. The Colonial fashion in mahogany and silver had been scrupulously observed in furnishing the white-paneled dining-room, where one rare old sporting print surmounted the mantel; the library, which gave a greater sense of relaxation, had deep chairs and sofas of Cordova leather, with small, convenient tables placed beside each one, walls lined with built-in book cases, and an abundance of current literature scattered about. The bedrooms, with their carved four-posters, low-boys and high-boys and braided rugs, were equally successful; the glassed-in galleries, the tiled bathrooms, the glittering kitchen, the immaculate basement—all were perfect. And in the remodeled stables two saddle horses and two automobiles—a roadster for Neal and a limousine for Anne—were already installed.

As they sat before the library fire the evening of their

reunion, after their delicious and beautifully served dinner, Anne commenced outlining her plans for the winter.

"I am going to start my days at home right away," she said, "that will give me time to get in three before Christmas, and I think this year we had better have an occasional Sunday tea as well. Now as to dinners—I thought I would ask the Hammels to set a day first and after that the Marceaus—and so on. The new cook is so wonderful—"

"I'll say she is!" interrupted Neal, still replete with dinner.

"Yes,—really when it comes to the three C's—cooking, clothes, and culture—we must admit the supremacy of France, no matter how patriotic we feel. Well, with Dora and Horace reënforced by Alphonsine and Madeleine, I see no reason why we should hesitate to ask *any one* here. There is just one hitch—I had a letter from Harriet saying now that we have a guest room, she feels sure we would like to have a long visit from her."

"The Hell we would!" said Neal with vehemence.

"And that she thinks she ought to do her best towards influencing Congress prohibiting the sale of tobacco in any form and limiting the sale of tea and coffee. She believes they are all harmful and she wants to lobby against them with this as a center."

"Good God!" ejaculated Neal with still greater vehemence.

"Well, what can I do? I can't decline to allow your own —and your only—sister to come to our house, can I?"

"No-o-o-o, I suppose not, but she will be a terrible nuisance, and as you infer, she would not fit in very well with your scheme of entertaining. Better have her come at once and get her visit over with. You can postpone your parties until after she is gone."

Anne sighed. "That may mean I can't wedge them in at all. You know how congested everything gets later in the season. The Hammels won't have a free evening. But my problems don't end with Harriet—my mother has written too. She says now that we have a spare room, she is sure that we would be glad to have Sol and Sam come and stay with us and go to George Washington University."

"Great Heavens, Anne! You can't put Sol and Sam and Harriet all in the same guest room!"

"No, but Harriet doesn't think of Sol and Sam and mother doesn't think of Harriet. And I suppose they all have equal claims upon us. Of course Junior won't need his room except during the holidays—I could crowd the three boys all in there, but I hate to—I want him to have that for his very own—I have taken such pride in fixing it for him. I hoped I was through with remodeling for a while, but I think I will have to have a room finished off in the attic. There is space enough for a fairly good one and for a shower bath."

"But if they start in a college course they will have to be here four years," said Neal, aghast.

"Of course. But as far as that goes, we do not know that the legislation Harriet is interested in will be disposed of this season."

"That's true too—well, we will just have to live in hopes. It's too bad, honey, just when you thought you had everything so nicely organized, but I guess it can't be helped."

His coöperative and helpful attitude made it easier for Anne to stifle her disappointment. She wrote to her mother saying that she would have a room ready for Sol and Sam by the first of January; and she wrote to Harriet to come at once, hoping that this aggressive lady would, by some miracle, prove sufficiently adaptable to her surroundings to be at least partially assimilated by them.

Her hopes were groundless. Harriet arrived in the middle of Anne's first "At Home." The day was stormy, and she wore a "serviceable hat," large black rubbers and a dingy brown mackintosh. Relieved of these, and of her dripping umbrella, she was disclosed clad in a high-necked, white cotton "shirtwaist," and a gray whipcord skirt, which was cut in multitudinous "gores" and finished around the botton with braid.

Anne had left her guests for a moment to see Harriet

217

comfortably installed in the precious guest room. She was conscientiously cordial but she faltered a little.

"I thought you might like to pour tea for me a little while," she said hesitatingly; "you could relieve Mme. Estavi at five. That will give you plenty of time to change your dress."

"I shall not take time to change," Harriet assured her briskly. "I shall come down at once. I see there are a number of people here and I certainly shall not lose this opportunity to talk about the evils of smoking, tea and coffee."

"Wouldn't it be better to wait and do that at some meeting?" suggested Anne. "At strictly social affairs like this, we don't bring up debatable questions."

"That shows you are not really interested in great causes," said Harriet, brushing her hair back flatly from her high forehead. "I shall have no such scruples. I am conscious of the frivolity into which you have led Neal, but I shall try to counteract such an influence. As to meetings, I shall attend those too, of course. In fact, I shall hold some here. I can see there is plenty of room for them in this large house which you have so extravagantly purchased, regardless of the fact that you already had a beautiful home in Hinsboro."

The first person whom Harriet approached on the subject near to her heart coming down stairs chanced to be the Brazilian Ambassador, who had inherited numerous coffee *fazendas,* the revenue from which permitted him to pursue his career unhampered by financial worries. Accosted by this strange-looking female, whose relationship to Neal he did not grasp, he leapt to the conclusion that he had fallen into the clutches of one of those "professional callers" whose presence is such a nightmare to both hosts and guests at many Washington functions, who wander about uninvited in search of warmth and food and amusement, and who are often very poor and very peculiar. Expecting that at any moment she might begin to remove fruit from the silver *épergne* on the sideboard, or stuff sandwiches into a paper bag, he tried to guide her gently toward the front door and expedite her departure.

218

Anne, catching sight of them just in time, and guessing the worst, whispered desperately to Senator Lassiter who, as usual, had sprung up from nowhere and was standing near her, and begged him to go to the rescue. Immensely amused, he shepherded Harriet skillfully to the sun-parlor and encouraged her to talk, conveying the impression that he agreed perfectly with everything she had to say. When, late in the afternoon, he was relieved by Neal, he left her with the happy idea that she had made a convert. The misleading philanderer, however, wandered off in search of Anne, laughing softly and claiming a reward.

"What thanks do I get for helping you out?" he asked, drawing up an easy chair and offering her a cup of steaming tea and a cigarette.

Anne, who was extremely tired after receiving nearly three hundred persons, accepted his ministrations gratefully.

"No end of thanks," she said with a smile, as she leaned back and blew little rings of smoke into the air.

"Ah—but I would like something concrete. Would you ride with me tomorrow morning or let me take you to a concert in the afternoon?"

"Neither. You know we went all over that thoroughly last spring, Blythe, after Neal went away. I won't play with fire."

"Oh, but this is such a tiny little spark! and you are going to need my help with that Tartar all winter."

Ann deliberated. In her determination that there should be no semblance of a repetition of the episode in Paris, she had leaned over backward in her observance of the proprieties. But after all Lassiter was extremely useful to her and she had perhaps been unnecessarily prudish.

"The concert, then," she conceded; "we are dining out and dancing afterward, and with all that, on top of all this, I will be tired and sleeping late. I don't pretend to come down to breakfast any more and the best time for riding is early in the morning. Neal and Nancy get in a canter together then."

Harriet felt aggrieved that Neal and Anne were leaving her alone on the very night of her arrival. It was impossible to make her understand that in a city where dinner lists were compiled weeks beforehand, they could not ask to bring an extra and unexpected guest with them to a formal dinner, and when she caught sight of Anne's evening dress, flaming red and fresh from Paris, her mounting disapproval burst all bounds.

"I never wore a sleeveless gown in my life or one cut below the collar bone," she began. Nancy unfortunately interrupted her.

"Perhaps you would if you had a lovely neck and arms like mother, instead of being scrawny," she suggested.

Harriet glared at the child. "Are you bringing up your daughter to be as fast as yourself?" she asked Anne. "I notice that you permit her to see you smoke. And I was horrified to observe that you seem to have contracted the habit. I am sure that nice Senator Lassiter must have been deeply shocked."

"Oh, no, he isn't. He gives mother most of her cigarettes," Nancy hastened to explain. "He says she doesn't know good kinds from bad, so he has to help her out."

"You mean to tell me that you, a married woman, presumably respectable—"

But Anne had disappeared. She felt she could not listen to another word from Harriet that evening. The next morning, however, her sister-in-law invaded the room where Anne, with nothing more substantial over her shoulders than the wisp of lace which served as a nightgown yoke, sat up in bed reading her mail and drinking her coffee.

"How do you expect your household to be properly managed if you don't get up in good season and supervise it?" demanded Harriet.

"Well, it is managed," answered Anne patiently. "I don't know of one where there is so little friction or where the servants do so much and do it pleasantly besides. Do be reasonable, Harriet; I worked hard for years; but my days of manual labor are over now. Alphonsine attends to the marketing herself—French cooks always do. The rest of the machinery I wind up just like a clock and I see that it does not run down. Beyond that I do not need to do anything."

The telephone beside her bed tingled. Anne picked it up.

"Oh, good morning, Blythe— No, I haven't forgotten. I'll wedge in a few calls first; if you are going to the Martinellis' we might start together from there—why, that's very kind of you. She is right here, I'll ask her—Harriet, Senator Lassiter says that he and his mother would like very much to have you lunch with them, informally, on Sunday. He says Madam Lassiter is interested in your views."

"I feel it my duty to go," Harriet replied, "though I do not approve of Sunday entertaining on general principles. But if it will help the cause—by the way, Anne, I should like a branch telephone installed in my own room. It will be extremely useful in mapping out my arrangements."

Thankful that her mind had been diverted, Anne gave the necessary order, and Harriet, placated for the moment, hurried off to map out her plan of campaign for the improvement of the nation. Before noon, it had been disclosed that she intended to use Horace and the limousine to facilitate her calls on all the members of both Houses of Congress, as she expected to influence these legislators in the right direction; that she had invited twenty zealots from the National Anti-Tobacco League to tea in order that they might arrange for a series of "parlor meetings" to be held every Monday morning in Anne's drawing-room; and that she had instructed Madeleine to fashion her a costume "symbolic of purity, peace and progress" from a bolt of white satin which she had found in the bottom bureau drawer and which the bewildered maid had already been instructed to make into "sleeps" for Madame.

Feeling that no amount of "supervision" would restore good feeling in her disordered ménage, Anne rose, poured oil on the troubled waters, and resolved to abandon all plans of her own for entertaining until a more opportune season.

By Christmas time, the entire family was thoroughly submerged by Harriet's domination. Without consulting Anne she had suggested to her parents and her brother, Arthur, that they should join her for the holidays; and the house, which had seemed so pleasantly spacious before the arrival of the correct and critical Conrads, had become so crowded that there was no breathing space in it either figuratively or literally. Anne welcomed the impending appearance of Sol and Sam as an excuse for clearing it out.

Harriet was too firmly entrenched to dislodge, but the others, with veiled comments on Anne's lack of true hospitality, departed on the same day that the boys arrived. But her brothers brought no solace with them. It was immediately apparent that they would have to be completely outfitted with clothes, that they would have to be brushed and bathed and barbered, before they could even present themselves as applicants for entrance to the university. They were so acutely unhappy themselves, in the alien atmosphere into which they had suddenly been plunged, that Anne's heart ached for them. She could not bear to listen to Harriet's sneers at "country bumpkins," or witness Neal's impatience with the "uncouth cubs." A dozen times a day she climbed to the attic chamber, to which they slunk away as much as possible, and coached them gently but firmly in matters of dress and deportment. They were so docile and tractable that it was pathetic, but she knew they were homesick for the ramshackle old house at West Hamstead, that they hungered for coarse accustomed food, that they would have been more comfortable in overalls than broadcloth, that they were stifled without the air of their native mountains. First Sam and then Sol came down with the "flu," and Anne, caring for them tenderly lest they should be more miserable than ever if abandoned to the mercies of a strange nurse, caught it herself; then it swept through the household like wildfire. Nancy, Neal, the servants, each was felled in turn. Alphonsine, the peerless cook, threatened to leave if a murderous American doctor entered her room again ordering her to open her window and admit the poison of the night air. Madeleine, the peerless chambermaid, contended that it was not her work to carry trays, that Dora must do that, even though poor Dora, at the moment this verdict was issued, lay prostrate on a bed of pain. Chaos and confusion reigned supreme in the stately house which Neal and Anne had felt so sure was to be the seat of culture and well-ordered living.

At length the invalids recovered, the situation shook itself into shape. Alphonsine and Madeleine forgot their grievances and redoubled their efforts to please; the boys began to adjust their difficulties and to enjoy life at the university. Harriet departed for Hinsboro well pleased with her winter's work, and assuring her brother and sister-in-law that she would be on hand the following season to "carry it further." Senator Lassiter saw her off at the station, and then swung back to Georgetown intent on taking Anne for a spin in his roadster with no one to observe just how long they were gone. He found her huddled over the library fire, looking utterly desolate.

"How do you manage to have so much spare time on your hands, Blythe?" she asked listlessly. "Don't you ever spend an hour in the Senate Chamber or attend a committee meeting or dictate a letter? Neal is so busy this season that he hardly has time to breathe—not that it would matter if you had all the leisure in the world, I haven't any, so I couldn't go to ride with you. I've got to prepare for more company. I've just had a wire. A Mrs. Griffin and her son, Roy, who live in Wallacetown, are arriving on the Colonial. They are old friends of Neal's and pretty important constituents. Now that we have this house, we have plenty of room—"

Blythe Lassiter shrugged his shoulders. "You will be a wreck if you don't watch out," he predicted. "Really, Lady Anne, you look frightfully seedy. The air will do you good."

"I don't need air. I need a little peace and quiet."

He left her reluctantly. It was several weeks before he found her alone again. Mrs. Griffin and Roy were not interested in "causes" and they were not seeking an education; but they had never been to Washington before and they did not know when they could come again. Therefore they desired to see it thoroughly. Their ambition was not limited by daylight or dark. The Lincoln Memorial at dawn, the lighted dome of the Capitol at night, appealed to them equally. They had somehow assumed that the cherry blossoms were already blooming; and since these were not in flower, they thought perhaps it would be well to linger on. If they did this, Mrs. Griffin could attend the sessions of the Continental Congress of the Daughters of the American Revolution. Meanwhile they took it for granted that they would have cards for the gallery at the Senate Chamber and House of Representatives, a letter to the Librarian of Congress, a permit to see the Bureau of Engraving and Printing; that they would be received at the White House. Mrs. Griffin wrote home to Mabel Hildreth how kind Anne was to them and what a lovely large house she had and hinted that perhaps George and Mabel and one or two of their children might be coming to Washington that spring, too; a hint upon which they promptly acted. Neither Neal nor Anne had forgotten how good Mabel had been to them that first year of their marriage when Anne was so sick. This was, obviously, the time to repay the obligation. Besides, George had become one of the leading farmers of the state; he had tremendous influence with the agricultural vote; he was not only an old friend—he was a constituent with whom to reckon. Then Governor Low, to whom Neal owned his appointment to the Senate, stopped off on his way north from a conference of Governors which he had been attending in South Carolina, and Mrs. Low joined him. Anne and Neal gave a large official dinner in their honor—the first one, in spite of all their plans which they had given that winter—followed by a still larger reception. The morning of these functions, Anne found in her mail a letter which she tossed to Neal with a little hysterical laugh.

"Just look at that," she exclaimed; "if it were not down in black and white I should not believe it—in spite of everything we have had to go through this winter—that any one would have the effrontery to write such a thing!"

Neal glanced at the offending sheet. "Dear Mrs. Conrad"—he read—"I do not know you personally, but I have always felt a deep interest in your state because my great-grandmother came from there; so I should like to attend the reception which you are giving in honor of Governor and Mrs. Low this evening. However, I see by the papers that you are not planning to begin receiving until half-past ten, which is rather late for one of my advanced years to start out for a party; so I hope you won't mind if I come at half-past nine instead."

"At which hour we will still be at the dinner table," said Anne still more hysterically. Suddenly she began to cry. Neal regarded her with alarm.

"Look here," he said. "Your nerves are all shot to pieces. It's this hellish winter you have had. You shall never let yourself in for another like it again. Family, or no family, constituents or no constituents, I won't have you landing in a sanitarium."

"I am not going to land in a sanitarium," sobbed Anne, "I am going to land in the nursery again. Of course I am desperately tired, and that does make me nervous, but one reason I am so silly and uncontrolled is that I am—I am just deathly sick besides— Oh, Neal, I am almost certain that I am going to have another baby!"

But she did not. The pleasant physician who had seen them safely through the "flu" and whom Neal summoned the day after the big dinner—which was such a tremendous success that it was long remembered as one of the outstanding events of the winter—confirmed her suspicions as to her condition; but when, after chatting merrily and casually with her for a few minutes, he went downstairs with Neal, he closed the library door and spoke frankly.

"There is no doubt that she is pregnant. Normally I should expect her to be confined about the end of October, but—I don't think things *are* quite normal. I will have another man in to look at her too, if you don't mind."

"If I don't mind!" Neal shouted. "You must do everything for her, *everything,* do you hear?"

"Don't take it so hard," said Dr. Harrison gently, "of course everything will be done for her."

Anne herself had no misgivings. After the first few weeks she was less troubled with nausea than she had been when Junior and Nancy were on their way; and when she

225

had had a fortnight of complete rest, she was up and about almost as usual except that she was careful—or tried to be careful—about getting over-tired. She shopped happily for the prettiest baby-clothes she could find, remembering with a slight pang how much simpler and scantier the layettes for the other children had been. She refurnished the guest room as a nursery—"and we will never have another guest room," she laughed, "as long as we live in Washington!" She jested about the "little Benjamin" they were to have so long after they had supposed that their family was complete; she acquiesced uncomplainingly to spending the summer in Washington where Dr. Harrison could watch over her. But, late in August, she was taken acutely and suddenly ill; and when she finally groped her way back from the Valley of the Shadow and stretched out her arms across the bed to touch the little bundle that she expected to find beside her, there was only empty space.

For "little Benjamin" had come too soon; and he had been stillborn.

CHAPTER XXIV

ANNE was very slow in recovering her strength. She had drawn so heavily upon her reserve that she had none left; and the debilitating heat and humidity of Washington in mid-summer served to retard her recovery still more. Dr. Harrison spoke frequently of the advisability of getting to a more bracing climate as soon as she was well enough to travel. But it was late September before she was able to leave her room; and by this time Nancy's school had opened and Sol and Sam had returned to college. So Anne would not hear of going away.

"I'll spend next summer in Hinsboro," she assured her long-suffering physician, "very quietly. The climate is bracing enough there, I assure you."

"The climate may be all right. In fact I have no doubt that it is, but I do not believe you will rest very much. Your husband comes up for election next fall, doesn't he?"

"Y-e-e-s, if he decides to run. I don't believe he has fully yet. But naturally he would like to. Having been appointed to the Senate I think he would like to prove that he could be elected."

"Quite so—and you would like to have him, I suppose?"

Anne flushed a little. "Yes, I would like to have him," she said quietly. "I am very proud of what he has done already. If he can do more, I shall be prouder still."

"And you wish to do everything you can to help him?"

"Of course."

"Then you had better begin by getting yourself in good physical condition."

Anne finally promised that she would talk to Neal about going away; but Neal, like most men, and especially like most husbands, while deeply concerned over acute illness, did not regard convalescence as a serious matter. As long as he felt that her condition was grave, as long as he could see that she was suffering, there was no medical suggestion which could have been made that he would not have insisted upon following. But now that she was up and dressed, now that she went out for a short ride in the motor every day, now that he saw her supervising Nancy's fall wardrobe with interest and shepherding her brothers into the social field, now that he heard her discussing dinners with Alphonsine, he assumed that she was "perfectly all right," and said so.

"Doctors always like to make mountains out of mole hills and drag cases out as much as possible," he announced, a little sententiously. "All this talk about 'nerves' and 'rest cures' and 'lowered vitality' sounds awfully important but personally I don't think it amounts to much. When you think of the families women used to raise and the amount of work they used to do—! Well, of course if you want another trip, I have nothing to say, but—"

Usually when Neal volunteered the information that he had nothing to say, this was preliminary to a lengthy argument. Anne, who didn't feel equal to arguing, cut him short politely but firmly.

"*I* don't want another trip, but I promised Dr. Harrison—"

"Well, I guess we can settle this ourselves without Dr. Harrison."

He spoke smugly. But in the succeeding weeks he watched her with secret anxiety. She was—he was reluctantly forced to admit to himself—very thin, very white and very listless. He tried to find satisfactory explanations for this: of course the loss of the baby had been a shock to her; but she would recover from that. Of course she had suffered a good deal of pain; but after all, her constitution was good, she ought to have excellent powers of recuperation. But did she? It began to look as if she did not. About the middle of November, quite as if it were his own idea advanced for the first time, he said a little gravely he thought it would be a good plan for her to have a change of air.

"It's nice and cool in Quebec," he told Anne, rather as if he were the discoverer of Canada's climate.

"It's nice and cool in Washington now," retorted Anne.

"Well, you could have gone away sooner if you had wanted to, couldn't you?" he asked almost angrily. "You said you didn't care—"

"I didn't and I don't unless you could come too—"

"Just before the opening of Congress? My dear girl, you know that is impossible. I am so driven at this time of the year I hardly know which way to turn. Besides . . ."

"Besides, you feel that this year, if you went away at all, you ought to go to Hinsboro?"

Neal hesitated, then drew in his breath and spoke with the air of one who was preparing for a deep plunge.

"Yes," he said at length, "I do. I have decided to run for the Senate. I would never be satisfied if I didn't and that means a real fight. I ought to have got started at it sooner. Of course the man that's in has certain advantages, but Fletcher, who is almost certain to oppose me, has millions behind him where I have thousands, and he owns the biggest newspaper in the state—whereas I haven't any contacts with the press worth mentioning, and even if I win the nomination—a very different proposition with the direct primaries than it used to be in the old convention days—the election won't be any walk-over this year. Business is bad. A good many mills are running on half time and others are closed, and the farm situation is really serious. Brown and all his bunch will play that up for what it is worth. He's a dangerous demagogue but he poses as the working-man's friend in the Senate."

"Aren't you their friend?"

"I've tried to be. But, according to Brown, I'm bound, tied and delivered to the 'interests.' The machine has ground out all my human qualities. Wall Street owns me body and soul. You would not recognize your husband, Anne, in Stetson's speeches—or on the front page of Fletcher's *Evening Inquirer,* as far as that goes. I don't suppose you keep up with the home papers, but if you did . . ."

"I do mean to, and I used to regularly. Lately . . ."

"Well, I am not complaining but I do think, Anne, you sometimes overlook the importance of keeping in touch with state affairs in your desire not to miss anything here. You are kind to every one who comes to Washington but you're not at home a great deal. Now if you could get to Hinsboro early this spring . . ."

"I can. I will."

"And make up your mind for a heavy summer—exert yourself. Don't act like a high-brow. I am not sure these trips to Europe and the private schools and all these servants are useful—politically speaking, I mean. A little of that stuff you tried to hush up—teaching school, living in a tenement and doing your own washing—has its points."

"I know. I'll try very hard, Neal, to do just what you would like and just the way you'd like it done."

"Well, if you feel like that, is there any reason why you should make a point of being rude to Mrs. Stone?"

"It was Mrs. Stone who made a point of being rude to *me!* The first day I met her, Neal—why, I told you about it!—and she has never lost a chance to snub me, insult me almost ever since. I can't think why she should hate me so when most people—well, most people like me. But anyway I can't accept her attitude lying down."

"You can't? Well, you better if you want me to stay in the Senate. It happens that Stone and Fletcher are thick as thieves. They roomed together in college. And Fletcher is making capital out of Mrs. Stone's dislike for you all over the state. You are pictured as an impudent, aggressive, ignorant little climber. The stories are terribly distorted, I know, but there is a grain of truth in them, and they are not doing me any good."

Anne sat very still. "An ignorant, impudent, aggressive little climber—" So that was the way she appeared to her enemies and Neal's. The perseverance, the patience, the self-sacrifice, which had enabled her to grow from a raw little country girl into a well-developed, self-assured woman were ignoble rather than admirable qualities when viewed with unfriendly eyes. She felt as if something cold and sharp had penetrated to her heart and coiled around it. But Neal, unconscious that she was stricken, went on talking.

"You say most people like you—well, it's never a good thing to bank on popularity, but I think you *are* popular —too popular. I don't want to hurt your feelings, Anne, and of course I know you don't mean to be indiscreet, but —well . . . Lassiter was here a good deal last winter. Harriet called my attention to it first."

"She would," Anne breathed between tight lips.

"And father and mother noticed it too. Probably the servants did, and other people. It was rumored around that you—that he—anyway when the baby was born, there was a paragraph in *City Chatter*—Miss Letts showed it to me—not that I believe a word of the scurrilous stuff or that she did—you know that, of course. You know that I love you and trust you, but I thought you ought to know . . ."

Feeling that he had perhaps said enough, Neal bent over the evening paper. The front page was printed with headlines about the tariff—that new bill over which he was working so hard. It was half an hour before he looked up and when he did, he noticed that Anne had left the room. He supposed that she must have gone to bed, as she often did now that she was so far from strong, but when he reached the Colonial chamber which she had made so beautiful, she was not there either. Well, then she must be helping Sol and Sam with their French. She often did that too—astonishing how she had mastered it. He couldn't get a can of hot water himself if the steward who happened to wait on him didn't speak English—clever, Anne was—and better looking every year—a great credit to him. He never would have got where he had without her. Complacently, he went to sleep.

In the morning when he woke she lay, as usual, beside him, her curls tumbled over the pillow, one slim bare arm thrust under her head. He never guessed that she had spent most of the night walking blindly beside the Potomac River, regarded with an anxious curiosity by an occasional watchful policeman and with covetous misunderstanding by an occasional night-prowler. But there was something about her that kept both from approaching her —something almost unearthly—something wholly tragic. The slimy serpent of slander had crossed her path as it crosses the path of almost every man and woman of destiny. And in the first hour of her agony—it seemed to her that her feet would never touch clean earth again.

CHAPTER XXV

"Yes, this is Mrs. Conrad speaking— No, Senator Conrad cannot come to the telephone. Oh, thank you, Mr. Baker, I'll take the figures—yes, I have it right, I think— Conrad thirty-two, Fletcher seventeen."

Anne hung up the receiver and went swiftly from the library to the shadowy hall. Neal, who cherished certain pet economies, insisted that all the lights did not need to be turned on at once. Anne, in the dimness could barely see him standing near the door, his white face strained and tense. She walked over to him and put her hand on his arm.

"Mr. Baker has just telephoned from Bakerfield," she said gently, "he said he wished to be the first to congratulate you. The result there is very encouraging."

"Bakerfield is only a small, unimportant place," Neal interrupted vehemently.

"I know. But perhaps the figures are an indication of what we may expect elsewhere. The vote is thirty-two for you and seventeen for Fletcher."

A harsh sound, something like a smothered growl arose from Neal's throat. As he had foreseen, the campaign had been a bitterly hard one. He had borne the brunt of it bravely, almost buoyantly, but on election night he had suddenly collapsed and, leaving his headquarters, had come home, refusing to see any one or even to speak with any one but Anne. Not that he seemed to derive much comfort from her presence. He sat crumpled in a heap or strode back and forth like a caged animal, and when he spoke at all it was savagely and despairingly. If the telephone had been a coiled rattlesnake ready to strike at him, he could not have manifested a greater horror at the suggestion of touching it. So taking her place beside it, Anne sat through the endless length of the dark afternoon, waiting for the tidings which sooner or later would come. Good tidings, evil tidings. Tidings of victory, tidings of defeat. She had no way of guessing which they were to be. She only knew that she must be there when they came. That until then she must comfort, cheer, cajole, caress—

In the gathering dusk, her hands clasped tightly in her lap, she reviewed the months that had passed since that night of desperation, when, bruised and bleeding, she had walked slowly along the Speedway confessing herself beaten, vowing that since she had tried so hard and failed, she would never try any more; and then suddenly, miraculously, finding the strength to vow that she had only just begun to fight. Turning from the gray Potomac, she had walked beside the still pool in which the columns of the Lincoln Memorial lay reflected in the ghastly light. There was peace there—peace not to be found in the rushing river. She sat down on the bank and clasped her hands over her eyes. Slowly, surely her sanity seemed to return —her balance to be restored. Let Maud Stone send her back to Hinsboro, humbled and humiliated, with Neal's career involved! Never, never, never! The hard bitter woman should be cheated of her triumph. Confess that a filthy periodical had the power to challenge her good name? Her dead baby seemed to rise from his grave forbidding her. Stretching out her hand she almost seemed to touch him. . . . Behind the slender shaft of the Washington Monument the sky grew vaguely rosy with impending dawn. She shook the tears from her eyes, threw back her head, and walked towards home. . . .

"State Headquarters? Yes, Mrs. Conrad speaking for Senator Conrad—two wards in Belford have gone for Fletcher by a large majority. Thank you. Yes."

Out in the hall again. Neal seized her arm and spoke before she could do so. "I heard you. The first two wards they have heard from! If I lose Belford *I* am lost."

"You haven't lost it! What do two wards amount to in a city? Nothing, nothing at all . . ."

Back to the telephone. Back, in memory to Washington —to Mrs. Stone. The suavity of her greeting the next time she met her enemy:

" 'Speak of angels and you hear their wings!' Miss Sharp has just been talking with me about you. She somehow conveyed the idea that I had the privilege of being intimate with you and she asked if I would not try to persuade you to let her publish a really *vivid* story about you."

"A vivid story?" said Mrs. Stone sharply, "about *me?*"

"Yes, I think they are so thrilling—those adventures of yours in Vaudeville, and your meeting with Senator Stone after you had been so unhappily married to the ventriloquist."

Mrs. Stone gasped. How Anne had unearthed these details of her early life, she didn't stop to inquire. She had taken every precaution, and she believed them to be known to not a soul in Washington. The capital, she felt sure, had supposed her "to the manner born." Her rigid insistence upon the rules of precedence, her arrogance in dealing with her inferiors in rank, the exclusiveness of her visiting list—Mrs. Stone, who had never heard of "Noblesse Oblige"—imagined that she had made of these an impregnable fortress for her social standing.

"Miss Sharp cannot write such a story!" she exclaimed with vehemence.

"It is written," said Anne calmly, "and she has had an offer for it from a very important syndicate. It ought to sweep the country! Of course she has been very careful to check up on the accuracy of the details. The champagne supper, for instance, in Senator Stone's suite the night you met him . . ."

Mrs. Stone's fortress was crumbling about her. She trembled. "How," she asked herself wildly, "could she have been foolhardy enough to offer attack when she herself was so vulnerable." Her lips shook as she spoke to Anne.

"I know that you and Miss Sharp are very good friends.

235

I have heard her say there is no woman in the official set whom she admires so much. If you can persuade her not to publish this story . . ."

"I never could understand," Neal often said to Anne that summer, "how Stone happened to withdraw his support from Fletcher. If he had not, the situation would have been very different, but as it is my troubles have been cut about in half . . ."

"Yes—Mrs. Conrad speaking. Oh, the report from the third ward—two hundred eighty-six to ninety-five in favor of my husband? Yes—I will tell him— Neal, did you hear that? You have carried the third ward in Belford almost three to one."

"Well, until I hear from the north of the state, that won't reassure me much . . ."

"And could you," she heard herself asking Clarence Hathaway again—Clare who was back from Stockholm on leave—a sparkling winter day when Washington was enfolded in one of its rare snows, "manage to be—well, a good deal in evidence this winter?"

"Of course, Anne, but just why?" She told him. Briefly, almost boldly. He whitened a little.

"It's a comedy of errors, isn't it, Anne? You don't care a rap about Lassiter, never thought of him except in the most casual way. And yet this ugly story gets started and you ask *me* to act as a foil when . . ."

"When I do care several raps about you. When I might have cared a good deal if I had not always loved Neal—if I wouldn't always love him until it *hurts*."

"Yes, I know—well, I will do my best, my dear. One may, I suppose, venture to seal a bargain by kissing your hand?"

"No, Clare, not even that."

"Well, then, not even that."

And Clare had played his part. Played it with such consummate skill that the "ugly story" was buried past any resurrection. Anne did not appear to avoid Lassiter in the least. Clare would not have permitted her to make such a mistake. She saw him as much as ever; but somehow he did not stand out, overshadowed as he was by Clare—the perfect pattern of all that a husband's best friend ought to be. Everyone in Washington not only said so but thought so. Reports of his perfection reached Hinsboro and Hinsboro too was impressed by Neal's good fortune.

"Headquarters calling. Figures from Chaselford, Summerdale, Medfield—just about a wash-out, Mrs. Conrad. Would you care for the exact figures?"

"Oh, no, thank you."

This time Neal was standing above her, his weight heavy against her weary shoulder.

"Bad news again? I knew it!"

"You're holding your own."

"Holding my own! Good God, I've got to do more than that!"

"You will, darling, you will. Would you not like a cup of cocoa or something?"

"No— No—don't leave that telephone. It may ring again at any moment."

But it didn't. The silence, like the darkness, grew oppressively heavy— Dora came in and suggested that it was past dinner time. Anne shook her head and Dora went out again. . . .

Roy Griffin, who knew so many lawyers; George Hildreth, who was State Master of the Grange; Mr. Goldenburg, whose one small shop had grown into a great chain with links all over the state; Low, who had appointed Neal to the Senate, and who had political wires running in every direction from his gubernatorial seat; would they all do their share? And, if they did, would it counterbalance Stetson's strength with the labor vote, where Neal had no strength? The *Wallacetown Bugle* and the other weeklies —a great many of them—if they were all friendly to Neal, would that make up for those two big papers of Fletcher's, which were hurling denunciatory editorials at Neal's head?

Spring came, glad and golden, magnolia-scented, to Washington, and Anne, asking herself these troubled questions, shook the beauty that was all about her impatiently from her consciousness, and strained with eagerness to reach Hillsboro, raw and wind-swept, and bleak as it was. But this was the year of the "Long Session," and Neal would not be at liberty to go home early in March. He would have to stay in the Senate through April, through May, through June. It was actually mid-July before adjournment came, at two o'clock one torrid morning when ugly feelings had been unleashed by fatigue and ugly words spoken by lips which were merely the mouth pieces for overwrought nerves. Neal, who had been steering a filibuster lost his temper that night and said unforgivable things to men who had been his friends for years. These unforgivable things were printed in the *Record,* and circulated through the country. Were they unforgettable too?

"Anne? Clare speaking from New York—how are things going?"

"Oh, Clare, I don't know. Not too well, I am afraid. Neal seems to be leading by a narrow margin in the country, but the city returns are slow in coming in, and those we have aren't very favorable."

"The later ones will be better. I'll call up again, say at midnight. Would that be convenient?"

"It will be a God-send. It's such a comfort, Clare, just to hear your voice."

"My boat sails at seven in the morning, but I've purposely not gone on board tonight. I want to hear that Neal's come through before I leave. Though, of course I know he is going to."

Junior wanted to go to a camp in the Yellowstone. Mme. Estavi was taking her little family to Europe for the summer and had invited Nancy to accompany them. But both children were kept at home. They added immeasurably to the picture—Junior's more and more famous smile; Nancy's sweeter and sweeter manners, made an indelibly favorable impression on wavering constituents who came to the house and so much had to be jammed into such a short time that not a single consideration could be overlooked. Neal's enemies had been at work all the time he

238

was chained to his chair in the Senate. And now only August, September and October were left in which to tear down what they had built. No one man, even if he were super-human, could achieve as much as Neal was expected to achieve—as much as he would *have* to achieve if he were to win. Of course the children must do their share, even though it was a tiny one. Anne must make them see —must never let them forget—how much that share might mean to their father. And she must do her share too. Must shield Neal, spare him, save him. But how, *How,* HOW?

She kept open house. This was hard on the servants, who could never be sure of a day off, and who, in spite of their faithfulness, became disgruntled and snappy; but it was harder on Anne. Should she provide for twenty at lunch, or two? The supply lists which she made out every morning covered several sheets of paper. And yet the refrigerator, the pantry, and the store closet were continually empty.

"That last case of ginger ale was used up yesterday—ten loaves of bread I'll need for sandwiches, and if you *could* help, Ma'am, and buy a part of the cake this time, we would appreciate it.—Well, three dozen chops might go 'round, but the last time the Mayor and his Council were here, you remember we didn't have so much as a bone left on the platter."

These were the echoes which reverberated from the kitchen. She listened to them and tried to heed them. But she did not feel she was always successful.

She went everywhere that she was asked, even when she was faint with fatigue. She picked up the threads of her old association, with her church, her historical societies, her pupils; she wore clothes that were spotlessly fresh, delusively simple. The Conrads thought she had too many, and told her so, but she did not dare try to do with less. She was gracious, cordial, democratic, dignified, tireless, decorative. What did it all amount to? If she had been an illiterate, ignorant slattern would it really have made any difference? How much "influence," after all, did a wife have in this frantic, powerful, hideous struggle of politics? Probably very little. Perhaps none at all. Still, she had done her best, and if only Neal did not feel she had failed him, it would not matter what any one else thought. But how *would* he feel towards her if he were not elected? She remembered the hard months after his campaign for the Lieutenant-Governorship, when he had been defeated. Was it going to be like that again? . . .

"Hello— Hello— Senator Conrad's house? The polls have just closed here in Weatherby. Allen, First Selectman, speaking—yes—two to one for Neal. We are banking on him, Mrs. Conrad, to come through in Belford yet. . . ."

Would defeat in the long run be such a calamity? She saw herself living in Hinsboro again, in the house she loved so much and into the building of which her very soul had gone—comfortable, happy, unworried—no more calls to make; no more "appearances" to keep up; no more "admirers" to contend with; time for her children, her music, her real friends. There was that little hedge she had always wanted to plant in the garden, the "Rose of Sharon" counterpane which she had always wanted to quilt, the breakfast nook she had wanted to build out of the pantry that had proved too large. How much simple satisfaction—how much real joy—she was denied because she could never "find time" for these things. Would she not be happier, no longer deprived of these homely pleasures?

And yet, even as she asked herself the question, she knew that she would miss the insidious charm, the fascinating excitement of political life as much as Neal. She could bear that philosophically, but because of her own feeling, she could gauge his. He must, he must go on.

She slipped to her knees. With the same simplicity, with the same ardor, that she had prayed on her wedding night, she prayed again now. For Neal—for Neal—for Neal. . . .

Still on her knees she reached for the telephone.

"Headquarters calling again, Mrs. Conrad. We've heard from the last five wards in Belford—["Oh, God—let him

240

win—let him win!"]—you must get your husband to the
telephone."

She spoke to him. Her voice sounded strange and distant, like that of a foreign woman calling from some far
shore.

"You will have to answer, Neal, this time." ("Oh, God
—let him win—let him win—let him win!")

She pressed the receiver into Neal's hand, threw her
arm around him. From the wire she could hear the crackle
of laughter—the tumult of triumph; and staccato sharp
the words that were being spoken:

"You old crape hanger you! What in Hell's the matter
with you? You have the handsomest margin—"

"What do you *call* a 'handsome margin'?" Neal shouted
through the receiver, clutching at Anne's shoulder.

"Well, if fifty thousand doesn't look handsome to you
—Come on down here, you old Son of a Gun, and
celebrate . . . ! ! !"

CHAPTER XXVI

WITH Neal Conrad's senatorial career every reader of any daily paper is familiar. There is the tariff, which bears his name; there is his speech on the British Debt Funding plan, which is used as a model in "elocution" for every school boy; there is his unshakable stand on the League of Nations which sent him, at the head of a special senatorial committee, to Geneva. All this, and much more, is so well known that it needs no further comment. Besides, this is not the story of Neal Conrad to which numerous famous biographers have already failed to do justice. It is the story of his wife.

And of his wife as the only hostess to achieve a real "Salon" in Washington; as the only American woman whose dress drew forth royal commendation at Buckingham Palace; as the only this and that in various conspicuous capacities, enough has also been said. Her dresses and her dinners have been described a thousand times. Why, therefore, attempt to describe tham again? It is neither the Beauty nor the Belle with whom we are primarily concerned—it is the woman . . . The woman who, on a certain hot afternoon in mid-June, boarded the Congressional Express with her husband, bound for the great National Convention in New York.

The lobby of the Waldorf Astoria, as they entered it, weary after their warm and dusty journey, was so jammed that they could hardly wedge their way through it to register. With every step that they advanced, some acquaintance stopped and seized them, shouting at them excitedly. With every turn they took, placards and posters of rival candidates—most of whom had their headquarters in the hotel—crackled above their heads. Scurrying bellboys, distracted room clerks, helpless assistant managers, strove in vain to perform their normal functions. Laden elevators sank and rose in the hopeless, endless endeavor to convey the mass of humanity which bounded into them like a phalanx from one floor to another. It was nearly an hour before they reached their suite; and Neal, mopping his brow and snatching up a glass of ice water, muttered as he drank, that he was "infernally late for the cursed committee meeting" and that he must be off at once.

"Committee meeting? *Tonight?*" Anne asked in astonishment. "Why, it's after ten now."

"Probably shan't get in before three," he informed her hastily. "Well, goo'-by. Better order yourself an orangeade and a chicken sandwich and have Dora see you unpacked and settled before she goes to bed. Try to get some sleep. You'll have a hard day tomorrow."

Refreshed by a bath and a cooling drink, Anne slipped into the lacy nightgown which Dora had spread out for her, and settled herself for slumber. Her hopes for repose were, however, entirely unfounded; a party of men who were occupying the next room, and who had apparently met in secret conclave, were either unaware or unconcerned of the fact that they could be overheard, and that they were disturbing the public peace. Their voices reverberated through the thin wall. Their lack of harmony rent the air. They were—it appeared—delegates from Chicago, in revolt against their "boss" and violently distrustful of each other. When Neal returned, haggard and hollow eyed, about five, he found Anne sitting up in bed, taut with nervousness.

"Neal, dear, just listen to that racket! It hasn't stopped for a single instant. I can't stand it! We'll have to go to some hotel where it's more quiet."

"Quiet! At a National Convention! Good God, Anne, you don't know what you're talking about. There *isn't* any quiet. Those fellows aren't really objectionable. They're just having a little friendly argument. You should have heard *our* committee. Turn over, old lady, and go to sleep."

"I can't sleep."

"Well, stay awake then, but I shan't."

Flinging his clothes hastily in every direction, Neal sank down beside her and was instantly dead to the world. Two hours later he was abruptly aroused by a heavy pounding on the door and staggered to his feet still drunk with slumber.

"Yeah,"—Anne, who had not closed her eyes heard him saying through a gingerly opened crack—"I guess so. All right, I'll be there right away." He closed and locked the door again and began to gather up his garments from the floor, and put them on.

"I hoped I'd have time for a shave and a shower," he muttered, "but I'm needed right away. You can get to Madison Square Garden all right alone, Anne, can't you? I've left your ticket on the mantelpiece. Don't lose it, whatever you do. And hang on to it when you show it. It might be snatched right out of your hand. Well, goo'-by."

It was only a little after seven and he was gone again. The hubbub in the next room had worn itself out. Anne began to grow drowsy but, almost immediately, she was shaken into consciousness by a band which, from the noise it made, appeared to be passing directly beyond the foot of her bed.

It was, of course, in the street outside. She went to the window and watched it go by, a glitter of braid and brass. Then resigning herself to the impossibility of resting, she rang for coffee and Dora.

At ten, clutching her precious ticket, she left her room, waited fifteen minutes for an elevator not already too crowded to take her in, threaded her way breathlessly through the crowd in the lobby, even denser than it had been the night before, and after another long wait secured a taxi. The driver turned at a most perilous crossing to transfix her with a piercing glance:

"You gonna woik fer our candidate, lady?" he queried; and giving his wheel a sharp twist, added, "You better— we're gonna keep you here 'til ya' do."

He set her down at an entrance which was apparently impenetrable and flanked with eight policemen. The

244

officers of the law seemed to regard her contemptuously. One of them spoke to her.

"Where's your button?" he asked abruptly.

Thinking she had misunderstood, Anne showed him her ticket, but, mindful of Neal's injunction, without relaxing her grasp on it.

"Naw—I don't mean that—ain't you got a button with a certain pitcher on it?" Anne shook her head a little bewildered. "Well, before you come back next time, get yourself one. But go along in now."

She found herself in the basement. There was a clatter of typewriters rising from a string of crowded press rooms, a clicking of telegraph instruments, messengers darting to and fro, a blondined young woman presiding over a cigar stand, delegates almost covered with badges and ribbons, more clusters of policemen. Beside large black letters, painted on squares of stiff cardboard, proclaiming themselves as guides to certain sections, steep staircases led to vague upper regions. Anne was so confused that it took her some time to find her own rabbit-warren. But at last, flushed and triumphant, she emerged on the platform and looked around.

The great oval of the huge structure rose about her, fluttering with flags—big flags, middle-sized flags, little flags, flags infinitesimally small. Out beyond her on the floor, the standards of the states, like giant markers on a flower bed, rose in the aisles beside the seated delegations. Alaska and the Canal Zone were, so to speak, blowing hot and cold together. So were Vermont and Texas; the Middle West was flanked, aggressive and immovable, by the solid South. The packed galleries towered tier upon tier, above the seething crowd beneath them; the boxes encircled the building like a crown; the press sections, stretching out in two whitewashed divisions, made her think of a great pale bird with its wings spread. Close beside her a radio announcer was broadcasting with the earnestness and enthusiasm that revealed the closeness of his contact with his unseen audience. Near the rostrum a group of men, who looked as if they had been up all night, were talking with their heads close together; the members of the

245

National Committee, bristling with self-importance, were securely seated in the most desirable places; back of them on the platform rows of women, in light summer dresses, fanned themselves and chatted with each other. A band, very spritely and smart, was playing "Three O'clock in the Morning."

Without further difficulties Anne found her seat, an excellent one between Mrs. Lassiter and Mrs. Lee. They greeted her cordially, and as she shook hands with them, she felt herself being playfully tapped on the shoulder and, turning, she was confronted with Mrs. Ranger and Mrs. Roper.

"My dear, isn't this too *thrilling!* Of course, we two were certain to be together. You know we're *never* separated. We're such *friends*. But I actually see the hand of Heaven in the rest of the arrangement. We simply *adore* National Conventions, don't you?"

"I have never been to one before," said Anne, who, for all her sophistication had never outgrown the habit of truthfulness.

"My *dear!* How quaint! Why, we haven't missed one since 1908, though none of them have been quite so *harrowing* as this is going to be. But I am sure our *dear* candidate will be victorious in the end, aren't you? Though these terrible New Yorkers will stop at nothing to prevent his nomination, *absolutely nothing*— I have it on the best authority."

A gavel thudded suddenly down. A Bishop began to pray, the national anthem sounded, Klieg lights blazed. A small, neat man with glasses balanced so precariously on his nose that he was forced to keep pushing them back toward his short-sighted eyes, read resolutions, figures and statistics. The Chairman of the National Committee introduced the Temporary Chairman, and this gentleman made an impassioned plea to God and the Convention to deliver him from the party in power. His fervor amounted to frenzy. He mopped his brow, and threw out his arms. But his audience remained calm. Anne saw several men looking at their watches, and in the press gallery, some bored looking reporters sauntered away from their seats. Anne, her own attention wandering, noticed the very fine sapphire that Mrs. Lassiter was wearing and realized that she was hungry. She had expected, of course, that Neal would come and take her out to lunch. But when the welcome adjournment came, she had still seen nothing of him, and Mrs. Roper and Mrs. Ranger bore her triumphantly away between them. The afternoon session came and went. The Permanent Chairman, efficient and belligerent, assumed control of the Convention with a few volcanic remarks. The Committees on Membership and Rules made their reports. The band played. The policemen clustered. The broadcaster continued to speak earnestly and enthusiastically into his machine. At last, genuinely worried, Anne approached Senator Lee, who had joined his wife, and asked if he thought "anything could have happened to Neal."

He laughed reassuringly. "My dear lady, your husband is one of the 'key' men. He can't be spared for window-dressing like this. He has to work."

"But isn't the work being done here at the Convention?"

Senator Lee laughed again. "Certainly not. What made you think it was? Because we sang the 'Star-spangled Banner' and shed tears about Shaw's administration? There is a bitter fight over the platform and a bitterer one over the candidate. Those are the real issues."

He appeared to be about to say something more along the same line but checked himself at the sight of Anne's clouded face.

"Don't worry, Mrs. Conrad," he added gently, "and be as patient with your husband as you can if he seems to neglect you; and—by the way— I wouldn't plan on getting away from here this week if I were you."

"But the convention is to end Friday!" said Anne, growing more and more bewildered.

"A week from Friday, perhaps, if we are lucky. But we probably shan't be lucky."

Senator Lee's prayer for patience was needed. Neal, not having appeared for lunch, did not appear for dinner either; having spent one night at a committee meeting, he spent two more in the same way. He did not go with Anne to the Mayor's Garden Party at Washington Square or the

247

Governor's dinner at the Ritz. He did not go with her to the Convention. He burst into their suite at extraordinary hours for brief moments, searching for clean collars and clamoring for ice water. Anne, consumed with curiosity and excitement, hungered for conversation and explanations. But she hungered in vain. Neal seemed hardly more aware of her than he was of the mantelpiece. It was there and she was there. That was all.

The bitterness of the fight on the platform became increasingly evident. The papers carried huge black headlines about it. The band played familiar tunes that were becoming to sound tiresome and silly, to fill in gaps in the program; a famous humorist cracked jokes that permeated from the press section to the rostrum; the Permanent Chairman bristled more and more. At last it was announced that no agreement having been reached, a majority and a minority report would both be submitted. There was a day of oratory and eloquence and hysteria; of plays to the gallery and appeals to sectionalism. It ended as it had begun, in confusion and hard feeling, and dramatic instability.

Anne, going back to the hotel after it was over, with a violent headache, found Neal sitting beside the marble-topped "center table" of their "parlor," with a sandwich in one hand and a pencil with which he was scribbling illegible characters on a plump pink Senate block in the other. There were dark circles under his eyes, and tired lines of fatigue about his mouth. But he was newly shaved and looked clean and cool in a light fresh suit. And as she entered he looked up with a smile.

"Hello," he said cheerfully, "the worst is over. I am a human being again. And I might say in passing, you have been a brick—as usual—during these last few days while I *haven't* been like a human being. Are you pretty tired?"

"Rather. It's all been so futile and ugly. I believe I won't go to the evening session."

"I'm sorry—I thought we might go together. The fact is —I am going to make a speech. There seems to be a sort of feeling that—well, that if I did I could straighten out this platform tangle."

"Oh, Neal, really? Then, of course, I'm going."

"Good! I hoped you would, and I thought we might have dinner—a real dinner—on the roof first. I hear it's cool and pleasant up there. Snap into a tub and out again and you'll feel better."

As she moved away, slipping her crushed dress over her shoulder, she had the curious impression which she had had a few days before when Senator Lee was talking to her, that Neal had intended to say something else and then decided against it. She turned and found that he was looking after her fixedly and suddenly she thought there were tears in his eyes. She went back to him.

"You are sure," she asked softly, "that nothing is the matter?"

"No, dear, nothing," he answered, and began to scribble again on the block of paper.

CHAPTER XXVII

THE speech which Neal Conrad made before the great National Convention in Madison Square Garden—clear, convincing, courageous, charming and incomparably dramatic, awoke the torpid delegates, soothed the angry alternates, and stirred the restive galleries in an applause that rocked the very foundations of the mammoth structure. Incidentally it also resulted in the immediate adoption of the majority report of the platform committee.

The following morning Senator Lassiter sought Anne out, an enormous bundle of newspapers under his arm—"I thought you might have slept late this morning," he said, smiling, "and so have had no time for these before you came over. It might interest you to look at them. Not only at the front pages, but at the editorial pages."

He nodded and left her. Anne unfolded the crackling sheets to be confronted with Neal's picture and heavy headlines which, in sharp staccato sentences, made it clear even to an unobservant public, how significantly he had scored. He had not only captured the right-hand column on the front page, he had also—she discovered upon following Senator Lee's advice—captured the "leader" on the editorial page; and not in one newspaper, but in all of them. She began to read avidly, flushed with pride.

Her attention was diverted by a stir among the delegates. The Permanent Chairman was announcing briskly that the names of the candidates for the office of President would be put in nomination, and that the roll of the states would be called by the Secretary of the Convention. This individual advanced to the front of the stage, and cried out, "A-l-a-b-a-m-a" as if he were challenging the South to mortal combat. A gentleman with a goatee and an expansive, immaculate waistcoat arose from the midst of the Alabama delegation, and replied, as if he were answering the challenge, "Alabama yields to California."

Pandemonium broke loose. The band, blaring its loudest, was completely drowned out by tin whistles, horns and rattles. States' standards waved, flags fluttered from the galleries, the chairman thumped and thudded in vain, and shouted to the ushers to clear the aisles. The portly gentleman who had appeared beside him with a manuscript half an inch thick, in one hand, raised the other hand with a gesture of impatience because he could not make himself heard. But for a quarter of an hour he was quite powerless to do so. When at last the din had partially subsided, he bellowed forth the opening sentences of his address three times.

"The man who I am about to name," he shouted over and over again. But he did not name him. He talked for nearly three-quarters of an hour, and still, as far as he was concerned, his audience was left in the dark as to whom he was describing. At last, with a crescendo of enthusiasm he revealed his secret. The uproar began again. Some of the delegates commenced to parade. Others, conspicuously silent even in the midst of the noise, sat stubbornly in their seats, resisting all efforts to drag them forth. The march continued without them until the most fervid enthusiasts had shouted themselves hoarse and sank down again exhausted. When this happened, the Chairman, who had been looking tensely on, as if prepared to spring from the platform at any moment, snapped his eyes in the direction of the secretary, and the secretary took up his challenge again.

"Arizona!" he shouted. Arizona, it appeared, was also in a yielding mood, and again pandemonium broke loose. Again a would-be nominator, clasping a bulky manuscript, stood impatiently beside the chairman, endeavoring to make himself heard. Again, when his chance finally came, he failed to take the Convention into his confidence concerning the identity of his candidate. Again, his final pronouncement was drowned by the whistles, the band, the sound of marching feet. This time it was the men and women who had sat still before who were parading, the ones who had been silent before who were shouting. The personnel was different; but the process was just the same.

By the time the fifth candidate had been placed in nomination Anne had resumed her reading; and when, exhausted by a tumult which, like the waves of a rough lake, seemed to be rising and falling without going anywhere, she decided that she might as well "see the thing through" since it must in any case be over very soon now, she realized that, when all possible names had been mentioned for the presidency, there still remained all possible—and impossible—names to mention for the Vice-Presidency.

Mornings of it—afternoons of it—evenings of it. The great principles of our party. The corruption of the unscrupulous politicians now in power. The leaders who, though dead, guide us with their sterling statesmanship. The country which our forefathers fought, bled and died to save. The Stars and Stripes, rippled by a gentle breeze, floating forever over a united country with no north, no south, no east, no west. On the Banks of the Wabash Far Away. The Sidewalks of New York. Way Down Upon the Swanee River. Ioway, Ioway, That's Where the Tall Corn Grows. Dixie. My Old Kentucky Home. The Man Who.

She had the terrible feeling which she had sometimes experienced on a long uncomfortable journey, that it was never going to end. She said so, dizzily, to Senator Lee.

He laughed. "The balloting will begin tomorrow, but we are a long way from the end of the Convention yet. Neither of the leading candidates can get two-thirds of the vote. There will be a dead-lock."

"And what will happen then?"

"One of them may withdraw, but I doubt that. It's more likely we'll have a compromise candidate."

"Have you any one specially in mind?" she asked, without much real interest.

Afterwards she remembered that Senator Lee had given her no direct answer, and wondered why. But with the first excitement of the balloting she forgot all about it. There was an indescribable thrill for her in hearing the

252

chairman of a delegation announce that his state cast twenty-four votes for a certain well-loved candidate. At least there was a thrill the first time she heard it. Even the second and third and the fourth. But finally . . .

For as Senator Lee had predicted, the balloting went on and on and on. She wondered how she could ever have thought the nominating interminable. It was this, instead, that was endless. One week stretched into another and many of the delegates, whose funds were limited, deserted their hotels and betook themselves to lodging houses and cafeterias. The heat folded down over the city like some thick impenetrable blanket. A spirit of weariness, of hopelessness, of hate, began to permeate the heavy atmosphere. And still the band played. And the Chairman rapped with his gavel. And the balloting went on.

CHAPTER XXVIII

"Darling Anne."

She had been drowned in sleep, the profound, prolonged oblivion of utter exhaustion; but Neal's voice, calling to her, brought her back in dizzy waves of memory to the consciousness of her surroundings. The brass bed with the picture of "still life" hanging over it. The pitcher of ice water on the mantelpiece. The faded flowers beside the riddled pincushion. Her bedroom at the Waldorf Astoria. The National Convention. The balloting. The Man Who.

"Anne," said Neal again. And again, "Darling." Her head was still heavy with slumber. But through it flashed the love-laden thought that he needed her. She sat up, pulling at a shoulder strap that had slipped away from her white shoulder, and pushing back the soft masses of her hair.

"What is it?" she asked.

"I wanted to tell you—how much I love you."

She laughed comfortably and stretched out her arms.

"Is that all?" she said lightly, "not that it isn't enough —worth more than anything else in the world! But you don't wake me up in the middle of the night usually to tell me so! You expect me to take it for granted!" Then with sudden apprehension clutching at her heart, "Neal," she cried, "there isn't anything wrong, is there? You haven't had bad news from the children?"

"No, no," he said soothingly. "The children are all right. It's just—" He broke off, and sitting down beside her on the bed, put his arms around her. "I think I haven't told you often enough perhaps—what you mean to me. I

254

have let you take it for granted. I have taken *you* for granted—or seemed to. I haven't really. I wouldn't have amounted to—to much of anything, without you. No one realizes that better than I. You've had all the qualities I've lacked—courage and endurance and talent and faith and vision. I've known all that, Anne, from the first moment I saw you, and I've loved you from that moment too. I've never stopped trying since that night we stood in the meadow and pledged our lives to each other—to give you what I promised you then—lace to wear instead of calico. Real lace. The lace—of a Queen."

"What are you trying to tell me, Neal?" she breathed.

"That the Convention is over, that the dead-lock is broken." His voice failed him suddenly, and he trembled violently, but he collected himself and went on. "When you told me you thought you wouldn't go to Madison Square Garden again, I didn't urge you because—well, I still couldn't be sure, though from the very beginning I have hoped—I have thought—I have had such good loyal friends working for me—I have known how events were shaping—" Realizing that he was becoming incoherent, he checked himself again, and again went on. "On the ninety-seventh ballot some one—a Southerner—voted for me. Then there were several scattered votes from New England. A whole Western delegation. When the count was ready I had nearly a hundred. On the next ballot there were over three hundred and then—and then— Oh, Anne, I'll never forget those banners—those marching feet—those lifted voices singing—cheering—shouting. They got me up on the platform and I—spoke to them. And afterwards they wanted me to go away with them. But I—came home to you—to tell you that I had been nominated President of the United States."

In the carpeted corridor beyond men and women passed, calling to each other excitedly. Porters wheeling trucks that squeaked, banged baggage hastily out of rooms that had suddenly been vacated and carted it away. The roar of the city lifted from the streets suddenly rushed through the dim room. The shrill voice of newsboys rose screaming above the blare of bands and the confusion of traffic.

"Extra—extra!"—"Dark Horse wins!"—"Conrad nominated for President!" "Extra! Extra!"

"But I," repeated Neal, "came home—to you."